# THE FIFTH BULLET

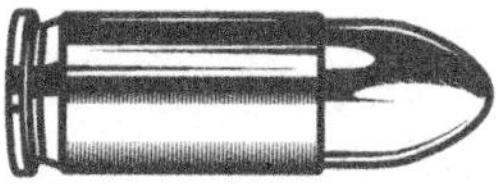

Martin, Thank you for all your great advice + for reading my book :)
Kathleen O'Connor

Kathleen O'Connor

**Print ISBN:** 978-1-0687951-0-7
**eBook ISBN:** 978-1-0687951-1-4



**Contacts:**
www.facebook.com/KathleenOConnorAuthor
kathleenoconnorauthor@gmail.com

Artwork by @oliviaprodesign
Images from by pixabay.com

# CONTENTS

# PROLOGUE

I'd never heard gunfire before, now I'll never forget it. Repetitive, thunderous shots torment me one after the other. I crumble as each one strikes. These ones aren't real though, just my ears playing tricks. I hug my knees close to squeeze the memory from my body.

It doesn't work, so I cover my ears with my hands and curl into a ball instead. Bile rises from my stomach, burning my throat and gargling with the air as I try to breathe as quietly as possible.

This treehouse was always my happy place; full of giggles and childhood adventure. Now it's my safe place. Looking around the small fort, memories catapult me back to when I last played up here. I thought I was too grown up for it at sixteen, but now I don't want to leave its sanctuary.

If mum hadn't insisted I climb above the treehouse to untangle Lyle's kite from the top branch, I'd be lying beside them on the grass too. The thought makes me gag and I throw up once more.

I know the men have gone and several hours have passed as it's dark now, but I can't move. Remembering what I saw through a gap in the wooden boards makes me heave again, but there's nothing left to throw up. I daren't move, so I just sit here shaking, next to piles of my own vomit.

When they realise they've made a mistake, they'll come back. *They'll come back*, I whisper to myself, flinching as I acknowledge my own terrifying words. They could be on the way already.

Panicking and with tears clouding my eyes, I fumble around the treehouse and gingerly descend the ladder. As my plimsolls feel for each rung, I hear myself whimpering as if it's someone else. At the bottom, I catch my breath in preparation for what I'm about to do.

In a dream-like state, I move across the lawn. Adopting a robotic distance is the only way I can walk past my motionless family, life spilling from them into the grass. I'm looking ahead and not down. The only sense in which I indulge myself is sound; the rustling of the grass beneath my feet and the kite still fluttering up in the tree in what's left of the evening breeze.

A thought seeps into my vaguely conscious mind, something I hadn't registered before. That kite saved my life...

# CHAPTER 1

## One Year Later

Bang! Bang! Bang!

My thumping heart is beating so hard, telling me to slow down and not to run so fast, but I can't. They're right behind me.

Bang! Bang! Bang!

I cry out, drawing strange looks from everyone around. The market is busy and hot. I'm running for my life, tears streaming down my face, yet no one is helping. I hear people right behind me complain as they're pushed out of the way by the two men in suits.

Fingertips brush against my back, grasping at what's left of my life. I lurch forward and cry out once more, expecting a sweaty hand to pull me back any second, but still I run free.

Despite the cobblestones tripping me in a sadistic attempt at sabotage, I'm able to weave an intricate path between the market stalls to get some distance from them. Dodging between people moving at a heat-induced, lethargic pace is like an obstacle course. My throat aches from the constriction of panic and I'm starting to see spots. Shadows chase me along the ground and I pump my arms harder in response.

The extra speed is almost my downfall, when an artist perched low on a stool appears out of nowhere, and I almost topple over him. Scrambling to stay upright, I see the doors to the indoor market, propped open with crates of colourful fruit. I run inside before they see me.

It's dark in here and the change in light makes my vision blur. The smell of raw meat from the butcher's stall reaches into my stomach, churning my insides around with a big meaty hand. Nausea almost forces me to stop and throw up, but I swallow it and frantically look around to find the quickest escape route.

I see it. A beautiful Persian rug hanging in an open doorway in the far corner, its golden threads sparkling in the sunlight, beckoning me over with a whispering voice that says: '*This way*!' I hurry towards it and slip outside.

The wall of heat hits me with such force that I recoil. Once again, my eyes adjust to the change in light and I stumble into the wall while blinded, scraping the skin on my shoulder across the jagged bricks.

In the small alley behind the indoor market, I run alongside a row of wheelie bins. My heart is still racing, so I take a deep breath to slow it down. The rotten smell of waste from the bins hits the back of my mouth, leaving a sour taste.

I look up and say a silent prayer for help aimed at the sliver of cloudless, cornflower blue sky. When I reach the end of the alley, my relief is instant as I turn the corner on the threat from behind me.

Then my heart sinks, heavy with regret that slows me to a walking pace while I revaluate. This street is empty. There's no traffic or people. No crowds to disappear into. A complete contrast to the busy market.

Many of the offices lining the street have mirrored windows shining silver in the sun, reflecting light onto the pavement. Daring myself to look behind, I quickly scan the road for the men in suits. No sign of them yet. They'll see me straight away here though, so I force my burning muscles to run once more.

I only get a little way down the street when a stitch pierces my ribcage, challenging the cramp in my thighs for which one can slow me down the most. I huff my breath out as far as I can, to ease the pain.

Each side of the street has an endless row of cherry trees, with bark so dark it's almost black. The reflection in the mirrored windows gives the appearance of more trees than there actually are, like I'm running through an enchanted, never-ending forest, as opposed to the reality of running for my life through the city streets.

I see myself among the trees in the glass and am comforted by the presence of my parents in my own features. My mother's long dark hair is swaying around my shoulders as I run, and my father's olive skin is a few shades darker, to which the sun has added a sprinkling of freckles across my nose. Thoughts of my parents remind me why I have to get away.

One of the offices has an underground car park. Shelter from both sun and sight is too inviting to turn down. Pushing through the cramp, I lift my knees higher to get underground as quickly as I can.

# CHAPTER 2

The cheery ringtone interrupts the laboured breathing as the two men emerge from the alley, looking both ways down the street for the girl. The taller of the two men looks at the caller ID and closes his eyes, releasing the air from his lungs in an exaggerated, condemned sigh.

'Marshall,' he declares his surname, as he wipes the sleeve of his suit jacket over his forehead to soak up some of the sweat gleaming against his dark chocolate skin. Saliva sprays the phone as he musters enough breath to speak the words he really doesn't want to say. 'No, Mr Garrett. She got away.'

Met with silence on the end of the phone, it allows him a few moments to contemplate the consequences they now face. Another sigh, this time of acceptance, brushes over the phones microphone.

Eventually, the reply is a chilling command. 'Don't come back until you've got her.'

The line goes dead and he closes his eyes in a long, drawn-out blink as he lowers the phone from his ear. 'We're in up to our necks, Reeves,' he says, putting the phone back in his pocket.

Still panting, Reeves spits his response. 'You should've just lied and said it weren't her!'

'Too late for that now. We're screwed if we don't get her soon.'

Deliberately ignoring his colleagues warning, Reeves taunts Marshall while loosening his tie. 'You could've run faster! I thought you were meant to be fit!'

'I am! It's the heat. I thought you were meant to be used to hot weather!' he bites back. 'Always bragging about being part Spanish and spending half your life at your aunt's house in the Costa Del Whatever-it-was.'

'There ain't no air here though, I can't breathe!' He bends over, leaning on his thighs for support, shaking his head. 'This kid's slippery.'

As Reeves' words sink in, Marshall wriggles inside the dense fabric of his suit as beads of sweat start a tickling race down his back between his shoulder blades. 'Mr Garrett ain't happy. We're gonna end up like the last people he employed to catch her if we ain't careful, and pieces of us will turn up all over this city. The sooner we get this job done, the sooner we can get paid.'

The mention of money instantly changes Reeves' demeanour as he stands up straight, finally catching his breath. 'I want that money.'

'Me too.'

I emerge from the other side of the underground car park like a butterfly breaking free of its cocoon to enter a world of bright colours and loud noise. The familiar old town buildings, even the unfamiliar faces of tourists, help me to get a grip on my emotions.

Blending in with the crowd gives me a shield of courage to walk instead of run. My legs and lungs need a moment to recuperate. I latch onto a group of tourists who give me cover as far as the bridge over the Cecelia River, where they all stop halfway to peer over the edge at a passing boat.

Walking solo to the end of the bridge, I turn down the grassy embankment. Pebbles and river rocks between tall blades of grass give me solid footing so I don't slip. The bridle path under the bridge leads me to the side entrance of The Archway craft market that occupies the old underground watermill. Two lanterns either side of the door invite me inside with flickering beacons of hope.

This was one of my mother's favourite places. The kiosks inside sell all kinds of handmade goods, fabrics and craft supplies. She loved making things and as I enter, I can almost feel her walking beside me.

People amble around the low-lit, cavernous rooms sourcing inspiration to fuel their creativity. More lanterns spread glowing light across the walls and the gothic decor makes me shiver at the thought of them chasing me down here. It's the quickest way to get through the city centre, but I get the creeps all the same.

A black Honda Civic is parked at the top of Yeoman's Hill overlooking the city centre. The occupants are leaning on the roof of the car.

Peter Lawrence is watching Layna cross the bridge and go beneath through a pair of binoculars. His ruddy cheeks tighten at the sight of her, so close yet out of reach. 'It's definitely her. We've got to get to her before they do.'

His brother Jamie jumps in. 'Yeah. Or there'll be nothin' left of her.'

'For sure. You know, she's not far from the river-bus station. She could get to the seafront from there.'

'Well, if she goes to the seafront, then she's probably going to that boat again.'

'Yep. The dock. Let's go.' Peter is already climbing back into the passenger seat before he's finished his sentence.

Jamie starts the engine and they pull away from their vantage point. The Honda Civic vanishes down the steep hill towards the seafront. It's somewhat symbolic of the intent of its passengers. What they are planning is something they can easily be sent down for.

Marshall and Reeves cross the bridge over the Cecelia River, frantically scanning the passing faces.

Reeves leans over the edge of the bridge and points below. 'Down there!'

Marshall rushes to the edge and looks over. All he sees is the river-bus passing by, no sign of Layna. He looks back at Reeves, his eyebrows furrowed in enquiry.

Reeves seems pleased with himself, so Marshall looks below the bridge again. 'Where, Reeves? I can't see her.'

'No, neither can I, but look! She's probably going on the river-bus to the dock!'

Marshall's shoulders drop with disappointment as he watches Reeves run to the other side of the bridge. He really thought they'd found her. After a shake of the head, he begrudgingly jogs along to catch up.

I stand stock-still.

A large woman wearing a red headscarf almost walks into the back of me and shoots me a dark look, accompanied by a tut. An audience of handknitted cuddly-bears look out at me from their kiosk with judgemental, beady eyes as I falter on my path and change course.

My gut instinct tells me not to go to the dock after all. If they realise I'm near the river, they could figure out that I'll use the river-bus to get there. Moving slowly through the dark tunnels that exacerbate my fraying nerves, I plan my next move. I could fool them by going in the opposite direction. My pace picks up in response to my new plan.

Lost in my thoughts, I don't notice the man until it's too late. Dressed in a smart suit, he strides purposefully towards me. His staring eyes burn a hole right through my body. My pulse points throb, berating me for causing yet more fear. I realise I've made another mistake by enclosing myself in the underground market. He could throw me into the dark river that runs alongside the kiosks and no one would ever know.

My tears magnify and distort his face as he gets closer. His sallow skin gives him a ghoulish complexion and I freeze to the spot, preparing myself for the end.

# CHAPTER 3

A compassionate smile spreads over his face, defying his cold, hard eyes. He twists his body to pass me, and greets someone behind me with a chuckle and a friendly 'hello'.

My knees buckle with relief. After a few minutes of gulping in the musty, damp air and looking around to make sure I haven't missed anything else, I continue on shaking legs like a newborn foal taking its first steps through an open field.

The Mercedes roars as Marshall takes his frustration out on the accelerator. Still out of breath from running all over the city centre, he leans back against the leather seat, feeling his shirt stick to his sweaty skin.

He turns the air-conditioning on full blast. Within seconds, the refreshing coolness takes effect. Sweat tingles across his face at the sudden drop in temperature. The tickling sensation makes his lips twitch, which he forms into words that he's been holding back. 'You'd better be right about this, Reeves.'

'I'll bet you fifty quid she's gone to the dock on the river-bus!' Reeves' breathing is loud as he clicks his seatbelt into place.

'You're on!' Marshall swivels to look behind while reversing out of their parking spot.

After adjusting his seat position to get comfortable, Reeves' fists clench in his lap at the thought of being wrong and having to start the search all over again. Behind his arrogant smile, seeds of doubt creep in, sprouting into insecurity over his guesswork. To distract himself, he focuses on what he'll do to the girl when he catches her, and his fists clench even tighter.

The murky green water of the Cecelia River laps against the side of the river-bus, as we saunter at an agonisingly slow pace away from the city centre.

I've positioned myself between two large families and keep my head down as we travel up-river in the opposite direction of the dock. My foot taps uncontrollably on the side of my seat and I fiddle with the buckle on my bag as the shadow of the bridge falls over the boat.

The children around me are laughing. The parents are chatting among themselves. It's all so normal, while my imagination is running wild, picturing a scene worthy of a film set where the men see me from the bridge above, jump over and land on the deck. I shake my head in defiance for the action to stop taunting me.

The shadow lifts as we pass through to the other side, and I dare myself to take a sneaky sideways glance out the window. No sign of them. Thank goodness. My neck and shoulders ache justifiably from the tension, so I knead them roughly, whilst evaluating the last hectic hour of my life.

That was close. I can't go back to Dave's shop any time, that's for sure.

As we travel further up the river, my muscles eventually relax with the gentle rocking motion and the hum of the boat's engine. Wistfully, I remind myself that tomorrow marks one year to the day since I left my home.

I've only been seventeen for three weeks. How can three weeks feel like such a lifetime? Time flies when your running from the people who killed your family, and who want to see you dead too, so you can't tell what you saw from the treehouse. That treehouse. The life-saving childhood adventure playground, so unassuming from its position at the bottom of the garden, but yet so poignant in it's throne of protection.

My house, once a place to feel comforted and warm, was transformed into a cold, empty shell that day. Everyone and everything that lived in its shelter is now gone. Destroyed by bullets and murderous minds. With each passing day, I no longer yearn to be back there. The tainted existence holds only nightmares. Gone are the happy childhood dreams borne from a blissful family life.

This time last year I was sitting at the head of the dining table, mum and dad either side of me and a ginormous chocolate cake piled high with mountainous icing peaks in front of me. Through the candlelight blaze atop, I see my little sister's face glowing as bright as the flames in pure delight, as she waited patiently for me to blow them out so we could all have a piece. Lyle, in typical younger brother style, motioned for dad to push my head into the cake. *Don't you dare!* Mum had scalded. We were celebrating my birthday late as I was away at a church camp for my actual birthday. When I blew out the candles, the recollection dies too, evaporating with a puff of waxy smoke.

As always, memories of my family weigh heavy on my shoulders, adding to the burden they already hold.

Union jack flags blow proudly in the sea breeze lining the promenade as the Mercedes flies past, breaking the speed limit twice over.

Reeves glares out the window, unaffected by the nostalgia before him; pastel-painted beach huts, palm trees climbing the cliff side, the steep rocky terrain tracing the coastline at the far end of the bay. His eyes are fixed only on the dock ahead.

It's busy, as expected, so it'll be hard to spot The Blue Star among all the fishermen and pleasure-seekers. Thinking ahead, he realises they are going to have to challenge Frazer Ryan, and looks over at Marshall to see if he has come to the same conclusion.

Marshall's expressionless face annoys him and he feels an outburst brewing in his gut. It bubbles up and spills from his mouth before he has a chance to control it.

'Why did he give the instructions not to hurt anyone?! It makes it so much harder! I could've just punched the lights out of that shopkeeper and it'd be one less place for her to hide out. Flush her out!'

Marshall shakes his head. 'Mr Garrett thinks that one day one of them will lead us to her. Leaving a trail of bodies all over the city will only get the police on our tail and nothing more!'

'Ain't that what he pays that bent copper for?!'

'My understanding is that he only has so much influence. I don't think he could stop investigations of several murders without someone catching on.' He lets that sink in before continuing. 'You really think you can punch Frazer Ryan's lights out?!'

'I know he's ex-navy, but he's old!'

'Still wouldn't wanna mess with him though!'

'We can take him.'

Marshall parks on a street leading up the hill away from the promenade and they walk back to search through the boats along the dock.

Red, white and blue bunting flutters, spoiling the almost silent forecourt of Somerton Classic Cars, where I'm wandering among those for sale. On the west side of the city, Princes Forest Retail Park offers me refuge from the dangers that are likely to be at the dock to the east.

For a few light-hearted moments, I imagine I'm a wealthy customer who can afford to shop for a car at a place like this. A smart burgundy saloon tempts me with its cream leather interior and crystal-clear windows. I peer in and boldly try the handle.

Suddenly, I'm aware that someone is watching me.

# CHAPTER 4

A wave of fear ripples through my body, spreading goosebumps from the back of my neck all the way down to my thighs. I look up at the window of the showroom and find myself staring into the icy blue eyes of a cool blonde woman. Our gaze fixes for longer than is comfortable, so I have the courtesy to look away first and slowly move away from the car.

I walk as casually as I can around the side of the showroom, conscious I'm still under the careful watch of the blonde woman inside. In an attempt to appear unconcerned, I put my hands in my pockets as I glance in at her. She has her arms folded in a defensive manner and the ice in her eyes has dispersed into inquisitive interest.

The back of the building doesn't have any windows. Out of sight, I force my shoulders into a relaxed position to appear calm. A brand-new truck shields me from the view of passing cars. One last deep breath full of fresh pine from the trees nearby and the salty sea air, gives me the courage I need to walk back to the entrance of the showroom.

I tidy my clothes, regretting I'm in scruffy denim shorts. The raspy strains of Bryan Adams flow from the sound system as I push through the door. Despite the sale of high-end vehicles, the showroom has a relaxed atmosphere and my worries about my appearance disappear when I see others wandering around in shorts too. We're in the middle of a heatwave, after all.

It's busy inside. Customers are sitting on large comfy-looking leather sofas waiting for their vehicles to return from the servicing department. Television screens entertain them as they sip tea or coffee. I brazenly approach the cool blonde, who has vacated her guard post at the window and is now behind the reception desk.

'There you are Miss Spencer,' she says in a clear and cheerful voice. Her blue eyes are now smiling at me, warm and friendly. 'Your courtesy car is ready for you now. Sorry about the delay.'

She hands me a set of car keys.

'It's a dark blue Audi A4 parked around the far side of the building.'

'Thank you so much. I'll see you in a couple of days,' I say, giving her a warm smile in return.

Through my eyes, I try to convey how thankful I am that she has come through for me once again. Angel has never let me down and I treasure our friendship more than I can tell her here at the reception desk.

Outside, the button on the key fob identifies the Audi in the corner when the lights flicker. I pull some shades out of my bag and settle in behind the wheel, thankful that my father taught me how to drive when I was young so I'd be ready for my test when I was old enough to take it. Not that I got to.

Suddenly, the car fills with my father's presence, ethereal and overwhelming as if he is sitting right beside me, guiding me through the operation of the pedals just as he did every day last spring. The tiny hairs on my arms stand to attention as chills wash over me, despite the humidity spawned from the hot summer day.

I rub my face vigorously with my hands, hoping to wipe away the tears before they fall and snap myself out of these ghostly daydreams. I re-focus on the job in hand and turn the air-con to full, hoping it will cleanse the air as well as my mind, as I check all the mirrors for any passing cars or people.

As I pull away, the bunting waves me off in the rear-view mirror, signalling a goodbye from my friend, who has once again come through with a car for me. I trust Angel with my life, but I remember a time when it was the other way around. It doesn't stop me from feeling bad as I leave her behind to face the music once more.

The cue hits the white ball with such force that it sends the blue one rattling into the corner hole without any doubt it would miss. Cliff Garrett stands up to his full height and re-chalks his cue with a delicacy that contradicts the strength of his shot.

'Wow. What or who's got under your skin today?!' Kevin asks, as he walks around the table weighing up angles and shot chances.

'I pay you to do my accounts, not to know my business.'

'You just don't seem your normal controlled self today, that's all. I know it's not a money worry, so it must be something else.'

'Just take your shot.'

As Kevin leans over the table, Cliff Garrett gently lets out a long, silent breath aiming upwards where his nine-arm chandelier hangs proudly above the snooker table. The dangling crystals sway with the movement of the air, reflecting prisms across the green felt to distract his opponent.

It works.

The ball grazes the edge of the hole and ricochets back into the middle of the table. To disguise his self-satisfied smile, Cliff pretends to check his appearance in the antique mirror hanging over the hand-carved stone fireplace, running his fingers through his salt and pepper hair.

Used to the flickering lightshow after hours of practice beneath them, Cliff takes his next shot with the same assurance as the last one. The pink ball vanishes into the hole, leaving him only one left for a win.

He steps away, leaving Kevin to do his ritual dance around the table looking for the best angles, and turns his back on the game to look out of the open French windows. They frame the spectacular view of his property, including the tumbling hills of Kings Park, with the glistening ocean in the distance. His eyes sweep across his territory with a mix of satisfaction and vanity.

The sound of the ball being potted and his opponent whooping turns his attention back to the table. He lost. Kevin is smiling at him, waiting for his response.

Fury and a quick, fiery temper erodes the admiration for his surroundings, and his mood changes with the blink of an eye.

'I DON'T WANT TO PLAY THIS GAME ANYMORE!' He snaps the cue in half over his thigh.

'It was your idea to play snooker...'

'I thought it would help me relax! I'm too riled.' He holds his head in his hands as he walks out of the room.

Kevin follows him into the hall. 'What's the problem?'

Cliff spins on the spot, turning to Kevin with such ferocity that he cowers, as if expecting him to land a punch.

Instead, he yells some more.

'The problem?! The problem, is that stupid girl is still on the loose! She could destroy me in a second with what she knows. I want her caught and I want her killed! I'm fed up of these incompetent clowns you keep hiring to catch her. You said increasing the reward was enough incentive to have her by the end of the day, but here we are two days later and she's still roaming free!'

'Okay, Mr Garrett. I'll talk to them.'

'I'm telling you Kevin, if they don't get her by the end of the week, these two are gone like the last lot and I'll do it myself! Last chance.'

'I know she's been a thorn in your side...'

'A thorn in my side?! More like a bloody dagger! A whole year she's avoided us! One year to capture one homeless, teenage girl. How stupid must these clowns be?! She's running rings around them, and making me look stupid!'

'I'll fix it, Mr Garrett.'

'You'd better, Kevin. Or else.' He let that sink in, accepting Kevin's silence as acceptance. 'I'm going for a swim.'

Relief escapes through her lips discreetly as the computer system accepts the information she enters for Miss Spencer.

Seeing her name next to the phoney record for Layna flushes her cheeks a guilty shade of rouge.

'Angel?!'

Her manager's loud, booming voice makes her jump out of her skin.

'What's going on here?' he demands.

# CHAPTER 5

'W-what d-do you mean?'

'You were supposed to order more brochures for the A6! Now people are going away empty handed!'

'Oh,' she breathes out with relief. 'I did order them,' she adds confidently. 'They're in the boxes in the store room. I just haven't had a chance to open them yet. I'll do it now.'

Her chair spins on its base as she leaves her desk and strides across the reception area to the store room. Out of sight, she uses the nib of her pen to break through the packing tape and takes a stack of brochures out of the box.

While organising them on the shelf in the reception area, she looks back to make sure no one is looking at her computer screen as she forgot to lock it. There's no one there, thankfully.

Remembering the time when, despite being a few years younger, Layna took a huge risk for her by helping her to run away from the violence at home, giving her all of her birthday and pocket money, and keeping her location secret, Angel's confidence returns. Encouraged by the knowledge that Layna would do the same again in a heartbeat, she would too, despite the risk.

From behind a pair of Jaeger sunglasses, Peter Lawrence bares his teeth as he watches Marshall and Reeves wandering along the dock. His forehead creases above the shades, as the two men gesture with hands out, indicating they haven't found her.

Normally he would be pleased Marshall and Reeves are doing all the legwork for them, but he isn't. His idea to follow them for a while to see if they would lead them to Layna has failed.

He puts the sunglasses back on the shelf at The Surf Shack, where he and Jamie are keeping their distance, trying not to draw attention to themselves. The colourful shirts, towels and beachwear irritate his black mood further.

From the corner of his eye, he sees Jamie looking around pretending to be a customer, unperturbed as ever, and it winds him up even more. Abruptly, he exits the shack, leaving Jamie awkwardly trailing behind.

Towering sycamores cast welcoming shadows of relief from the sun as I enter the park.

I glance back at the car in its space opposite the entrance as I pass through the iron gates. The anxiety of leaving Angel's courtesy car flutters through my veins, despite the relaxed atmosphere of the park swaddling me up in its normally comforting blanket.

Last time I was here, it was autumn and the sycamore seeds rained down around me, spinning like tiny propellers. Sycamores remind me of my father laughing at me when I was small and told him I wanted to catch some 'helicopter seeds'.

Today, the air is clean but for the invisible pollen particles tickling the back of my nose. Heat seems to collect in the open expanse of the park and I feel for those who are trying to play tennis in the court ahead. Equally, a brave group of boy's battle under the oppressive sun in a game of basketball. A smaller boy is trying to hold his own against the bigger boy's and I find myself rooting for him as I walk past, before exiting the park at the opposite end.

I'm thankful for the affluence of this small town of White Hills, as the large, detached houses are set back from the road so no one can easily observe me through twitching curtains. It's a quiet area and all I can hear are my own soft footsteps and the occasional cry of laughter blowing in on the wind from the park.

Turning the corner onto another leafy street, I come across a house called The Three Pines, as declared on a plaque on the wall. I slow my pace and look up at the house. I'll bet the occupants are at work or a charity function of some sort. The gates are open so I head up the drive, feeling the crunch of the gravel beneath my feet.

As I approach the front door, I glance up at the top floor windows and find myself looking at a crow that's standing guard on the edge of the roof. From its defensive stance I half expect it to swoop down at me to protect its domain, but its eyes are transfixed on an entrancing half-moon in the bright blue summer sky.

Ignoring the feathered guard on the roof, I look around to make sure there's no people about, then slowly walk around the side of the house. Shielded by bushes, I'm free to 'break and enter' at my will. The basement window is slightly ajar, as though they are inviting me in. I bend down and push the window open as far as it will go. Being so small, I just about fit through and slide down into a dark room.

The sound of chillout beats designed to mimic those played by DJs at summer resorts fill the interior of the Mercedes.

Knowing Reeves as well as he does, Marshall is quietly traversing a battle of wills with his inner voice that's encouraging him to pull the trigger on Reeves' tempered bullet. Knowing what the outcome will be, he should stay quiet, but he loses the battle and revels in the enjoyment of the moment. 'So you owe me fifty quid, Mr Reeves!'

Reeves smashes his palm against the dashboard. 'I hate playing these games!'

'You made the bet, Reeves!'

'Not that game, these games!' His thumb points over his shoulder to the dock in the distance.

'Well, that's what Mr Garrett wants...'

Reeves cuts him off, not yet finished with his outburst. 'But it ain't getting us anywhere! He don't want anyone killed, but it don't mean we can't shake things up a little. Bit of encouragement to talk, you know.'

'You wanna chance it and get on Garrett's wrong side that's up to you.'

'This guessing game does my head in! That list of people and places the last two left us is useless! We might as well burn that bit of paper and start from scratch! All it did was get them killed.'

'It's not so bad. We were almost there at the shop, that was on the list. She turned up there eventually, didn't she? And we would've caught her too, if you hadn't got distracted by that tall, bronzed brunette! We've just got to figure out where she'll logically go next if she's still in the city centre where we saw her.'

Reeves sinks into his seat and rubs his forehead, creasing his skin into premature wrinkles. After a few moments his boiling temper simmers down and he makes another haphazard guess. 'My money's on the bar owner.'

'Nah, it's too far from where we saw her.'

Reeves shrugs his shoulders, not trusting himself to speak without ranting again.

Marshall's lips purse in reconsideration of Reeves' suggestion. 'You know, you might be on the right track. We could put the squeeze on the bar owner. She might not be there now, but she'll probably go there again at some point and even if he don't fold, one of his customers might.'

He flicks a glance away from the road at Reeves to gauge his response. The flaring nostrils and moody, scowling face sitting atop an angry red rash splaying down his neck, vanishing under the collar of his shirt, tells him all he needs to know.

Eventually Reeves nods slowly. His mood visibly shifts as he interprets Marshall's suggestion of 'putting the squeeze on' as a free pass to dish out some of the aggression fuelling his temper.

Marshall pulls into the next road to turn around and they head back into the city.

The occupant of The Three Pines is on the doorstep, inserting the key into the lock. He steps over the threshold and closes the front door quietly.

Looking all around the house from his vantage point in the hallway, he checks to see if anyone else is home. The only sound is the ticking from the grandfather clock in front of him.

Ignoring the rule of not wearing shoes on the marble floor, he walks through the hall and into the kitchen. The door to the basement is on the far side. He opens it and descends the stairs.

At the bottom, he unlocks another door using a key that only he has, and enters the room. Feeling along the wall for the light switch, he flicks it on.

# CHAPTER 6

'You have a pretty good jump shot for a computer genius!'

'Thanks Layna. I'm not as good as Todd Mayberry though. He's nearly six foot already but he's the same age as me. He only has to reach out and the ball's through the hoop.'

I'm sad for Corey feeling so inadequate at being the smallest boy on the basketball court, and try to reassure him. 'It's not all about how tall you are, Corey. You've got brains. That far outweighs height! You were giving them a run for their money out there in the park.'

'Thanks. How can I help you? It's been a long time since I last saw you.'

'I need some more cash. I'm down to my last tenner.'

'Sure. Let's log on and check the funds.'

Corey takes a seat at his desk and turns on his computer. I shake my head in marvel at what he's doing for me. He was only twelve-years-old when he set up the fake bank account. Apparently, he had been doing it since he was eight. I never asked how or why. One unanswered question does still puzzle me though.

'You know Corey, I still don't understand why my parents bank account isn't frozen.'

Corey's hand abruptly stops moving the mouse and he speaks to me without turning.

'Me neither.'

I can't see his facial expression, but he sounds just as puzzled as I am. Then he turns to face me and I see he doesn't look worried at all.

'Let's just be thankful it's not.' His brighter tone is somewhat reassuring. 'And don't think of it as stealing either, this money is meant for you, remember?'

'Yeah, I know it is...but. Well, ok then, I do need the money.'

Corey smiles at me and as he does the necessaries online, I look around the basement room now that the light is on and I can see properly. The wall behind his black desk has been painted red since I was here last. There's a second computer, half concealed in a cabinet, and I dread to think what he's up to on that one. He's added a mini fridge and upgraded the size of his TV to an enormous screen that swallows up a whole wall, and is connected to several game consoles. The speakers look like they can blow a hole in the earth. I'm impressed.

Corey's voice shatters my daydream of being a teenager with sole access to a room like this.

'All done. Should be ready tomorrow, usual place.'

'Thanks Corey! You're the best!'

I playfully ruffle his hair, then immediately regret the action as belittling. Although I trust Corey, having my fate in the hands of a quirky thirteen-year-old is a gamble at the best of times, but Corey puts my mind at rest.

'If only the guys at school knew I had a friend as cool as you, I'd be Mr Popular no matter how awful my jump shot is.'

'Remember, Corey, not a word!'

I leave the room using the same method that I entered.

Racing around the streets, over-cooking corners, the Honda Civic is just about keeping up with the silver Mercedes.

Peter sniffs unsatisfactorily as he figures out where Marshall and Reeves are going. The Calypso Inn is miles from where they last saw her. He shakes his head in disbelief, as they watch the silver Mercedes park right outside the bar.

Jamie feels Peter's frustration emitting from his pores. The bitter, angry fumes fill the car, ready to combust at any moment. He readies himself for the certain explosion, regretting letting Peter drive.

Peter grips the wheel white-knuckled as he yells. 'Are they really that stupid?!'

Jamie knows it's a rhetorical question, even though it's directed at him. Before he can think of a response that won't further aggravate his brother, he's thrown forward as Peter slams on the brakes among the city traffic.

'She's not gonna go there again after what happened last time, is she?!'

Another rhetorical question which Jamie doesn't respond to. Peter wants affirmation, but he's loathed to point out that last time she was here, it wasn't Marshall and Reeves after her, it was the duo before them. Knowing this will spark another outburst, he grinds his teeth to keep his jaw firmly shut.

'Garrett's really scraping the barrel with these two, I'm telling ya.' Peter's voice changes to quieter, menacing calculation. 'I've got a better idea.'

He pulls hard on the steering wheel to turn around. The cars behind all skid to a halt and beep in frustration.

Jamie's brain shifts in its cavity under the sudden change in direction, sending him into dizziness that makes him feel queasy. He grips his seat as he's thrown around the car like he was part of some racing car experience day.

Peter laughs at his own bad driving, taking delight in annoying the other road users. After doing an illegal U-turn in the middle of a busy intersection, the Honda races past the road sign for White Hills.

# CHAPTER 7

The green and yellow neon sign reflects the words Calypso Inn across the top of the silver Mercedes.

Marshall expects a bit of trouble here. The bar is known for being the kind of place where everyone sticks together, whether they know each other very well or not. He looks over at Reeves and is assured to see he has his game face on. His eyes are shining with anticipation and his dimples frame a big cheesy grin, meaning he's clearly in the mood for a bit of trouble of his own.

They leave the car and go down a flight of stairs to the basement bar, pushing the doors open with force to announce their arrival. Caribbean music and laughter escape through the open doors.

Behind the bar, Farrell Gregory stands tall and proud as he shares a joke with some of his customers. His shoulder length dreadlocks tickle the side of his face as he laughs heartily and there is just a hint of his childhood Jamaican accent left in his response to the joke.

He looks up upon hearing the doors burst open. Recognising Marshall and Reeves from Cliff Garrett's clan, he calls out to them. 'Sorry, there's no room at The Inn!'

People sitting around the bar chuckle at his joke.

Reeves laughs along, playing the game, before responding. 'You're a funny guy, Farrell. Let's see how funny you find this!'

He pulls a sharp knife from his pocket and grabs the hair of a woman sitting at the bar. Pulling her off the stool backwards, he holds the blade to her throat.

Several people leap out of their seats, ready to jump into action.

'HOLD IT! One move and this young lady will have tasted her last cocktail!'

Everyone freezes initially, before slowly backing away to indicate compliance.

He spits the next words into her ear. 'Did it taste good, sweetheart?' He's so close he can smell the coconut shampoo in her hair as she whimpers. 'Bet you never thought it'd be your last one now, did you?'

The woman cringes as condensation from his breath forms over her ear. Her legs give way, so Reeves hoists her up to full height by her hair, feeling her baby-soft afro curls slipping through his fingers as he does so. He squeezes tighter to keep his grip.

Everyone sees what's happening but nobody dares move. The cheery steel pan music chimes away in the background, at odds with the disturbance ensuing among the potted palms and picturesque beach scenes covering the walls.

Reeves tightens his grip on the woman as he speaks. 'Good. I can see you all understand.'

Marshall takes over the show. 'Now, who here is a regular? I bet pretty much all of you spend every pathetic second of your lives in here. So tell me, who recognises this girl?'

From his inside pocket, he pulls out the last school photograph taken of Layna, and holds it up for all to see.

Farrell's nerves jangle in the pit of his stomach. He thanks God for every second of silence after the photograph is shown. He will never give Layna up, but can't be sure his customers will be so loyal, especially under a test like this.

No one speaks, so the only sound between pan chimes is crying from the woman as the cold, serrated edge of the knife scratches the skin on her neck. Her legs are still shaking visibly and her hair is tangled in Reeves' fingers. A few strands tear out from the roots under her own weight.

Her cries force Farrell to break the ice. 'We haven't seen her! Don't take it out on this poor girl!'

'Somebody please help me!' Her voice is quiet, barely more than a whisper.

Reacting to her small, desperate plea, Reeves twists the knife a little, making a slight nick in her skin. A small dot of blood forms, rolling down her neck like a teardrop, staining the top of her blouse.

The other customers gasp in unison, followed by a few screams, and collectively they all inch forward instinctively trying to save the woman.

'NO! Don't even think about it!' Reeves stops them in their tracks by jolting her to prove his strong grip.

Farrell rubs the small, soft hairs at the back of his neck with his hand, helplessly trapped behind the bar. He deliberates about his chances of leaping over the counter and getting to the girl in time, but concedes the guy is likely to cut her throat before he can reach her. He lets out an exasperated breath and tries to be the voice of reason once more.

'STOP THIS NOW! Take it out on me if you want but she has nothing to do with Layna!'

Ignoring his words, Reeves looks Farrell dead in the eye and grins widely while he draws the knife around the young woman's throat. He laughs aloud at the blood shooting through the veins in the whites of Farrell's wide eyes.

Farrell leans over the counter, flailing his arms towards them but they are just out of reach. 'NO! NO! Stop!'

Reeves laugh deepens, a proper belly laugh, as the woman takes a slow, rasping breath of disbelief at what is happening to her. The knife makes just a small cut in the skin all the way around, not deep enough to do any real harm, but it immediately seeps blood.

# CHAPTER 8

Piercing screams drown out the happy music in the background, but still nobody dares to take any action as Reeves' knife is still embedded in the woman's skin.

Reeves continues with his sick humour. 'Don't worry, it's just a scratch. Someone get her a plaster!'

Marshall sniggers and looks around for someone to enjoy the joke with, but is only met with hostility. He lowers his eyes, internalising his laughter.

One of the barmen, Davies, makes a move from the side of the bar where he has been watching, weighing up the odds of taking Reeves out. He's stopped in his tracks when the shiny, pointed edge of a large knife appears on his chest. He looks along the handle, up the arm and into the face of Marshall.

No longer laughing at Reeves' joke, he's shaking his head, warning Davies not to try it. Davies holds firm, staring him down, but doesn't move. Marshall looks away first, shooting a look at Reeves as a reminder not to go too far.

Reeves twists his fingers in the woman's hair and she squeals in response. It pains him to drop it at this point, but he throws her by her hair across the room and into the crowd of customers.

She falls into the arms of an elderly man with a white beard, her grandfather. He holds her tight, glaring over her shoulder with a dark look, as everyone rallies around her.

While they are tending to her, distracted from any thoughts of retaliation, Marshall quickly jumps in before Reeves tries anything else. 'Your customers are more loyal than I expected, Farrell! But ask yourselves this.'

He looks around the room to make sure the whole of 'The Inn' are still listening. 'Are any of you willing to lose your life or the life of someone close to you over one useless bar owner and some girl you don't even know? Next time we come, we expect one of you to start talking. So be on the lookout for her.'

'Good luck, Farrell!' Reeves raises eyebrows and smiles to deliver the sarcasm intended.

Marshall follows suit, with a jolly, high-pitched sentiment. 'We'll be back to visit you all again soon!'

Climbing the stairs to leave, Marshall half expects to be pounced from behind and is surprised when they make it back to the car unscathed.

The mood is high as he starts the engine and pulls away. Laughing at their own audacity, jubilancy fuels a fast-flowing conversation in which they make plans to go back again and follow through on their threat.

The inside of the Calypso Inn is fairly relaxed, given what just occurred. Farrell is dishing out free drinks, while some of his customers break any tension left with well-timed humour.

The woman dabs at the line of broken skin with some wadding from the first aid kit. Her grandfather is at her side, reassuring her that it's not deep and will heal.

Farrell swirls brown liquid around in his own glass, before taking a sip and feeling the heat burn his tonsils. He knows everyone here well enough to know that beneath the calm facade, many are seething, making unspoken pacts of revenge. He has a feeling that if Marshall and Reeves ever come back to the Calypso Inn, as they promised they will, they'll probably never be seen or heard from ever again.

# CHAPTER 9

In the round, sphere-shaped world of binoculars, the focus falls on a boy playing basketball in his back garden. Peter shakes his head in judgement. The kid is never going to make any basketball team.

Inside the car, Jamie fiddles with the radio volume, while his brother spies on the boy. He sees Peter lower the binoculars and make a move back to the car.

'Anything?' he asks, hoping not to stoke an angry response.

'Nah. The kid's mother just called him in. If the mother's around, then Layna definitely ain't around, that's for sure.'

'So what now?'

Peters reply is flat and empty. 'We re-think.'

Jamie starts the engine and pulls away. He squints into the rear-view mirror at what he thought was the boy clocking them from the upstairs window. He can't be sure though, so he doesn't say anything to Peter.

A sense of relief washes over me as I exit the park and see Angel's courtesy car just as I left it. I had a horrible feeling I'd find it clamped for some reason. As I'm about to get in, the hairs on the back of my neck prickle, telling me someone is watching me.

I keep my hand on the door handle but slowly turn to scan the street behind me. In what feels like slow motion, my eyes eventually meet those of a man behind me.

He leans on the counter of his ice cream van, his eyes glued to mine. For a second, I fear he'll leap through the window, a menacing action that seems out of place in the midst of his pink van full of sprinkles and joy. After staring at me for what feels like an eternity, he winks. Then two children come over to be served, so he looks away.

Feeling perturbed at how easily I became a target, my senses are on high alert as I spot another danger coming towards me from the opposite direction. I turn quickly and walk away from the car, trying not to show my face.

The parking warden is checking all the cars along the street. She has a friendly, round face, but I'm not fooled. It takes a tough nut to do that job, so I walk as fast as I can.

The last thing I need is to be caught driving a car I don't own. I'm sure Angel will arrange for Somerton Classics to corroborate 'Miss Spencer's' courtesy car story and I have ID in that name too, but it's risky and I don't want to drop Angel in it. I make a very quick decision to leave the car where it is and go to my next destination by train.

The boy eats hungrily, hoping to grow bigger and stronger, like some of the other boys at his school. That way he can be a match for them physically, as well as mentally, especially at basketball.

'Slow down, Corey, you'll make yourself sick!'

Doing as he's told, he slows down, knowing that the quicker he complies, the less attention his mother will pay him. She obliges by turning her back to put some pots and pans into the dishwasher.

Swallowing the misery lurking at the back of his throat along with his next bite of food, he avoids eye contact with her whenever she flashes a glance his way to make sure he is conforming. He wriggles around on the kitchen chair, battling the urge to eat as quickly as possible so he can get out of the kitchen and back to his den in the basement.

A queue of taxis snakes its way around the circular path leading to White Hills train station. Some tourists nearby are taking pictures of the quaintly decorated building. For as long as I can remember, it has been painted white with black gables and hanging baskets of colourful flowers.

It's late afternoon and the sun is still beating down hard on my shoulders as I walk across the bouncy tarmac of the car park towards the entrance. There are more tourists inside, all looking lost, as it's an old-fashioned station with none of the usual electronic boards. It's easy for me as I know my train always leaves from platform two.

With no ticket machines either, I take my place in the line for the ticket desk. My usual habit of discretely scanning faces and reading body language for anyone that stands out around me kicks in while I wait. Then something worrying catches my eye.

In the newsagents opposite, the headline on the newspaper rack makes me do a double-take and sets my heart racing. It says; *Have You Seen This Woman?* Cliff Garrett has tried some extravagant tricks to flush me out over the years. Irrationality consumes me as I worry it could be referring to me.

The ticket clerk is motioning for me to move forward. I ask for a return ticket to Albany Cove and hand over my last ten pounds, then hurry over to the newsagents to investigate. I flick through the paper and find the full story on a two-page spread.

A photograph of a tall, slender woman with fair hair and a pale complexion confirms my paranoia. She's been missing since a night out with friends last week. The poor woman's family must be fraught with worry, making me feel equally guilty and foolish that I even considered it could be referring to me. I throw the paper back onto the shelf as if it's burned my fingers with shame. In defiance of my own emotions, I strut over to the gates and saunter through as if I haven't a care in the world.

No matter what time of year I come to a train station, the platforms are always cold. It's a welcome relief from the sun, as I inspect my fried shoulders and see the angry, red skin preparing to peel off in protest.

After a short while, a train ambles up the tracks and I board the second carriage. I find an empty table for four and settle in next to the window.

I love this journey to Albany Cove as the train passes right through Princes Forest, winding a path alongside the Cecilia River in the valley. The river glistens as the train rides alongside it. I lean my head against the window, entranced by the sparkles dancing across the water and begin to relax in the quietness of the carriage.

At the first of only two stops on the way to Albany Cove, a tall, athletically built man in a suit studies the train from the platform, before choosing Layna's carriage for his journey. He sits on the opposite side of the carriage and looks over at her staring out of the window, deep in thought. Now that's very careless, he thinks to himself.

Before the train sets off, the man leaves his seat and goes to the next carriage. He speaks into his phone in a hushed voice, before finding a new seat.

Recognising there's not much he can do here on the train, he decides to follow her, so he can catch up with her in a quiet place. An abandoned newspaper offers concealment, where he can observe her carriage for the rest of the journey.

# CHAPTER 10

The train starts off from the next station so gently, that I barely feel it. The optical illusion plants the idea that the platform is moving instead of the train.

Eventually, the buildings give way to the greenery of the countryside once more. The track gets so close to the river that I just want to open the window, reach down and run my fingers through it. To feel the cold, refreshing water would help me feel alive, instead of this numb state of existence I've fallen into. Then we hit a bump on the rail, making me sit up sharp, a warning for me to snap out of it.

I don't know what's come over me recently, I'm never this easily distracted. Never letting my guard down has kept me alive. There's no one else in the carriage though, so no harm done.

After only a short while, the train slows through the built-up town centre into Albany Cove station. When the platform appears, I stand up and stretch while waiting for the doors to open. A fair few people disembark from the other carriages. I fall in line with them to the main exit.

Outside the train station, another line of taxi's are waiting with anticipation. I ignore the pleading eyes of the drivers and walk straight past.

Using his height to look over the heads of those in front of him, he watches the girl exit the station and tries to keep up without making it obvious he's following her. Then an obstacle appears in his way. A large one.

The mean-looking security guard demands to see his ticket. Peering over the guard's shoulder to see what direction she went, he feebly admits that he doesn't have one. Looking back into the guard's unamused face, he offers an equally feeble smile. Forced to buy a ticket belatedly, he loses track of Layna once more.

The evening sun shines blinding light over the grey pavement, luring me up the steep hill with its offer of rest and shelter at the top. My heavy legs remind me that I always seem to be climbing this hill at the end of a long, tiring day.

Bursts of colour from the awnings of all too familiar guesthouses and cafés along the way encourage me to keep going, despite the burn building in my leg muscles. The blue and white one indicates I'm half way. The yellow one above the lighting shop, full of twinkling chandeliers, marks three quarters of the way.

Just as I think my thighs can ache no more, my saviour appears at the top of the hill, the magnificent Hotel Indigo. Lit from behind by a spectacular sunset of russet and cerise, I daydream about falling asleep in one of its plush, comfortable beds.

Finally feeling the terrain straighten out under foot, I turn into the front garden that's shadowed by tall lilac trees growing in manicured borders. Wide steps lead me up to the entrance.

The woman behind the front desk has blonde hair in a low chignon beneath a bright red pillbox hat. Her jacket is the same shockingly bright shade of red, with royal blue shoulders, cuffs and stitching. I have to remind myself that we are not on a plane and this isn't a flight attendant. Her make-up looks professional and she offers me a welcoming smile through matching red lips. I envy how she still looks attractive in such an ugly uniform and her perfect white teeth catch my attention as she speaks.

'Good evening, Miss Abraham.'

'Good afternoon, Miss La Croix.' My reply sounds calmer than I feel.

A slim, spindly young man behind her, who I've seen here before, stops delving around in a cabinet to stare at me. I study him too. To match his thin physique, he has thin hair in a shade of dark blonde or light brown, depending how the light catches. He's also dressed in the same tragic combination of red and blue, and seems extremely interested in my presence.

Tiffany confirms my fake reservation under the name Miss Abraham and hands me the key card to my hotel room. I head to the lift, eager to put some distance between myself and Tiffany's nosey colleague.

Tiffany watches the young man watching Layna all the way to the lift. She speaks without breaking her smile. 'Stop staring, Henry.'

'I wasn't staring.'

'You still are!' She playfully nudges him out of his trance.

Henry busies himself with some paperwork he needs in order to take over Tiffany's shift, but snatches the odd side-glance over at Miss Abraham while she waits for the lift. His heart flutters with each glance and he struggles to hide the clumsiness he develops when she is around.

Amused at Henry's crush, Tiffany smiles, but it's also one born of relief that Layna is okay. She sneaks her own secret glance over at her, captivated as the vision morphs into that of Layna's mother, Rosa. When she worked here, Rosa stood waiting for that lift many times. They're so alike, it's hard for Tiffany not to think of them as one in the same.

Waves of gratitude sweep in from a distant shore whenever she thinks of Rosa, without whom she'd still be confined to cleaning hotel rooms, imprisoned by inhibiting shyness. She takes a deep breath, full of sadness and grief that turn her smile upside down, and blinks away the tears diluting her eyeliner. Never having the chance to thank Rosa for everything she did for her, she makes up for it by helping Layna.

She loiters at the end of her shift finding more things to do so she can be sure the coast is clear for Layna before she leaves. Once the evening entertainment is in full swing in the dining room down the hall, she finally logs off her computer, knowing Layna is safely tucked away in her hotel room. She grabs her bag and coat from the back office and leaves the hotel.

Henry watches Tiffany leave and settles in for the night shift on the front desk. As he waits for the computer to load his settings, he fantasises about being the first person to see Miss Abraham in the morning. There probably aren't many guys that can say that. A pleased expression spreads over his face, until he remembers he doesn't have any friends to brag to.

His feelings of inadequacy battle with the exhilaration he feels at seeing his crush again. With his thoughts jumping between the two, his heart rate increases as he struggles to keep up. The power of these thoughts surprise him in the physical reaction they cause. He slides around in his seat, like the action will stop his mind from taking over his body in this way.

To calm himself, he tries to focus on some admin, but it doesn't work. His mind still wanders back to Miss Abraham. Her hair looked sun-kissed with burgundy streaks. She had freckles decorating her cheeks. She never dresses particularly flashy but she always looks stylish to him.

Instead of replying emails, he idly types her name into the hotel checking system. He hits the search button and waits.

# CHAPTER 11

Chloe La Croix is just finishing her last fingernail. The dark red polish glides over the remaining section and she readies herself for the compliments from the customer.

It's taken until these last couple of nails for her hands to stop shaking. The semi-famous actress, Elizabeth Mayhew, put her at ease chatting about her latest endeavours on screen.

'Amazing, Chloe! I'll definitely be recommending you to everyone I know. They look fantastic!'

From the corner of her eye, Chloe sees her manager Veronica giving her a thumbs up from the other side of the room. Elizabeth strides out of the salon in a flurry of expensive perfume and newly polished nails, leaving Chloe a huge tip.

Chloe takes a second to adjust her clothes around her stocky frame in the mirrors along one wall. She runs her fingers through her short, choppy hair, twisting the ends in different directions.

Veronica comes over and puts an arm around her shoulders. She speaks to her through the mirror, rather than looking directly at her. 'Well done, hun!'

She thanks Veronica via the reflection.

'And well done Mrs Kline for recommending you to Elizabeth! I hope she does tell all of her friends. Our profit line will go through the roof!'

'I still can't believe she asked for me personally!' The glint in Chloe's eyes conveys the underlying message to Veronica that she is the key to the salon's success in Elizabeth's circle.

Perched on the edge of the bed in a charming guesthouse near the Hotel Indigo, the man runs his hand over the silk embroidered bedspread, enjoying the softness on his fingertips. He holds the phone to his ear in the other hand.

Standing up tall while listening tentatively to the man on the end of the phone, his toes, on his now shoeless feet sink into the luxurious thick pile carpet. He walks over to the window and pushes aside swathes of chenille and chiffon drapes to peer outside. The lights across the town glow against the dark sky, duplicated in the reflection of his pupils in the glass.

The sight of his own face breaks the spell and he abruptly turns back to the room. He runs a finger over the graceful curvatures of the Louis XV furniture, dislodging a tiny cluster of dust caught in one of the grooves with his nail, before his turn to speak in the conversation draws him away.

'Yes, I almost caught up with her, Mr Brooks, but I had a bit of bother with a security guard in the train station, so I lost her.'

His thumb and forefinger frame his chin as he absorbs the reply before offering a reply of his own. 'Yes, sir, I'll keep trying. I'll scour the town tomorrow. It's not a very big place, so I feel quite optimistic about finding her. I'll let you know... bye.'

Under a canopy of coconut husk, the warm evening air ushers Chloe through the entrance of the Monkey Nut Café. She spots Tony amidst the colourful, inviting tiki hut decor. Smiling, she slides into the booth next to him.

'There she is! You look lovely, babe!'

Without even thanking him for the compliment, she launches straight into the story of her victorious day as nail technician for a famous actress. '...and the best part is that she is going to tell all of her friends to come to our salon too! Veronica was well pleased. Maybe she'll promote me from junior to senior nail technician!'

'You deserve it, babe. Make sure you start hinting about that promotion right away.'

'I will.' She leans her head on his shoulder indicating thanks for his belief in her. 'She's going to star in The Crown In The Sky, you know!'

'What's that?'

'It's a period drama. She'll have her own make-up artist and a wardrobe assistant all to herself because her costumes will take the most work.'

'I see.'

'...and she just got back from The Maldives. The production company sent her there to get a tan. She said the water is so clear and there were turtles on the beach outside her cabin!'

Latching onto her enthusiasm, he makes a suggestion. 'We could go on holiday too, somewhere exotic and luxurious. Find our own piece of paradise, hey?'

'Oh Tony, could we? I've always wanted to go abroad. Tiffany goes all the time and she's always bragging about Monte Carlo or The Seychelles.'

Then she checks herself. 'Sorry, Tone, I don't mean to sound like a whining, jealous little sister.'

'No, you don't, babe. I told you before, I understand completely. Was the same with my older brother, so I know how you feel. We'll go on our own holiday and I'll treat you to a whole new holiday wardrobe too, so you can keep up with that fancy sister of yours!'

'Really?'

'You're great at your job, I'm so proud of you. You deserve a holiday. Then you'll have something to tell all those famous people when you're doing their hair.'

'You mean nails.'

'Yeah. They're lucky to have you.' He kisses her forehead. 'I'll book something for us and then you can ask for leave.'

'Okay. Oh, Tony, thank you! You're too good to be true.'

'You're everything to me Chloe and I want to give you the best. We'll find a tropical island where we can hire a skippered yacht and go off to a private beach, watch glorious sunsets. We'll get side-by-side massages in the spa, eat lobster and caviar. Honestly, babe, you'll love it.'

Chloe is already lost in a daydream, listening to his melodic, calming voice, full of promises of paradise. He hands her the drink she's been neglecting while talking. Feeling the cold condensation on the glass against her sweaty palms, she wraps her lips firmly around the straw, smiling at him through her eyes. They fill with water when the citrus hits the back of her throat. She blinks away the fuzzy tears before he thinks she's crying and looks into his earnest face. He's waiting for her to answer a question she didn't hear.

'Uh, yes, that's right.'

His cheeky grin tells her she got away with it.

'You should have seen the nail colour Elizabeth chose. It's called Blood Red. Maybe she'll wear it for the filming.'

Stupid cow ain't even listening to me. He swallows a few times to suppress the irritation and to keep his tongue in check. He's glad the holiday suggestion worked, but the sound of her voice is grating his nerves to shreds.

To distract himself, he reaches for a buffalo wing from a sharing platter that just arrived at the table, flicking off one of those edible flowers used for decoration. She only has a few pieces as she is too busy talking about all the places she wants to go on holiday, so he eats the majority himself.

The waiter brings the card machine over to the table for payment at his signal. As the receipt prints, he hands the card back. 'Thank you, Mr Reeves.'

# CHAPTER 12

The aroma of chicken casserole emits from the dish in the centre of the dining table. Even its delicious, sensory stimulation cannot lift Chloe's mood. Everyone else says the smell is making them hungrier.

'You're acting as if she's bloody royalty! It's only Tiffany!' She gestures at her sister as if she were a lifeless object.

'Stop with your silly rivalry!' Her mother's scowl makes her feel five-years-old again. 'Besides, she doesn't come for dinner that often, do you love?'

Chloe answers before Tiffany can speak. 'Only every bloody week!'

'Oh, shush! There's plenty of casserole for both of you.'

'I already told you I'm not that hungry. Tony bought me food after work.'

'When are we going to meet the famous Tony then?!' Her father's playful expression suggests he doesn't believe there's a Tony at all, that she's made him up to sound grown up.

'Why don't you invite him round for dinner?' Her mother's suggestion is stern in contrast to the seemingly friendly invite, that reeks more of calling her bluff.

Fury coils in her stomach, ready to spring, but she curtails it enough to answer more calmly than she feels. 'He gets busy with work, but I'll ask him.'

The percussion of cutlery clinking against the plates fills the long gap in conversation that ensues, until Tiffany ends the silence. 'How's work, Chlo?'

'Really good actually. Elizabeth Mayhew, the actress, came in and asked for me personally to do her nails. Veronica might promote me to senior nail technician, and Tony said he'd take me on holiday too.'

The rapid-fire play made by Chloe catches Tiffany off guard, as she flusters over what to respond to first. Before she can get a word out, she's beaten to it.

'That's nice love.' Her mother throws a bucket of cold water over Chloe's parade with her dismissive manner, drawing a scowl from her youngest child. 'Didn't you once have that singer Elijah Robinson stay at the hotel, Tiff?'

Once more, her mother plays a trump card for Tiffany and Chloe slumps in her chair, leaning one elbow on the table for support and gives up the game that she never seems to win.

'Room 427. Geez, Henry. You've got it bad.'

'Sorry, did you say something?'

Henry jumps and clicks his mouse at the screen to close Miss Abraham's record. He squints at the dark corner near the main entrance looking for the owner of the voice.

Jim, the security guard, steps forward into the light and Henry's relieved that he's only hovering in the corner to hide the fact he's eating a sandwich while on duty. He's still looking at Henry, expecting an answer as he takes another bite.

'I'll be going for my break around midnight.' The lie inflames his face, bright enough to rival his uniform.

Jim nods his acknowledgement, then turns away, seeming not to notice.

The bubbles feel cold against her skin, before hot water soothes the bumps forming on the surface. After a long day at work and dinner at her parents' house, Tiffany sinks down into the tub and lets the scented candles take over her senses. Flames paint the calm, pale turquoise walls with majestic patterns and relaxation music full of sensual tones sends her muscles into oblivion.

Her mind takes longer to switch off than her body, though. She's so proud of Chloe, but disappointed she didn't get to tell her this evening. She reaches a bubble-covered arm out of the water to make a note to invite her to lunch this weekend in her diary that's balanced on the bath rack.

Thoughts of Layna permeate through the hot, moist air and into her conscious mind. Helping her with a bed for the night is the least she can do. With the knowledge she has done all she can for tonight, her brain waves slow and she drifts off into a blissful, water-induced sleep.

He carefully creeps along the quiet corridor. The carpet is soft beneath his feet, absorbing his footsteps. Henry looks around, breathing heavily, unsure how he got here. He rubs his sweaty palms on his trousers as he reaches room 427. Standing outside, he listens for any movement.

Knowing Miss Abraham is just on the other side of the door turns his legs to jelly. Butterflies flutter around his stomach and he struggles to stand still, such is the turmoil in his body. He visualises her sleeping peacefully, wrapped in the hotel's crisp white sheets. Closing his eyes, he loses himself in the moment, allowing the serene vision of her asleep to race his heart into overdrive.

A woman's voice startles him and he falls over his own feet as he spins around.

# CHAPTER 13

'Who's out there?'

Cold sweat patches form under his arms and on the front of his chest as he tries to think of an excuse to be there. His lips start to move but no sound comes out, as he looks for the owner of the voice.

Critical eyes peer through a tiny opening in the door. She's alarmed at finding an intruder, but her face changes as she sees his uniform. She opens the door a little bit wider, revealing hair wound around curlers and a wrinkled face heavy with sleep.

Henry uses his best boy-next-door voice. 'It's just me, Mrs Lowe.'

'Well, I'm a light sleeper so keep your noise down!'

'Okay, sorry to bother you.' Sincerity masks the astonishment from his voice. He'd barely made a sound.

Turning hot on his heels as she closes her door, he hurries down the corridor, overcome with embarrassment. He returns to his position at the front desk where he remains for the rest of the night, no longer trusting himself to be around Miss Abraham.

Chloe pulls back the duvet with such force that it lands on the floor. Cursing, she scoops it up into a ball and dumps it back on the bed.

Unable to sleep due to the anger wreaking havoc through her mind and body, she stomps around her room for a while, taking her temper out on various objects.

Her parents words and more importantly, tone of voice, continue to taunt her, fuelling her tantrum to a level never reached before. She has a one sided, silent debate with them, telling them everything she wished she had said at the dinner table. Then ridiculing herself for not having the guts to do it at the time.

Not being able to settle enough for sleep, she strides into her ensuite and strips off her clothes. Switching on the shower, she puts a hand out to check it's up to temperature before stepping under its hopefully calming stream.

At first it works. She enjoys the feeling of water cascading over her body, washing away all that is eating away at her. But it doesn't last. After a few moments, she ends up scrubbing herself red-raw, taking her anger at her family out on her own skin.

Peaceful sleep is far away in the distance. I know I'm having a nightmare, but I can't wake up. Constraining sheets wrap themselves around my arms and legs, holding me captive in my bad dream.

It's pitch black. Water swirls around my rowing boat. I'm alone and my family are each in a boat of their own. The lake is huge and I'm blinded by cloak of night. I can hear everyone talking, but I can't see them. I chip away at the dark, menacing water with my oars, hoping not to disturb any creatures lurking beneath.

Every now and then, I hear my family calling my name, pleading for me to come and save them. Their voices are hollow and echo off the water, making it impossible to tell where they are. I shout back to them. 'I'm coming Mum! I'll find you Lexi! Be brave Lyle! Where are you, Dad?'

The lake is still, yet I feel a current pulling me away. My arms ache and I can't row anymore, yet I still call out to reassure them I'm coming. My eyes strain, looking all around into a never-ending, black abyss.

Out of the darkness appears the edge of another rowing boat. I've found one of them!

As it gets closer, moonlight appears in the night sky shining its beam across the lake, eventually falling on the face at the helm. It's Cliff Garrett.

I wake up with a start and sit up, gasping for breath. I'm still looking all around for the rowing boats until the hotel coffee maker on the dresser reminds me where I am. I can't go back to sleep through fear of lapsing into the same nightmare, so I get up and switch the coffee maker on.

# CHAPTER 14

The red sports car pulls into the parking spot perfectly between the lines on the first try. Tiffany enters the Hotel Indigo with her usual verve, but slightly earlier than normal.

'Morning Henry! How was the night shift?'

'...Umm...yeah, it was very quiet.'

'Good. You can shoot off home if you like. I'll take over.' She slides behind the desk and almost brushes his hand off the mouse before he has finished clicking to log off.

'You're eager!'

'I just want to get an early start today,' she says, sitting in the seat before he has fully removed himself. 'See you tomorrow,' she adds, delivering the dismissal through a smile and staring intently at him.

He takes the hint.

As he disappears into the back office, she forces herself to be patient enough to wait until he's left the hotel entirely, before she can continue with her quest.

When he appears from the back office only a minute later in his normal clothes and carrying his bag, she lets out a sigh of relief as he says goodbye on his way past. A few clicks later, Layna is successfully checked out and the system is manipulated into thinking the bill's been paid.

As if psychic, Layna emerges from the lift at that very moment and smiles, giving her a delicate wave as she heads out the main door. She waves back, before relaxing into her swivel chair.

For the first time in several days, Jamie wakes up in his own bed. Reaching out from beneath the sheet, he grabs his watch from the bedside table. Seven thirty. He turns over, hoping to get another few hours, when he is startled by a loud knocking on his door.

'Come on, Jamie-boy! Time to go hunting!'

Peter's jubilancy is challenging at this hour. With a heavy heart and even heavier legs he drags himself out of bed and heads for the shower. He already has a headache forming at the thought of another day supporting Peter's vendetta. But he promised his mum he'd stay close to keep an eye on him. And that's exactly what he will do.

The cry of seagulls gives away their position above the shroud of fog draped over the town of Albany Cove. Henry looks up but can't see them. The long street of small terrace houses, each with a different colour door and matching drainpipe, leads him home from the Hotel Indigo.

A tall man in a grey suit is standing next to the front gate of a luxurious guesthouse called the Golden Birch that spans three of the terrace houses knocked together. He's talking into his phone.

As Henry gets closer, the man quickly puts the phone in his pocket and calls him over. 'Excuse me? Have you got a sec?'

'I'm sorry, I'm awful at directions. I send people the wrong way all the....'

Then the man stops him mid-sentence with his palm and pulls a picture out of his pocket. 'Have you seen this woman?'

Henry's heart drops from its cavity into his gut and then back up again, before drumming away at a volume he is certain the man can hear.

'Miss Abraham?' The words came out before he could stop them. In a bid to take back control, he sucks in his stomach, tightening his core, while he decides what to say next. 'Um...why are you looking for her?'

'She's an old school friend. I heard she might be in the area staying at the hotel you work at and I was hoping we could reconnect.'

'Oh, um, I recognise her but she hasn't stayed with us in over a year.' His lie felt justified. This man's fake friendliness and knowledge of him being a hotel employee despite him not being in uniform set several alarm bells off all at once; an acute warning that this isn't the innocent encounter he's portraying.

'Oh okay, well, thanks anyway.'

Equally satisfied over the man's disappointment and the successful delivery of another lie without flushing this time, he says a quick goodbye and continues on his way. As he walks, his shoulders hold square and his chest puffs out in pride, like a lion protecting its herd.

Marshall has to hold the phone away to protect his eardrum from Reeves' ferocity. Despite the distance, he can still hear the words as they leap out of the phone.

'Why'd you hang up on me?!'

'Coz the kid was coming towards me! Anyway, he said he ain't seen her in a year, so I'm coming back.'

'Told you you're wasting your time there.'

'Alright Reeves! I'll see you soon. Oh, by the way, she's using the alias Miss Abraham.'

Walking downhill away from the Hotel Indigo takes me under the fog that's formed over the higher ground. The moisture in the air sticks to my skin, preparing my already burned arms for another muggy summer day.

Just as I did on my way here, I count off how far I've come by the shops and colourful awnings as I descend. Albany Cove reaches down into a valley where it eventually meets the coast in the distance. I can see the train station tucked away among the buildings in the town centre. The steep hill tips me forward and I have to lean back to stop myself being forced into a jog.

When I finally reach the station, I use my return ticket and take a seat on the wooden bench. Commuters, all with dull, empty expressions that doing the same journey every day brings, replace the tourists of yesterday.

It's not long before the people around me start to move forward, jostling for position as the train approaches. I stand up but stay back to let them fight it out among themselves. There are not many seats left when I finally board, but I find one next to a man hiding behind his newspaper.

# CHAPTER 15

The man has hardly moved since the train set off, not even to turn the page. I feel unnerved and wish there were another seat but the train is packed now.

I begin to plot how I can get his attention to see if he's hiding for a reason. The ticket inspector appears at just the right time, so I use his emergence as a genuine reason to instigate conversation.

'The ticket inspector's here.' I say in my most helpful voice.

With a flurry, he pulls his newspaper away from his face and thanks me for letting him know. I relax into my seat knowing he is just a random commuter engrossed in the finance pages.

The morning scenery passes by in the window opposite. Fog blends the woodland into the sky perfectly. It almost looks like smoke from a forest fire dramatically engulfing its surroundings. The train winds a rickety path through and, despite it being rush hour, I know it won't take long to get back to White Hills so I can collect the car.

The classroom is quiet but for the tapping of keys by fingernails coloured in various marker pens and chewed skin from teenage angst.

Corey's fingers haven't typed a single word yet. The bullies at the back of the class, lurking in plain sight in front of his teacher, suppress his desire to top the class with his school project about volcanic eruptions. With his back exposed to them, he feels vulnerable and wishes he got to class sooner for one of the seats on the back row.

Remembering what they did to him at the start of the school year makes him feel sick. The memory happens faster and faster each time it taunts him, like being on the waltzers at the fair. With every spin, he zooms in on the face of each boy in turn, as they stand over him in the changing room. Then it's the face of the headmaster, and then his parents. They are all smiling, even the headmaster, as he arrogantly talks his way out of any embarrassment being brought on the school. The air whizzing past his ears carries the sound of his parent's laughter, making a joke about how '*boys will be boys*'.

The sick in his stomach is about to make an eruption of its own, so he asks to be excused to use the toilet. There, he empties the content of his stomach and splashes his face with cold water at the sink.

Staring at his mottled, bloodshot reflection in the mirror, Corey thinks of the sweet revenge he'll get after school. Every time he hacks his father's company, and the parents of those boys, depleting funds and deleting important files, it mends a tiny piece of his broken heart, and gives him the boost of confidence he needs to get back to class.

As he walks, he presses his lips together, silently vowing never to tell Layna where the money he gives her really comes from.

It's too early for the creepy ice cream van man or the parking inspector, so I climb back into the Audi unobserved and grip the wheel with relief. Public transport gives me the heebie-jeebies as I know it's the most likely place they'll look for me. The shelter of the car brings a renewed energy fuelled by a feeling of safety.

I turn on the engine and let some air in by winding down the windows, before I make all the necessary checks to move off. Driving away from the park, I merge onto the main street, allowing the flow of traffic to carry me to the other side of town. I have another tricky task to complete here in White Hills, so I put the radio on to distract myself from the anxiety I feel brewing.

Henry can't sleep, and it's not just because of the daylight shining through gaps in his curtains across his face. His whole body tingles while he stares bug-eyed into his fantasy world, one where he is calm and mature around Miss Abraham next time she comes to the hotel. She'll be impressed and they'll strike up a conversation, leading to dinner in a posh restaurant and then home for drinks.

But he can't bring her home. The heavy knowledge of reality weighs him down like an anchor into the deep ocean of his mattress. She'll want someone with a swanky apartment, full of modern furniture and a mini bar, not someone who still lives with his mum and sleeps in a room that looks like a child's.

From his elevated position on the captain bed he's had since he was twelve, his tired eyes inspect the posters all around the room and eventually fall on a rugby ball on the shelf, where it's been since he got it. The present from his mum was surely an attempt to make him more of a 'proper boy' with a bit of rough and tumble on a rugby field. The constant side-eye she gives him is enough for him to know she thinks he's severely lacking in the 'masculinity' department. He knows it. He thinks it. But it hurts all the more that even his own mother thinks it too.

With his infatuation suppressed by feelings of inadequacy and self-loathing, he formulates a plan to move out and find some of the maturity he lacks by living at home with his mum, still sleeping in his childhood bed. Next time Miss Abraham comes to stay, he wants to be in a position where he can ask her out.

# CHAPTER 16

I lean on the ornately carved enquiry counter breathing in the musty smell of old books, wood panels and furniture polish.

The librarian behind the counter is wearing a knitted cardigan with a heavy nametag pulling at the threads, declaring her name is Virginia Rose. Waves of auburn hair fall from her half-up, half-down hairstyle and she doesn't quite meet my eye from behind her glasses as she speaks.

'May I help you?'

I clear my throat. 'Yes please, do you have any books on the origins of basketball?'

'Yes, we do. Why don't you try one of our most popular titles, the Biographical History of Basketball by Peter C. Bjarkman? You'll find it on row S, shelf three and then follow the alphabetical order.'

'Thank you very much, that's really helpful.'

'My pleasure.'

The teal carpets are almost threadbare and I feel the outline of the floorboards beneath through my plimsolls as I navigate my way around the shelves. The book I need is tucked away at the back. A cheque for one hundred and fifty pound slips out of the inside cover, made out to Power Plus Ltd, a fictitious company created by Corey.

'Nice work, Corey,' I whisper.

A hand appears on my wrist. The grip is tight and vice-like. I almost drop the cheque as I instinctively jump back and look up into the enquiring face of Virginia Rose.

'Sorry to startle you. But I found the map you were asking about, dear,' she says, pushing it into my hand. 'Sorry it took so long,' she adds curtly, before scurrying away.

'Err...no problem,' I stammer. '...and thank you.' I have no idea what I'm thanking her for, I didn't ask for a map.

She speaks over her shoulder as if she doesn't want to be seen with me. 'You're entirely welcome.'

My brow tightens in confusion as I look over the pocket sized fold-out she gave me. Distracted, I put the book back in the wrong place on the shelf while I try to figure out the meaning behind it. Alone in the aisle, I slip the cheque into my pocket and take the map over to the study area where I sit down at one of the desks to investigate.

A woman at a nearby desk looks a little sheepish. A slight movement on the chair next to her tells me why. She's snuck a dog in, a tiny dog, in her shopping bag. I offer her a sweet smile of allegiance, indicating I'll keep her secret. Her stony face doesn't smile back though, so I look away and focus on the mystery Virginia presented me with.

It's an ordinary street map, but one whole street has been filled in with orange highlighter pen. I don't get it. I look over to the enquiry desk, but Virginia has vanished. I flip the paper over, checking all sides for a clue, and notice an additional symbol on the key at the side. It has a line added in the same orange highlighter with the words No 78. The highlighted street is Barley Lane, located near to the beach in Orchard Valley, a small town I remember visiting when I was about ten-years-old.

My parents have friends who live there, but we didn't visit them very often. Virginia is also a friend of my mother, but I don't think she knows the couple in Orchard Valley, so I struggle to make the connection. I look around for her once more but she's nowhere to be seen.

The woman with the dog has also gone, so I'm alone in the study area, bemused and with no one to ask about Barley Lane. I gather my things and head back to the car.

Outside, the air is now deliciously warm and full of the sweet smell of freshly cut grass from the playing field behind the library. The woman and her dog-in-a-bag are sitting on a bench beneath a huge cedar tree. When she sees me, she gets up and walks to the edge of the car park.

I get back into the Audi, but before I start the engine, I look at the map in my hand once more. 78 Barley Lane. A knot of uneasiness forms under my ribs. Virginia is a timid, kind-natured soul who gave us books every time she visited our family. She doesn't plot inexplicable map locations, act shadily or take risks normally. When she set up my link with Corey, she was a nervous wreck and it almost broke her innocent conscience, so I'm alarmed at her change in behaviour.

As I drive out of the library car park, I worry someone got to her. Equally, I worry when the nosey woman with the dog watches me drive away with more interest than is natural curiosity. I shift my weight in the driver's seat to find a comfortable position to alleviate the ache of anxiety around my ribs. Falling into the traffic once more, I take the shortest route back towards the city, to the Calypso Inn.

The alley behind the shop looks like a scene from a slasher film. Strewn with rubbish, offensive graffiti over the walls and the smell of urine strong and pungent. Jamie kicks a few used needles out of the way and tries not to think about the prospect of an attack by...well just anyone here.

His voice bounces of the brick walls, as would his screams should they become the stars of such a horror flick. 'Why don't we go round the front Pete? Doesn't look like there's access to the shop from back here.'

‘No J, too many people about on the street. This way is better. The access is over that wall. Give us a leg up!’ he demands.

Jamie hooks his hands together so Peter can get on top of a wheelie so he can climb over the wall behind it. Jamie’s hopes of not having to follow are dashed when his brother holds out a hand to pull him up too. They both mount the wall as if it were some gallant, hero-carrying stallion set to charge of into a sunset after defeating the bad guys. Before dropping to the ground on the other side with a thud that crushes the fantasy under the force.

‘Let’s try the back door.’

Crouching down, they approach the door like two panthers about to set upon their prey. Peter reaches up and tries the handle. Its locked.

Jamie is relieved. The dread of a confrontation has made him an anxious wreck. But he doesn’t show it on his face.

‘Damn.’ Peter spits.

‘Looks like we’re gonna have to go around the front after all, Pete.’

Peter doesn’t reply but begrudgingly makes his way back to the wall, where they repeat the leg-up up tactics to climb back over. Peter almost crashes through the lid of the wheelie bin as he lands on the other side, sending it across the alley with him on top, surfing the rubbish wave as he tries to keep balance.

'That was close!' he yells, as the bin comes to an abrupt halt when the wheel catches on a stone. He jumps down and pushes the bin back to the wall for Jamie to use. Brushing the escapade off their clothes as they walk, they make their way back through the alley to the front of the shop.

The lights are off and the door is locked. They peer through, trying to make out any kind of movement inside.

'Is this definitely the shop Garrett's guys almost caught her at?' Jamie asks.

'Yeah, definitely. The guy who runs it used to work with Layna's dad.'

'How do you know that?' Jamie enquires.

'It says the owners name on their website. His Linked-In profile says he used to work at Minster's. That's where Layna's dad used to work after he left the military.'

Jamie is silenced by his brothers attention to detail in their quest to find Layna. It seems Peter's determination is undwindling. After a few moments chewing over their situation, he attempts to flatter Peter's ego for the idea to come here, and shrug off the fact that it's another fail. 'It was yesterday morning they were here, you'd think he would have opened as normal today.'

Without realising, Peter buys into it. 'They must've scared him good and proper! No sign of him though, is there?' Peter concedes. 'He probably shut the shop up sharpish, and has gone into hiding!'

'So where shall we try next?'

# CHAPTER 17

The black and white cat licks its lips, eyeing up the uneaten sandwich on the plate in front of its owner.

With her palms together in prayer, Virginia closes her eyes, pleading for forgiveness. 'I'm sorry Layna. I know you said not to....'

Trembling thighs beneath the table trigger her to get up and move around. She busies herself feeding Jester and Cleo a snack, then dusts the knick-knacks on the Welsh dresser. A framed photo of Layna's family draws her eye and she picks it up. The happy family smiling at her forces tears to drop onto the glass, before she smears them away with the duster. 'Please forgive me, Rosa. I was only trying to help her.'

With tear-stained, wet cheeks, she drops into the armchair, exhausted from her emotions. Jester and Cleo jump up and snuggle in, sensing her sadness.

'Do you think I've done the right thing?' she asks them.

Two pairs of critical cats' eyes condemn her.

The Mercedes cuts through the chalky-white limestone verges as if it's the only car on the road. Marshall smiles as the other cars move out of the way and allow him through, enjoying the power trip.

The sign for White Hills flashes past, prompting Reeves to air his thoughts. 'Not sure about this kid, Marsh. We might be wasting our time.'

'Yeah, but the Lawrences watch him all the time so he must be involved somehow.'

'I guess. Good thing he's just a kid; he'll probably break with one punch!'

'Are you serious?! I was thinking more along the lines of buddy up to him. We've seen him play basketball in the park. We could start a game and ask him to join in, let him win a few shots and get him on side.'

The snort of disgust echoes in the back of Reeves' throat as he looks out of the side window, a gesture meant to dismiss Marshall's idea, but leads to a double take of a vehicle coming in the opposite direction. 'STOP THE CAR!'

Startled, Marshall tugs on the wheel involuntarily, causing them to swerve at speed. 'What the....'

Reeves cuts him short. 'Turn around now!'

'Reeves, have you lost your mind?! We could've crashed!'

'That was her! Driving that Audi. Go back!'

'What do you mean her?!'

'I mean Layna, Marshall!'

'What're you talking about?! Layna can't drive! No one's ever mentioned that before.'

'I'm telling you that was her!' He turns in his seat trying to get another look, but the Audi is already out of sight.

'You sure?'

'Yeah! Get off at the next slip road and turn around.'

Reeves' response convinces Marshall enough for his foot to ease on the accelerator on the approach to the slip road. 'Okay. You'd better be right, Reeves! But even if it was her, we'll never catch up now.'

'But she's going back to the city! If she goes anywhere near The Calypso Inn, it'll only take a couple of questions to someone who took our message to heart, and we'll have her!' The Mercedes' suspension is thoroughly tested as Reeves bounces around in his seat like an agitated toddler on a long journey.

Marshall humours him with a wry grin. 'Yeah, we'll see, Reeves.'

Backstreets form a labyrinth behind the Calypso Inn, so I have plenty of options on where to park out of sight. I put my jacket on and sling my bag over my shoulder. Then I pull my hair through the gap in a baseball cap like a ponytail and walk with my head down. The warm air swirls around me as I approach the Calypso Inn, and I hold onto my hat for fear of it lifting off to reveal my identity.

Feeling the beat of tropical music as I descend the stairs to the basement, I enter the bar as casually as I can and sit in a corner table at the back. Being lunchtime, there are more people here for food than there are drinkers.

Farrell isn't behind the bar. The woman serving is Shirleen, his ex-girlfriend. I hope that doesn't mean he's not here and she's covering for him. I'm biting my lip with angst when another member of staff appears at my table asking what I'd like to drink. I don't recognise this man, so he must be new. He's tall and muscular, and immediately I worry someone has infiltrated Farrell's circle.

He disarms me with a charming smile and I realise that he's a relative of Farrell's; the resemblance is undeniable. Despite his lack of dreadlocks, the smile is the same and so is his friendly demeanour.

'Something fruity with a twist of lime,' I answer him, playfully, contrary to the nervous knots in my stomach.

He laughs with a smooth, velvety tone. 'Can you be more specific, my love?!'

'You must be new here.' All the other staff are aware of the code drink order I gave.

He nods. 'Yeah, quite new, but I've been here long enough to know you're not a regular. I'm Davies.'

'Nice to meet you, Davies,' I don't offer my name in return. 'Ask the manager, he knows what drink I'm referring to.'

'Okay, my love. I'll be right back,' he says, smiling at me as he leaves.

I watch the light catching his shaven head as he disappears out the back and feel more hopeful that Farrell is here, otherwise he would've said. Opening a cocktail menu, I use it to hide my face until a dark shadow in the shape of a large man falls over my table.

'You've got some balls, girl!'

I breathe out, relieved to see my friend and I'm put at ease by his humour. 'You've only just discovered this?!'

'Well, no I've always known you're a gutsy gal! But look, you can't stay here. Come with me now.'

Something in Farrell's voice makes me leave the shelter of my corner table immediately and follow him to the hallway out the back of the bar, out of sight of the customers. It's dark as the walls are red embossed wallpaper and the only light source is a cheap bulb on the low ceiling, casting a coral hue over Farrell's face.

'It's not safe for you here. They were here, Garrett's latest duo, making all kinds of threats. You know I will never give you up to them, but I can't promise my whole clientele will have the same loyalty to you.'

His childhood Jamaican accent seems stronger with the seriousness in his voice. My heart races as I look around for an escape route. 'I only came to ask if you could cash this for me.'

I hand him the cheque.

'Wait right here.'

Farrell disappears back into the bar area and I'm left hopping from foot to foot, wringing my hands together, eager to get out. The clock on the wall is playing tricks on my mind. With each tick, the hands go forward, then backwards, time literally standing still.

Eventually Farrell reappears with a wad of cash, which he thrusts at me. I start to thank him but he pushes me backwards, ushering me to the back door. 'What are you doing?!'

'Saving your bacon!'

He slams the door in my face.

# CHAPTER 18

Peter is talking in riddles. 'Come on, Jamie-boy, figure it out! What places have we almost caught her before?'

Jamie squirms in his seat, as if changing position will help him to figure out what Peter is talking about. 'It was all different places,' he offers weakly, knowing it's not the answer Peter wants.

'Yeah, but they all had something in common. It's obvious!'

The sound of the radio distracts Jamie, filling the empty space in his head with the nasal tones of pop music. The blankness manifests through his face, like he's struggling to answer a million-pound question on a game show. His lack of answer riles Peter, as he knew it would.

'COME ON!'

'I don't know what you mean, Pete.'

In a rare moment of empathy, Peter gives Jamie a hint. 'I mean what *types* of places?'

Sweat gathers in the creases of Jamie's forehead, sticking them together in a permanent frustrated frown. It feels like a trick question, so whichever answer he gives is bound to anger his brother.

Peter rolls his eyes. '*Busy* places!'

Jamie does a slow nod, still not quite understanding the relevance of the answer. 'So how does that help us?'

'She's always in busy places, right? Not hiding out somewhere quiet. Nah, people are too nosey in quiet places. So what does she do? She gets lost in crowds!' he says, revelling in his own cleverness.

'Surely that makes it more difficult for us to spot her.'

'Don't think so negative, Jamie-boy! It helps us because we just have to hang around the busiest places until we see her! Think train stations, shopping centres, bus stations...'

Jamie swallows the words down with a gulp before his mouth can blurt out that it's a terrible idea. Last time he told Peter a suggestion wasn't any good, he got a fist for his trouble, so he keeps quiet and allows him to bask in his 'great plan'.

Music fills the air around the open-top jeep, leaving sound-trails as Davies and I blaze through the city streets. The mid-afternoon sun heats the leather seat to a scorching temperature that feels like it's melting onto the back of my thighs.

We seem to be heading out of the city but I can't be sure as Davies won't tell me where we're going. Every time I ask, he just smiles and avoids the question. So far, he's told me the story of how he got this jeep, how he came over from Jamaica to work for his cousin Farrell, and how he hopes to open his own bar in the future, all in an attempt to fill the conversation without answering.

The speed at which we are travelling doesn't alter as the jeep traverses a winding road along the cliff tops outside of the city. I can't enjoy the scenery as I'm so nervous. When the next song finishes, I try again with Davies. 'So where are we going?'

'You'll see!'

His beaming smile is infectious and although I'm annoyed at him for eluding the question again, I can't help but smile back as I press on. 'What's Farrell up to?'

'You'll see!'

He laughs this time, before singing along with Sheryl Crow's Run Baby Run. I wonder if he realises the significance of the lyrics he is singing.

Not knowing where I'm going makes me fidget and I keep adjusting my seatbelt even though it was fine in its original position. I try to peel my legs off the leather seats. All the secrecy means that Farrell knows it's something I won't agree to if he told me, so I can't settle until this journey is over.

Corey'd had enough. The school was oppressive and triggering. Every day, he faces his demons to attend but today he's run out of fight.

The walk home is therapeutic. He takes his time, breathes in some fresh air and collects his thoughts. He really hopes that Virginia and Layna don't find out what he's doing. The last thing he wants is to upset his favourite librarian and his cool older friend.

Virgina asked him to help Layna, and he does, he justifies to himself, just not in the way she thinks he is. Layna needs money. And he needs to steal from his father's bank account and the parents of his tormentors at school, because it feels so good and in a strange way, healing. The revenge tastes sweet on his tongue.

He's used his skills to bypass multiple companies supposed security systems and gone undetected quite easily. So far. He smiles to himself, which a passing elderly gentleman misconstrues as a greeting and returns the gesture. Another person I've fooled, Corey thinks.

Despite his jubilant exterior singing along to the radio, Davies is keeping a close eye on his rear-view mirror, making sure no one is following them. After his latest glance confirms they are safe with no one tagging along behind, he sneaks a look at his shotgun rider instead.

She's so self-assured and confident for someone so young and with such troubles that Farrell has given her a bundle of money and asked him to take her to a safe place. He'd told him very little of her background but obviously feels responsible for her, so if she's in trouble, he'll do anything he can to keep her safe too.

She keeps asking him where they are going, but Farrell told him not to tell her until they get there. Apparently, she's nervous about where she can hide out and probably wouldn't have agreed to come with him if she knew. So he did his best to allay her fears without really answering her questions. The smirk she gave each time tells him she is playing along good naturedly.

After climbing many a hill and entering a residential area, he turns the Jeep onto a street overshadowed by yew trees. Half way along a row of bungalows, he stops outside one with a neat front garden full of potted plants and turns off the engine.

# CHAPTER 19

I watch the rocking chair sway back and forth gently in the conservatory full of bright tropical flowers and huge jungle-like plants. Through the steam from my hot cup of tea, the concerned eyes of Farrell's grandmother are watching me as if she's trying to read my mind. I have my feet tucked underneath me on the cane chair, in a bid to appear more relaxed than I feel.

Farrell would never put his grandmother at risk, so he must be certain there's no way they'll find me here. At first, I wasn't sure she was happy to have me stay. Her face was hard and set in an unreadable expression. As soon as she spoke though, I heard the same friendly undertone and saw the soft heart that's apparent in all of Farrell's family.

Through the tea-mist, Ava Gregory is trying to read the facial expression of the young girl Farrell bought to her for help. Though she seems more settled than the nervous, timid girl who arrived, she's still gazing off into a distant world where her troubles clearly consume her.

Farrell didn't explain much on the phone, just that he was sending a young girl over who needs a place to stay for a while. As yet, she hasn't yet been able to gage exactly what's going on, though she can see the sadness and fear in her eyes. She hasn't tried asking her any questions so far, as she clearly needs time to adjust to her new surroundings.

She puts her knitting down and quietly potters around the conservatory watering her plants and picking at non-existent weeds to give the girl some space.

Something about being in this lush, sensory conservatory slows my brainwaves to a pace matching the trickling water fountain in the corner. When Ava first led me in here, it was like entering paradise. She told me how she purposely keeps the temperature and humidity high as most of her plants are from the Caribbean. The seductive, intoxicating aroma forces me into a state of relaxation I rarely afford myself.

I watch her sprinkle water over a pot of yellow flowers. My mind leaps to a place where I really don't want to go. I rub my fingers over my forehead, as if it will somehow halt the memory forming inside my mind. Yellow flowers remind me of the last time I saw my family. Mum's favourite flowers, freshly picked from our garden, in a vase on the patio table.

I don't want to have this memory, yet it's playing out on the inside of my eyes where only I can see. Yellow flowers.

Yellow flashes. Bullets. Screams. Yellow bile, with yellow pain. Yellow roses around the grave.

Yellow was the day my life changed and I feel a tear escape, tickling my freckles and landing on the back of my hand. I look up to see droplets from Ava's watering can trickling over the delicate petals and down the stem, mimicking my own teardrops.

Ava feels the pain emitting from Layna's aura, circling around the conservatory, looking for solace among the soothing plants and flowers. She wishes she could help the girl more than just providing a bed for a few nights.

'Are you sure the police can't help you, child?'

Sad, troubled eyes gaze at her as she shakes her head. 'Too many informants.'

'Maybe we can arrange for you to stay with our relatives in Jamaica?' she offers.

'Thank you Ava, but I can't leave the city as my family are here.'

Confusion stops Ava from continuing with her problem-solving quest. She could have sworn Farrell said she didn't have any family. Tears shine in the girls eyes. She doesn't want to make her cry, so she doesn't ask anything more. She gets on with watering the plants but continues to think of ways in which she or Farrell can help, feeling a sense of obligation passed on from her grandson.

The Mercedes creeps around the backstreets near the Calypso Inn, looking for the dark blue Audi or Layna. As the silver nose of the car peeks around the next corner, Marshall and Reeves both lean forward and see the young woman in denim shorts at the same time.

Reeves points. 'That's her!' and makes a move to open his door before the car has even stopped.

'Wait Reeves! Wait till she turns round, we need to be sure!'

'It's her! That money's ours Marshall! And I won't have to spend any more time with that dumb cow in Albany Cove who talks about nail polish all day!'

'She's turning around!'

It's not her. They both drop back into their seats at the same time, defeated.

'I knew it was too good to be true,' says Marshall.

Reeves punches the inside of the door.

'Steady! This is my car!'

'Alright! But let's stay nearby. I'm still one hundred percent certain that was Layna driving and she could still come here.'

'But you're always a hundred percent sure, Reeves! And half the time it turns out not to be her at all! So you'll forgive me if I can't get too excited until I see her with my own eyes!'

Marshall uses one of the parking bays next to a garage to turn the car around in order to park up. As he spins the wheel, he exhales his disappointment and distrust.

Reeves closes his eyes and rubs his face with his hands, leaving them in place for a moment, enjoying the sensation of travelling blind. But then he's thrown forward with force when Marshall slams on the brakes and they skid to a halt.

'WHAT THE HECK?!' He uncovers his eyes and looks at Marshall, who is staring through the windscreen with his mouth open.

Reeves looks out too, and grins, which in turn becomes a throaty chuckle. Marshall joins in and sinister laughter takes over the sombre mood.

The Audi is parked straight ahead of them, tucked away down the opposite end of the road. They park on a nearby backstreet under the cover of an old stone arch, where they can watch the Audi discreetly. There's no way it can leave without them seeing.

Marshall turns off the engine and they settle back into their seats, preparing to wait it out.

# CHAPTER 20

A bowl of piping hot pasta appears on the desk in front of Henry. Oozing with red sauce and melted cheese, his stomach responds with a rumble as he struggles to remember when he last ate.

'You need pick me up, no?' Fabien the chef offers in his broken English, accented with French.

'Thanks, Fabien.'

On his second nightshift in a row, the lack of sleep in between has left him slumped over the front desk. It's taking all his effort just to push the mouse around. He picks up the spoon and watches the pasta shapes desperately cling together as he tries to pry them apart.

At this moment, an idea strikes him, snapping him into a bolt upright position like a steel rod splint shot down his spine. He drops the spoon, pushes the bowl away and types the room 427 into his computer. The information displayed has him reaching for the key and hurrying towards the lift.

As the doors close, encapsulating him in another fantasy-fuelled escapade, he looks down at his feet with shame. 'What are you doing, Henry? You're acting like a school boy.'

The lift pings for the fourth floor and he steps out. The feeling of déjà vu consumes him as he inches along the corridor and slips inside room 427 before Mrs Lowe, or anyone else, can confront him. He locks the door from the inside and leans back on it, eyes wide and body trembling.

Headlights illuminate the dark backstreet. The engine of the Audi A4 purrs quietly against the faint hum of the city at this hour.

'Yeeeeaaaaah!' Marshall's low, rasping celebration harmonises with the Mercedes engine as he starts it up in readiness to follow.

'That's definitely her. Same hair. Same colour top as this morning.' Reeves claps his hands together for dramatic effect.

Marshall edges the Mercedes forward out of its hiding place, and they follow at a safe distance. The Audi leads them onto a main road.

'Hunters Way. How apt!' says Marshall.

Reeves sniggers. 'Hope she turns down a quiet street again, somewhere no one will hear her screams!'

Smiling eyes reflect from the rear-view mirror into the dark interior of the car. Davies told her this top makes her eyes sparkle. Thoughts of Davies's smile send a giddy feeling from her stomach down to her toes, making her foot jolt on the pedal.

Her smile fades as she realises the silver Mercedes behind her has followed her around the same roundabout twice after she missed her exit. Driving especially slow for a fifty mile an hour road so the Mercedes can catch up, she squints into her mirror to see who's driving.

Oddly, it hangs back, and an uneasy feeling makes her adjust her driving position in preparation for a chase. She decides to test them by driving around in circles in a nearby residential area at a monotonous speed. Sure enough, the Mercedes follows at the same pace.

'It's over, Reeves. She's clocked us.'

'No, keep going! I'm tellin' ya, she didn't notice. Too busy trying to navigate the roundabout to see us.'

'I don't know, Reeves. She's driving really slowly.'

'It's just cause she's lost. Look, she's turning into a quiet residential street!'

'You wanna stop her here?! You're outta your mind, Reeves! Too many houses. Someone will hear!'

'We don't have much choice right now do we?! In a few more streets she could be on the dual carriageway and we'll have missed the chance to pull her over.'

'Well...yeah but...'

'No buts, just pull her over! Or run her off the road! There's no one around, everyone's in bed!'

'What if she screams?!'

'We'll say we're undercover police doing a traffic stop! Just do it now, Marsh!'

Marshall presses hard on the accelerator. Overtaking the Audi, he blocks it against a high curb at an angle that also prevents the driver's door from opening fully.

# CHAPTER 21

Reeves is out of the car before Marshall. He tries the door to the Audi. It's locked. 'Open this door, darlin'. Games over!'

Marshall joins him just as the window winds down.

Slowly, the face comes into view. Although she bears a remarkable resemblance to Layna, it's not her.

Unwilling to admit defeat again, Reeves presses her. 'Where's Layna?'

'Who?'

'Ah, come on, love,' says Marshall. 'What were you doing at the Calypso Inn?'

'I work there!'

'You work there?' Reeves' voice is quiet in resignation.

She mocks him with her response, moving her head side to side. 'Yes, darlin', I work there!'

Marshall and Reeves exchange a look, before muttering incomprehensible words of supposed apology and they back away from her car.

Lights pop on all along the street and curtains twitch as people look out to see what the racket is.

Having jumped out of her car the minute they pulled away, the waitress is still yelling at Marshall and Reeves as the silver Mercedes leaves the scene. Gesturing, she hopes they see in their rear-view mirror what a fuss she is making.

As soon as they're out of sight, she climbs back into her car, ignoring the enquiring eyes of the neighbours she woke up. She turns the car around and heads back to the Calypso Inn, keeping an eye out for the Mercedes along the way.

After parking the Audi back in the same spot, she goes inside to find Davies. 'I think I fooled them!'

'Well done, Carmel! Hopefully we bought her some time.'

The Mercedes turns into the St Ives Hotel, where it goes all the way around the circular water fountain in the front, right back to the exit onto the road.

'What are we doing in here?!'

'Turning around, Reeves! I wanna get out of the city!' He swings a hard left onto the main road, throwing Reeves against the door, reminding them both to put their seatbelts on.

'Alright fine, but put your foot down!'

'Calm down! I don't want to get caught speeding!'

'I can guarantee one of them nosey neighbours has called the police and they're probably on the way already!'

'Yeah, and if they're looking for a silver Merc and see one speeding past, we might as well hand ourselves in now! Even if it's only a report of a small roadside incident, as soon as they look at your rap sheet, and mine, we're done!'

'Yeah, yeah, okay. Just get us away as quick as you can.'

The smell of fresh linen should be relaxing, but I'm enthralled in another terrifying nightmare. The pillow is bouncy beneath my head as I thrash around trying to force myself to wake up.

The visions are blurred but the voices are real, so are the faces that appear with clarity amidst the hazy backgrounds. News reports and memories twist together inside my mind, and I helter-skelter around each one until I'm dizzy.

A female reporters' voice, accusatory and stern, tells the world that the oldest daughter is missing, presumed to be the shooter. Me. She means me. I try to yell back at her that she's wrong, but no sound comes out.

A male reporter declares a charity event a success due to a sizable donation by a generous businessman, Cliff Garrett. His arrogant face basks in the glory, until he slowly starts to go fuzzy, morphing into a girl's face. Stephanie Lawrence.

My beautiful friend, smiling and care-free. Then a bullet hits her forehead and the smile is gone. The men's voices counting out the three Raye children, certain they got them all. Finally, I wake from the anguish, crying aloud.

Sitting up, I come face-to-face with Farrell as a boy, all goofy and happy, carefully framed and hanging proudly on the wall opposite. I untangle my fingers from the stringy tassels of the candlewick bedspread and concede I'm far too on edge to sleep.

I should've listened to my gut when Farrell called to say his waitress, who just happens to look like me, had an encounter with Garrett's men. Thankfully she is ok and no harm came to her. I had wanted to leave right away but Ava's face and pleading voice forced me into an emotional tug of war; pleasing those who have been most kind to me or my natural instinct to run. Not wanting to hurt her feelings, I've tried to settle for the night, but I can't. Davies is taking care of returning the courtesy car, so I leave Ava a thank you note and set off on foot.

The offbeat rhythm of the reggae anthem ringtone disturbs the stillness of the dark room. A hand fumbles for the source, knocking over a glass of water on the bedside table.

'Hello?'

'Davies? Grandma called. Layna's gone!'

He sits up, immediately awake. 'Gone where? What time is it?'

'It's 3.30am and I've no idea. Gran found a note when she got up to use the loo.'

'She can't have got that far on foot.'

'Yes, she could. She avoids public transport so she walks for miles around the city every day. And it looks like she's been walking for a few hours already.'

'Any idea where she'll go?'

'I'm not sure, she has a lot of hiding places and I only know a few of them.'

'That girl needs help.'

'I know.'

# CHAPTER 22

It's the crack of dawn and my legs are damp from the sweet morning dew that's settled across the field, caught on the petals of tiny wildflowers cupped like hands. Strands of tall grass lick at my legs, and I'm thankful for the dog-walkers who created a pre-trodden trail for me to follow.

The countryside offers me a sure-fire capture-free journey knowing they will not be looking for me in a random field in the early hours of the morning. It's so refreshing to be free of the anxiety that usually weighs my shoulders into a rounded slouch, and I find I'm walking taller with my head held high.

It doesn't take long for the sun to rise just high enough to spread light throughout the pale dusk. I hear its voice echoing through the rays, calling my name, telling me to keep going towards the golden rivers forming across the sky. Staring hard at it, I use its power to draw me through the field, to the city creeping into view on the horizon.

The sound of a car door slamming right next to his head wakes Jamie from his fitful sleep with such a start that he chokes on the saliva in the back of his throat. Pain shoots down his neck from sleeping with his head leaning against the window.

A woman has parked in the space next to them. She's already yelling at the kids in the back seat as she gets out, exasperated as only a mother juggling a lack of rest and being in the confined space of a car with toddlers can be.

Sleep fog clouds his mind as he tries to remember where they are. He looks around and recognition takes hold as he sees the row of log cabin style retail units under large western frontier signage. The Goldmine retail park is where they came last night following Peter's idea of looking in busy places.

He looks over at Peter, who's out cold, slumped against the door, while rubbing his neck to ease the pain. Pressing his knuckles into the muscles forces the cramp to eventually release.

Peter is stirring at the disturbance. 'Tell that woman to put a sock in it, J.' His coarse voice is full of sleep and agitation already.

Jamie fires up the air conditioning, hoping to freshen the air and the mood at the same time. When Peter wakes up annoyed it doesn't bode well for the day ahead, and he'll take the brunt of it as always. He tries sweetening his brother by giving him the power over their next move. 'Do you wanna stay here, Pete, or go somewhere else?'

He replies through a wide, mouth-splitting yawn. 'Let's try The Oceanside.'

The splinter enters my skin and all the little sensors on my leg inform my body of a foreign object. As I jump down from the stile, I inspect the wound site and see that it's gone in at such a close angle that it's too hard for me to dig out here and now. I leave it lodged in my leg and ignore the soreness forming.

The woods ahead look impenetrable and foreboding. I consider if I can afford the extra time it will take to walk several miles around them, or whether I can cut through and hope it's not as dense as it looks. I can't see any trails, so I'll be doing the groundbreaking myself. The morning sun is fierce already, tipping the decision in favour of cover from the trees and the shortest route.

The inside of the woods is at least cool and shaded, and the heady scent of forest earth is calming. I try to avoid the sharp branches and prickly leaves but inevitably, I'm scratched all over. It's so quiet in here but for the sound of the birds chattering high up in the trees and the unmistakeable sound of a brook that I eventually find through a cluster of wide trees covered in ivy.

At the edge, I look around for a way to get across. There's a set of rocks sticking out of the water downstream that I use as stepping-stones. After a few hairy moments with slippery moss and a wobbly rock that tries its best to tip me into the water, I make it to the other side.

A bird lets out a sharp cry above my head just as my foot touches solid ground. My heart jumps sending shockwaves down my arms and legs, and I almost fall backwards into the water. By gracelessly flapping my arms, I regain my balance. I look up at the fluttering in the tree canopy above, just as a few leaves float down around me, having dislodged from the branches in the fracas.

Unnerved, I run quickly, barging my way through the bushes like a seasoned explorer, unafraid of what lurks beneath or getting stung by nettles. I'm able to make good progress at this pace and eventually reach the edge of the wood. Without picking up any more splinters, I climb over the fence and feel the bounce of grass in the field on the other side beneath my feet.

The view overlooking the bay area is spectacular from the field on top of the cliff. To get down to the bay, I walk towards the horizon, where the blue ocean meets the blue sky, picking off all the sticky burrs in my hair and on my clothes as I walk.

The strong smell of roasted coffee circulates the tables outside the café across from the Calypso Inn. Marshall and Reeves keep a watchful eye on the bar as they sip the hot liquid.

Invigorated by the caffeine, Reeves thinks aloud. 'She has to have been here. It's too much of a coincidence for my liking. And I'm still certain it was Layna driving that car the first time we saw it.'

'Nah, it was the girl from the bar.'

'Think about it though! I see a girl that looks like Layna driving a car that just happens to go to the Calypso Inn? I think the only coincidence is the barmaid looking like Layna.'

'But Layna wasn't old enough to have a driving licence when all this started and she couldn't have got one since she's been on the run.'

'She coulda got a fake one,' Reeves holds his hands out to emphasise the easiness of his suggestion. 'I could get one tomorrow if I wanted.'

'True. I do think there's something in it.'

Reeves slurps his coffee noisily as he watches Marshall's invisible cogs churning over the second-guessing game. He can feel him coming around to his way of thinking.

'I'm not saying you're right, Reeves, but just for a second, let's say you are. What would happen now?'

'What do you mean?'

'Well, barmaid-girl goes back to Farrell and tells him she got pulled over by two guys who thought she was Layna.'

‘Right.’

‘Farrell tells Layna what happened. Layna hears that someone who looks like her was stopped, so...,’ he rolls his hands around indicating Reeves should finish his sentence.

‘So... she needs to look different?’

‘Yeah!’ said Marshall with a grin. ‘It’s a long shot, but if that’s right, you know where she’ll go!’

‘Yeah, that salon! Let’s go!’ Reeves’ eyes are bright with excitement and he stands up before he has even finished his short sentence.

They head back to the car with renewed optimism. The Mercedes leaves its space and gets into the lane for The Oceanside Shopping Centre in the South Bay area.

So enchanted are they by the notion they have a new lead, and a good one, neither of them notice a battered old Volvo moving into the line of traffic just a couple of cars behind them.

# CHAPTER 23

Ten-foot arch windows capture a view of the lustrous ocean in the South Bay. I look out as I ride the escalator up to the second floor of The Oceanside Shopping Centre. The beach looks busy already, full of colour and life against a backdrop of beige sand.

As I reach the top, I look down at my clothes, dishevelled from my battle with the woods. The embarrassment burns from within as I enter the trendy salon, Essence. The reception desk is in the middle of the room. I lean against it and watch all the beautifully put-together stylists at work, further fuelling my insecurity over my own appearance.

I catch the eye of an attractive older lady whose hair is piled up with highlighting foils. The rest of her hair is jet black and I wonder what colour is developing to add contrast. Behind her, the tall and slender stylist works quickly and efficiently as she finishes the last strand. She hands the lady a magazine, then turns her attention to me.

As she approaches, I'm at odds as to where to look first, either the glittery silver belt breaking up the otherwise monotone black outfit, or the flock of shocking pink spiked hair. Tattoos cover her arms from her wrists to her shoulders.

She gives me the once over, and the look on her face tells me she knows I've literally been through a few hedges backwards. Her lip-gloss shade matches her hair and catches the light as she speaks. 'Morning, Miss Browne!'

'Good Morning, Maisie.'

'What'll it be today?'

'I fancy a bit of a change.'

'Follow me,' she says, with a flick of her pink spikes gesturing towards the curtained end of the salon, where they cater for those with medical conditions such as cancer or alopecia in private. It's the perfect place for me to undergo a transformation. Maisie slowly pulls the curtain across the rail so we are hidden from view.

Jamie has to circle the car park twice before finding a space. The Oceanside Shopping Centre is heaving. It'll be hard to find just one young girl among the crowds, but he still goes along with Peter's plan without complaint. Once parked, they go inside and Peter sits at a table in a roped-off section outside a café just inside the door.

Before Jamie can sit down, Peter gestures towards the counter inside. 'Get us some drinks J.' Then he gets straight to work scanning the faces coming in and out of the main door.

As always, Jamie does as he's told and approaches the counter inside. After only a few moments in the queue, a scream outside forces him to abandon his position next in line and hurry out of the café.

The table where Peter was sitting is now empty. A brawl is happening nearby, with Peter in the centre, hands gripping the forearms of a young girl who was seemingly walking past outside the roped section when he accosted her. She's screaming on the top of her lungs and several people are trying to pull him off her, including her group of friends who are all shouting as they tug at his arms.

For a second Jamie stands in shock. Peter's rage has literally made him blind. Blind to the fact that this was not Layna, and blind to the fact that even if it was, he cannot simply grab her in the middle of a busy shopping centre without people reacting and trying to stop him.

As the realisation dawns across Peter's face, Jamie snaps out of his shock to seize the opportunity to step in. 'Come on, Pete. That's not her. Let her go.' He has to shout above all the other voices vying for the right to be heard.

Peter releases the girl, offering a feeble apology as he lets go. 'Sorry, I thought you were someone else...'

Why he thought that was acceptable has Jamie questioning his brother's sanity more than ever before. The people around would have reacted the same way even if it was Layna.

As the onlookers disperse, glaring at Peter as they back away, Jamie takes a hold of his brother's arm to indicate he has control over the situation so no one needs to call security or the police. He speaks quietly to placate the outburst. 'Come and sit down, Pete.'

'Really thought that was her...' Peter's response is quiet too, as he slowly lowers himself down into his chair.

Jamie feels the dirty looks from customers at the surrounding tables, as they also settle back down in their seats. He allows their judgement to bounce off him and stares at his brother. Watching the emotion screw Peter's features up into creases defined by grief and anger, he can't help but feel sorry for him.

'Just take it easy, Pete. Even if it was her, we can't be grabbing her in the middle of a crowd like this. You've gotta be more careful, hey? I'll get us some drinks.'

Peter nods but doesn't speak. He just taps his middle finger nervously on the table.

Jamie keeps his eyes locked on his brother as he rejoins the queue to be served.

On the third floor of The Oceanside Shopping Centre, the vintage sweet shop has the scent of effervescent sugar powder that instantly transports anyone who enters back to their childhood.

The girls sandals clip clop across the replica Victorian tiled floor and up to the counter, where she requests a special box of chocolate truffles and a bag of sugar-coated sweets. She looks all around as she waits, taking in the old fashioned fairground style artwork across the top of each shelf and the Olde English writing used to label each display.

The shop assistant uses a portable step to reach up to the shelf behind the counter for the box of truffles. With an exaggerated show of precision, she places them onto a pile of luxury wrapping paper before looking up at her customer.

'Are they for you or a gift for someone?' she asks.

'No, they're for a friend.' The raven-haired girl replies curtly, as if the shop assistant had asked some wildly inappropriate personal question.

'Shall I wrap them for you?' The eagerness displayed through wide eyes and beaming smile, still fully evident in the shop assistants demeanour.

'If your quick about it.' Another curt response.

Only then does the shop assistants enthusiasm for providing a good service wane a little. Her next actions are rather more subdued, as she pulls the lever on an antique cash register and the tiny bell rings as the drawer opens. She then passes the card machine across the counter, leaving the raven-haired girl wondering what was the point of the till register.

The shop assistant hands her the bag and offers a more meagre smile as she thanks her for the purchase. The woman practically snatches the bag, without so much as a thank you, and leaves the shop in a hurry. The smile vanishes from the shop assistants face as she watches her go, wondering if everyone is going to be that rude today.

# CHAPTER 24

I'm adjusting to my life as a blonde inside The Glacier restaurant, on the fourth floor of the Oceanside Shopping Centre. The view over the bay is even better from here and I sit back against the bench seat, comfortable in the knowledge that even if Cliff Garrett, or one of his goons, walked in right now they won't recognise me.

I take a bite of my toasted cheese and onion sandwich. In mid-chew, a voice interrupts and I'm left with cheese strings hanging unceremoniously from my lips as I look up at the woman at the next table.

'Aren't the plants in here unusual?' she says.

I look around as if noticing for the first time the many planters that fill the gaps between the tables and benches. 'Oh um...yes, they are...' I say through pieces of toast, trying not to spray the crumbs over my table. Dabbing at my mouth with a napkin, I hope the green from The Glacier logo doesn't transfer to my skin via the grease.

She doesn't look away and raises her eyebrows in expectance of me to expand, but all I really want to do is finish my food and get out of here. I look out of the window to indicate my part in the conversation is over. Her disgruntlement at my dismissal is evident in her loud sniff of discontent. I hope she's just a lonely woman looking for conversation, but she's making me nervous.

I eat the last piece of sandwich in one mouthful instead of two that I'd normally use for a bite of that size. Then I down my bottle of Appletise, feeling the fizz travel up my nose, and I leave the restaurant.

The Mercedes navigates the busy car park at The Oceanside Shopping Centre with ease. Finding a space is the difficult part.

Eventually, someone pulls out and Marshall cuts in front of another car that was waiting first and grabs the spot. Ignoring the honking horn of the annoyed driver, he turns off the engine but leaves the air-con running.

Turning to Reeves, who is already looking at the many faces coming and going, he expresses concern for their plan. 'Now we're here, I'm not so sure this'll work. If she's changing her appearance at that salon, then the possibilities are endless.'

'I'll know her when I see her.' Reeves declaration is so self-assured that he even surprises himself.

'I don't know that we will,' says Marshall, with a tilt of his head to emphasise the point.

'Trust me. I will.'

Marshall looks up at the main doors. 'Shame we couldn't get closer to the entrance. But at least there is only one way in and out.'

'Just keep an eye on those spaces as well, we can move closer when someone leaves.'

---

A few rows away, the battered Volvo grabs another parking space as soon as it's vacated. Without the luxury of tinted windows, sun fills the car with glaring light but The Watcher can still see the Mercedes from where he's parked.

His air-con hasn't worked for years, and while it was once state-of-the-art, by today's standards it would be considered useless warm air, even if it did work. Instead, he uses his handkerchief to wipe the sweat pouring down his face.

With fingers sticky from the moisture on his skin, he grips the red-hot steering wheel, poised to make a move. He keeps his eyes locked on the Mercedes, waiting to see if they get out.

---

The Forte Lane department store on the third floor of The Oceanside smells of expensive perfume and has suede upholstered chairs dotted around for customers to rest or place heavy bags while they shop for more. Classical music plays in the background, creating the perfect ambience of white noise required for making decisions over such extravagant purchases.

To match my classy blonde hair, I need a classy outfit. I head to the personal shopping department in the far corner where an eager-to-please gentleman in a smart suit skips over to me.

'Hi Jacques, how are you?' His name is actually Jack but he prefers the French pronunciation as he thinks it sounds more flamboyant.

'Miss Curtis, you look ravishing!' He kisses the back of my hand but keeps his sparkly eyes fixed to mine.

'Thank you, Jacques.'

'You simply must allow me to select a gorgeous outfit to match your new style!' He offers me the crook of his arm.

'I'm in your capable hands,' I say, as I slide my hand onto his arm.

# CHAPTER 25

I leave the Forte Lane department store with my scruffy old clothes hidden in a large gift bag, cunningly disguised as purchases.

Jacques, as always, had great pleasure in 'dressing me up' for the new look. The sparkle in his eyes when he's designing an outfit for someone never ceases to amaze me. It makes me wonder what life would be like to have such a passion about something.

In my world, I never have time to sit and contemplate what I would do if this was not my life. I suppose I'd be at college or in the sixth form maybe. But I have no place in the world as it is. I just hurry from one hiding place to another, and suddenly I envy Jacques, Maisie, and Angel. They've all found their 'place' where they can enjoy living their lives.

Shaking my head from this whimsical thinking, I almost lose my blonde wig, so I pretend to run my fingers through my hair to adjust it back into place. I ride the escalator down to the ground floor with a new confidence, courtesy of my disguise.

As I exit the Shopping Centre, I feel the warmth of the sun through my wig. Looking down at my outfit, I hardly recognise myself in the elegant sand-colour trousers and silk top with a gold, rust and brown swirling pattern. The oversized sunglasses had a price tag of more than the rest of the outfit put together.

I tiptoe away from The Oceanside in my new strappy gold sandals and head to the South Bay area to blend in with the crowds.

The warm water flushes over his dry throat, but has no effect on quenching the thirst. His sodden handkerchief is rendered useless as he mops his dripping face.

Still poised as he replaces the lid on the water bottle, he doesn't take his eyes of the silver Mercedes for one second. He can tell they are up to no good, because no one goes to a busy shopping centre, takes the time to park and then doesn't go inside.

Figuring they are watching the entrance, he watches them too. If they try to harm the girl, he will wring their necks.

Through my tinted world of shades, I pick a path through the sunbathers crowding the beach in the South Bay. The gold sandals dangle from my fingers to avoid getting sand in them. Colourful umbrellas, muted by my sunglasses, tempt me into buying one and hiding behind it for the rest of the day. It's not a bad idea, but I first need to take care of tonight's shelter issue.

I'm startled by screams. As I spin my head quickly to look around for the danger, I almost dislodge my wig again. Then the screams turn to laughter coming from a group of children and I breathe out the fear that inhibited my body for a few seconds. The unmistakable sound of the Punch and Judy show reassures me that everything here is normal.

Half way along the beach, a tall and tanned lifeguard is reprimanding a group of teenage boys for playing a very aggressive game of football on a part of the beach teeming with families and small children. I catch the gist as I walk past. A small toddler was hit with the ball and knocked over. One of the boys had also fallen on top of an elderly lady. The lifeguard orders the boys off the beach immediately.

Concrete steps lead me up onto the promenade towards the Georgian townhouses along the seafront. I loiter outside a gift shop in the ground floor of one of the houses and pretend to look at the tacky souvenirs on display in the window. Among the keyrings and fridge magnets, a Jack-in-the-Box makes my heart flutter. My sister had one of those.

Feelings of sadness consume me once more. I can't help but picture my family sitting in the living room, with Lexi only about four or five, playing with this Jack-In-The-Box in the middle of the floor. She laughed so hard each time it popped out and did it over and over again. The infectious laughter from the memory helps me to snap out of my sorrow, and I see from my reflection in the window that I'm laughing aloud but only to myself.

Having dawdled at the window as long as I can, I move along to the next building. I peer in the glass-fronted office at the man behind the desk. The door is wedged open and he doesn't notice me as I enter. An older couple are sitting in the corner, where she is nursing a sting from a jellyfish on her ankle. A lifeguard is explaining to her what to do to take the pain away.

The other lifeguard behind the desk is now looking up at me. As I approach him, I feel the sweat beneath my wig making my scalp itch. It reminds me he may not recognise me as a blonde, so I take off my sunglasses. He smiles at me, relaxed now he's on a well-deserved break after dealing with teenage tearaways on the beach. His skin is almost as brown as his hair for spending most of his days near the water.

'There you are Miss Johnson!' He walks over to a crate on another table. It holds all kinds of lost property and I can see a few wallets, sunglasses and a single flip-flop. 'I found your keys,' Brent says in a believable manner as he hands them to me.

'Thank you so much, I don't know what I would've done.' I say, feigning relief. I could win an Oscar, with all the charades and characters I portray.

'No problem, take care now.' His eyes hold firm with mine.

I put the keys in my pocket and leave the lifeguards' office. The sun reminds me immediately to put my shades back on. I cross the road to The Surf Shack to buy the biggest umbrella I can find, and head back to join the masses on the South Bay beach.

The gift bag swings by her side, spilling sugar crystals into the bottom creases from the vintage sweets wrapped loosely inside. She doesn't notice the man staring at her from a car as she walks past.

Taking a seat on a bench that has a view out to sea, she settles back for her ten-minute break. The salon is busy today and she flicks off her shoes to let her toes breathe.

A man joins her and, without a word, she holds out the sweet bag. Jacque's eyes bulge as his fingers fumble around for the biggest one.

'Thank you, my darling Maisie!' He savours the sugar as it melts on his tongue. 'And job well done to you, I hardly recognised her again.'

'Thanks Jacques, I'm glad you got to see her too.'

Reeves sits up straight. 'There! There she is!'

'Where?!' Marshall also sits up straight and reaches for the door handle, ready to jump out of the car.

'Not Layna, that hairdresser girl. Bright pink hair, you can't miss her!'

'Tssk. I thought you meant Layna! That hairdresser had blue hair last time.'

'Well it's pink now and it's definitely her. She went over there and is sitting on that bench with a bloke.'

'Oh yeah, I see her. She ain't with Layna then.'

'Not yet. Let's keep watching her.'

The spoon clatters onto the ceramic tiles of the mosaic table. Jamie spins around in his chair as the waitress picks it up, cursing her own clumsiness. He turns back to Peter, who hadn't even registered the sound having recaptured his tenacity to look at every face that enters the shopping centre. Jamie tries to follow suit, to keep up with his brother's dedication to finding this girl.

'Crowds are thinning out now, ain't they J?' Peter speaks without looking at him.

'Yeah, should make is easier for us to spot her if she comes here. Shall I get us another drink?'

'No, J!! Why don't you get it?! She only hides in busy places! If there's less people about, she won't come here, will she?!'

'Oh yeah, I see. Sorry Pete.'

Peter, compelled by temper once more, is already walking off.

The sun falls lower in the sky above The Oceanside Shopping Centre. And as such, shadows fragment the glowing evening light around the car park and across the roof of the Mercedes.

Marshall rubs his eyes, squeezing out the ache around the sockets. Scrutinising every face has given him eyestrain. 'I think we're done here for tonight, hey Reeves? It's getting late. She won't go to the salon now.'

'No, she probably won't. I think we should come back early tomorrow though. There's still a chance she'll go there.'

'Yeah, I agree. Until tomorrow then.' Marshall reaches for the key to switch on the engine.

'Or not!'

'What d'ya mean? Reeves, that cheeky grin! It's giving you away. Something opposite to what your dimples are trying to proclaim.'

Reeves can only laugh in response.

'I almost daren't ask, but what've you got in mind?'

'Head to the Hotel Indigo.'

Marshall's wide-eyed response makes Reeves laugh again.

Without another word, Marshall looks behind to reverse out of the parking space.

The Volvo backs out at the same time and slowly follows the Mercedes out of the car park and away from The Oceanside Shopping Centre.

By keeping distance of a few cars, The Watcher is able to follow them discretely. His breathing is laboured, drying out his already dehydrated lips. He peels his sticky grip from the wheel to make a left turn, then a right.

At the next junction, the Mercedes turns left, heading out of the city. After a few moments of hesitation, he follows it.

# CHAPTER 26

The sand of the South Bay spills over my feet from between my toes as I walk along the beach behind the remaining sunbathers who refuse to leave until the sun has vanished entirely from view. I keep my eyes on the sand to make sure I don't tread on anything sharp left by those who had picnics on the beach.

My slow pace comes to a complete halt in front of the beach huts as I watch a luxury yacht out in the bay. I can just about make out the shapes of the people onboard enjoying their laid-back lifestyle on the waves. A long, deep breath helps me exhale away my envy.

Before anyone notices, I turn about-face and use the key Brent gave me to enter beach hut number thirty-one, and shut myself inside. The mint green paint is flaking off both the outside and inside, dry from the harsh combination of salt and sun. Shards of light pierce through the wood panels, turning the dust into shining, floating crystals and the cobwebs into iridescent tapestries. My sophisticated blonde disguise will be hard to pull off after a night in here, but it'll have to do.

I survey my living quarters for the night. It's cluttered with beach equipment like windbreakers, deckchairs and sun loungers. I add my umbrella to the hoard of buckets, spades, beach balls and towels that are piled high in the corner, beneath the spider's lair. I'll soon get used to the odour of dust and mildewed wood.

Opening out a sun lounger, I calculate the hut is just about big enough to accommodate its full length, then I lay some of the towels over the dusty cushion. After making sure the door is locked from the inside, I settle on the lounger. Carefully at first, in case it collapses with me swallowed up inside. Once I'm sure it'll take my weight, I lean back and try to relax.

The Hotel Indigo has quietened down for the night. The guests have retired to their rooms and all Tiffany can hear is whistling from Jim the security guard as he returns to his position by the main door. His relaxed demeanour tells her that he found nothing out of the ordinary on his round of checking all entrances and exits.

Two men approach the door.

'Have you got some late arrivals, Tiff?' asks Jim.

'No, I'm not expecting anyone.' Concern spreads beneath her heavy make-up while she prepares her speech to declare they are too late to book in for the night.

As they enter, one approaches Jim at the door and starts to tell him of a problem in the car park. Jim disappears outside with him, seemingly to investigate a car that has been broken into.

Tiffany strains to hear which car it is, hoping it isn't hers, and doesn't quite register the other man until he's right in front of her. He's dressed sharply in a dark grey Armani suit with a white shirt beneath and is leaning, actually posing, on the counter.

Thoughts of her car are put on hold as she offers the man a professional smile. 'How can I help you?'

The man moves around the counter as he takes something out of his pocket. 'Yeah, perhaps you can. We found this on the ground next to the car that was broken into.'

Tiffany leans in, wondering if it's something of hers. He unfolds the rag in his hand and she looks up at him, confused.

There is nothing in it.

Before she can say anything, the rag smothers her mouth and nose, and the man grips the back of her head with his other hand to stop her pulling away. Her screams are muffled as he forces the rag further into her mouth. She claws around in the air for a something to grab hold of as he drags her out from behind the desk.

'There's no one else here sweetheart, it's just you and me.'

Reeves looks around the lobby to make sure he is good for his word, before looking back into her frightened eyes. 'My, my, I can see why your sister has such a bee in her bonnet about you! I wouldn't wanna be the ugly duckling little sister either!'

He drags her over to the lift. Once inside, he hits B for basement and as the lift starts to move, he smashes her head against the wall, making the lift shake unsteadily on its cables. She goes limp and doubles over. Reeves watches with glee while she's crumpled in half. So much so, that he was unprepared for the punch she landed on him after springing up to full height. He's stunned by her strength as it sends him reeling backwards and blood trickles from his nose.

'Bitch!' he yells, going to work on her in a manner only seen in a professional boxing match. At first, she tries to fight back but he ducks and dodges all of her meek attempts, eventually landing enough blows to stop her fighting back and it becomes a one-sided match. She has no chance against his punches as they hit her one after the other.

Reeves laughs loudly, relishing every second, as the lift comes to a stop and the doors open. Dragging her up from her cowed position in the corner, he works quickly to bind her hands with a plastic zip-tie that he had ready in his pocket.

He grabs the rag that has fallen on the lift floor in the battle and shoves it into her mouth so far that he feels her gag. Then he takes a bandana from his pocket and wraps it around her mouth to hold it in place, tying it tight at the back of her head where it catches strands of loose hair.

Outside the Hotel Indigo, Marshall makes a big show of pointing out things on the ground, leading Jim all around the car to show him the evidence. It'd only taken them a few seconds to smash the window of a random car and throw the contents of the glove box around, but he strings it out as long as possible.

'Oh, there's some more over here look...'

Jim follows him and inspects the items closely. Now that the darkest dusk has taken over the sky, it's getting harder to see, causing them both to squint.

'Do you think it's a guest's car? Or one of your employee's?' Marshall doesn't wait for a reply. He chatters away, hoping the conversation will keep the guard out here as long as possible.

# CHAPTER 27

'Come on, beautiful. Snap out of it!'

The voice is not familiar too her. Tiffany comes to with a whirring sound inside her head, made worse when a rough hand taps her cheek. After a few seconds, the stars waltzing around her head begin to fall back into place one at a time. Instinct tells her to get up quickly, but her body won't respond, so she's surprised to feel her feet lift off the ground.

With force, she's thrown out of the lift, opening her eyes just in time to see the cold, filthy tiles of the basement floor just centimetres away. She closes them again and braces herself for the impact.

Falling head first, her forehead cracks on the tiles; her bound hands useless to break her fall. Eventually, her body catches up, landing in a heap. Searing pain shoots from her head down to her toes as she tries to sit up.

The man is laughing at her and for a fleeting second, she thinks someone will hear him and come to her rescue, but then remembers there won't be anyone else around at this hour. Her heart sinks with the knowledge, but her survivor-mode continues to fight through the pain to try and think of another escape option. Within seconds she realises there *are* no other options, and fear grips her as she realises she might die down here.

Tears fill her eyes, blurring the vision of the man looming over her. Her lips feel like they've been split into a smile too big for her face with the bandana tied so tight. The rag is wedged too far down the back of her throat, activating her gag reflex and making it hard to breathe, let alone shout out or make a noise of any kind.

'Why?!' She has to use the extreme back of her tongue to form the word but it still only comes out as a muffled sound.

The man doesn't understand her, but something he said in the lobby jumps back to mind, answering her own question. Chloe. He said something about her sister. Before she can unscramble the clue, the man yells at her.

'WHERE'S LAYNA?' he demands, still smiling with joy from tossing her to the ground like a ragdoll.

Her bright blue eyes, glassy with tears, stare back at him, conveying confusion and terror all at the same time. More importantly, he sees the recognition upon hearing Layna's name.

'Oh, how I love taking a pretty face, like yours, filling it with fear, like yours, and watch that prettiness fade away.' He laughs again. 'Give it up, sweetheart. She'll only get you hurt and she ain't worth it. Trust me.'

He squats down, cradles her head and strokes the side of her face with the back of his fingers. She whimpers and tries to pull away. 'There, there...' he says. 'You really are a pretty thing, ain't'cha?'

Then he shouts, enjoying the reaction as her eyes widen in fright. 'TALK TO ME, YOU STUPID BITCH! BEFORE I REALLY LOSE MY TEMPER!' His voice bounces off the bare brick walls of the basement.

He backs away for a moment to plan his next move. Before he can think, she squirms away on her back, pushing with her legs. He grabs her ankles and pulls her back towards him, laughing once again as he does so.

Tiffany closes her eyes again, as she slides across the floor towards the man who she now understands is after Layna, but somehow tied to her sister too.

Her eyelids are forced open roughly by fingers with hard skin and sharp nails. She stares into two evil cesspools, the scariest eyes she has ever seen. Surrounded by bloodshot veins, like rivers feeding evil into a lake of blood. They send a dark message that more violence is coming.

The rag suppresses another yelp as the man grabs her wrists and yanks her up from the floor with such ferocity that her head whips back. The whiplash shoots down her neck.

He pulls her over to the lift doors and presses the button, but when the doors open, he doesn't take her inside. Instead, he reaches in and presses the button for the ground floor, sending the empty lift away.

Only now does she realise that was her only feasible escape route, but it's gone before she could utilise it. Shaking and with the pain in her neck getting stronger, she still tries to pull away. The thought of being stuck down here with this vile man makes vomit rise from her stomach, where it sits in her oesophagus.

Despite being wobbly on her feet, she tries kicking out at him. Catching her stiletto heel on his shin. She tries to do the same again but misses, catching his knee instead, then she braces herself for his response.

# CHAPTER 28

'Right then, you feisty little bitch!'

He grabs hold of her roughly and turns her around so she isn't facing him and can't kick out. With his free hand, he takes out his knife, the same one he cut the woman's throat with at the Calypso Inn.

He holds it in front of her, pleased for the effect it has, with her squirming around trying to get out of his grip. Behind the rag, she is crying through racking, silent sobs, only evident by her body thrusting with each wail.

Knowing he must be getting close to breaking her, he pretends to bring the knife up to her face but then moves it away and uses it to force the lift doors apart, revealing the lift shaft inside. He looks up at the bottom of the lift sitting at the floor above them.

Raising his eyebrows, he looks back at her. 'Now that looks very precarious!'

He puts his knife away and grabs the tops of her arms with both hands, shaking her firmly. 'You ready to talk yet?'

She shakes her head, so he pulls her towards him and spits as he talks. 'You'll be sorry!'

He pushes her into the lift shaft, face against the back wall. Straddling her from behind so she's unable to wriggle free, he takes another plastic tie from his pocket, loops it around the tie on her wrists and then around a metal rail on the wall. He steps outside the lift shaft, looks back and admires his work.

'I only have to press one button and you're done, sweetheart! Nod your head if you know where she is.'

Tiffany shakes her head.

Even though Layna was here, she has no idea where she is now, so she couldn't tell him even if she wanted to. Nor would she, anyway. She made a promise beyond the grave to Rosa that she would protect Layna with her life.

Saying a silent prayer for help, she pleads with God for something, someone, somehow to come and save her from this awful man. His disgusting, evil eyes have left an imprint on her psyche, telling her he means everything he says and she is likely to die down here in the basement.

The thought makes her panic and in desperation, she tries pulling her wrists back in the hope that the plastic will break. It's no good, the ties only cut into her skin. She looks back at him. He is laughing again, enjoying her predicament as only its creator could.

'Well, I'd love to hang out here with you, darling, but duty calls. Told you you'd be sorry.'

Entering the lift, he punches her in the back of the head, using the same force he would on a punch bag, as she can't get away. Then he walks away from the lift.

After exploring the basement for a few moments, he finds a staircase leading up to the ground floor. At the top, he opens the door and checks the lobby. There's not a soul about. He exits the stairwell, closing the door behind himself, and walks through the lobby with the bravado of somebody who's meant to be there, in case anyone should appear.

On his way past the front desk, he sees the security guard through an open door to the back office with a phone to his ear. Assuming he's calling the police over the car break-in, he smiles and heads outside to find Marshall.

Tiffany's ears are ringing from all the punches she took. The whiplash in her neck is making her dizzy as it travels up around her skull and down her back.

She cries out loud, but the sound is absorbed by the rag. Her mind is racing to calculate how long she has left before someone comes to the basement in the lift. She might make it all night, but Mary-Ellen, the room attendant, will be bringing the laundry carts down here in the morning to the laundry room along the corridor.

Her body gives up holding her weight and her legs buckle. Unable to sink low enough to curl into a protective ball, she dangles from her wrists. The ties hurt as they dig in, but it's not as painful as the knowledge that she might die before someone finds her.

# CHAPTER 29

After Jim reports the car break-in, he returns to his post at the door. This time though, he stands just outside so he can keep an eye on the car park.

He scans the area through the dark, sees the two good Samaritans leave, and decides to circle the car park on foot just in case the vandals are still loitering. He whistles as he walks so that anyone hiding in the dark shadows between the cars will hear him coming, as he doesn't want to startle someone into a defence attack.

The dust is gentle as it settles across my skin. I fight off many urges to sneeze, breaking my sleep into segments.

Drifting away once more, I find myself outside my old house. At first, it looks the same as it always did but then it turns into a ghoulish vision. Blood spills over the roof and drips down the sides, covering the windows and the doors. Tarnished with the evidence of lost lives, it's no longer the house I can call home.

I haven't touched the house, yet when I look down, my hands are covered in blood. I stare at them for a few moments before remembering I must get away. I try to run down the street but my legs won't move. I grab a hold of a lamppost and drag myself a little way. Crying and falling to my knees, I grab hold of the grass and bushes in the front gardens, hauling myself just a little farther along each time.

Eventually I make it to the corner. I reach up and grab a hold of a trellis covered with thick, scratchy brambles. The thorns latch onto my skin, snagging tiny pieces away. A spider crawls across the back of my hand, angry that I have disturbed his living quarters amongst the branches.

Then I snap awake and slap at the back of my hand with the other one. The spider from the corner of the beach hut must have come to explore and crept into my dreams. I jump up and shake my clothes down in the dark space, hoping to remove him from my person.

As freaked out as I am that a spider was crawling over me, I'm also thankful for him waking me from another awful nightmare.

---

The house is in complete darkness but for a few table lamps around the edge of the room. Poker chips scattered over the dining table among bowls of crisps and cans of beer suggest a game in full swing. Cigarettes and testosterone make up the heavy atmosphere that has each player breathing faster than normal, cards held close to heaving chests.

'How long have you been having these mini tournaments, Ellis?' Brent's voice cuts through the smoky low light.

'For more years than you've been born, son. Even before I became a lifeguard, in fact.'

'Well thanks for inviting me. My uncle was mad jealous when I told him I had a game. He was a professional poker player for years, retired now. He taught me all I know.'

'S'alright, lad. We relish the challenge from you youngsters. Don't we fella's?' he asks the rest of his cronies around the table. 'Keeps our game fresh! You two are both working out well.'

He gestures to Brent and Cavan. 'Cavan's a good player and your uncle taught you well, son.'

Marshall is definitely playing a game, but not the kind these guys thought he was here for. He places his next bet and concentrates hard on his real quest; buddy up to Brent.

With not just money as his motivation, the internal duel with Reeves over who has the best tactics is a driving force. He can't wait to see the look on Reeves face when he comes up trumps, literally!

'There's a man who's enjoying his game!' says Ellis, having read his expression.

'I'm having fun! Poker's my game. I enjoy playing mind games.'

The guys all laugh along. Including Brent. It pleases him to gain ground with him as he's convinced it'll be one of the guys that'll lead them to Layna in the end. The women are too strong-willed.

He makes a play knowing it'll win Brent the game.

# CHAPTER 30

The shrill sound of seagulls, lewd and unrelenting, wakes me from the light dozing I've been doing for the last few hours. My back is stiff and my tongue is stuck to the roof of my mouth, such is the dry, dusty atmosphere I've slept in.

I pull my aching body up into a sitting position and reach for a bottle of water from my bag. As I quench my thirst, I watch the dust particles moving slowly through the air like a snow globe. Knowing I've been breathing that in all night makes my nose twitch.

As I try to stand up, my body creeks from a lack of proper support on the sun lounger. My feet are dead but I manage to shuffle over to the door. I need to know if it's safe to leave unnoticed, so I unlock the door and open it just a tiny bit to look out.

There is no one on the beach yet; the white sand is unspoiled. In silent glory, the morning sunrays cascade down from the sky, landing on the crest of waves, where they're gently washed ashore. It's so beautiful.

I've always loved the beach and moments like this remind me why. When it gets crowded later it'll be a completely different place, but for now, it's all mine. I grab my bag and head out to create the first footprints of the day.

The Honda Civic has the choice of spaces in front of the door to The Oceanside Shopping Centre.

'Here we go again, Jamie-Boy!' Peter unclips his seatbelt and stretches his arms out in front, pulling them further than is comfortable to stretch his shoulder blades.

Before he switches off the engine, Jamie seizes on Peter's good mood and musters the courage to make a suggestion. 'I know you wanted to come back here again today, Pete, but do you think we're better off focusing on transport hubs? You know, like you said yesterday she's got to get around. We could go to the city train station, it's close by.'

'Don't make any difference, Jamie-Boy. She's gotta buy stuff like food and what-not as well. She could show up in any of the busy places.'

'Fair enough.' Jamie switches the engine off and opens his door.

'Nah, stay in the car J. There were too many nosey people yesterday. We can watch for her out here.'

Jamie closes his door, shutting in the dread of another day in an enclosed space with Peter. He turns the radio up to keep the mood light and watches as cars begin to flow into the car park, quickly filling the spaces around them.

The Mercedes pulls into the only available space at the far side of the Oceanside Shopping Centre car park.

'I knew we should've got here earlier, Marsh!'

'Sorry, I had a late night at the card game! You know, because your plan to break the woman at the hotel didn't work? So I had to work the lifeguard instead.' Marshall basks in the glory of rubbing Reeves' nose in it.

Reeves, deliberately ignoring the jibe, presses on. 'We needed to get here earlier to get a space closer to the entrance. We'll never spot her from here.'

Marshall drops his quest to stir Reeves up and joins the conversation trail Reeves has started. 'Particularly as we don't know what she'll look like if she's going to that salon.'

'Just focus on small women and facial features. She can't change those!'

Marshall opens his takeaway coffee and takes a sip. 'You're very optimistic today!'

'Today's the day Marsh, I can feel it!'

'You said that yesterday, Reeves!'

'Yeah, but today I'm sure. Can feel it in the air, brewing like a fruity little beer that you savour the taste for hours after you drank it!'

'You're enjoying this way too much!'

'Aren't you?! You're getting paid to throw your weight around! And the big pay out at the end will be sweet.'

'Yeah, that's what I'm holding out for. Want out of all this really.'

'You what?! What're you gonna do?'

'I'm working on a business plan. If this money comes through, it'll be all the funding I need to get Cavantech Enterprises off the ground!'

'You going straight?! Come off it.'

'I'm serious. Got big plans, Reeves!'

'Yeah? Well, we better get this girl caught then, ain't we?'

The panorama of the South Bay is both wonderful and disappointing at the same time. The viewfinder on top of the cliff shows me a beach that's getting busier by the minute, but no sign of Brent. Normally he makes himself easy to find when he knows I'll be giving keys back.

Concluding that he must be in the lifeguard office, I give up my charade as a tourist and head down the hill away from the viewfinders. Half way down, a man comes towards me. I notice immediately that he's overdressed for the beach in an Armani suit. He stares hard at me as I walk past, then turns around and starts walking behind me.

Immediately my skin pricks and adrenalin rushes through my limbs, making them throb with fear. I feel his footsteps getting closer behind me. I close my eyes and hold my breath.

A rush of air whispers against my cheek and shoulder as he hurries past. I open one eye and see him running for the bus that's almost about to leave its stop on the promenade. I breathe out.

Realising I have come to a complete stop, I persuade my legs to move again, gradually recovering from the false alarm with each step. Insecurity from the encounter makes me worry that my wig is not on straight, so I try to adjust it discretely.

I'm still breathing hard as I reach the promenade. I can see from here that the doors to the lifeguard's office are closed. A quick glance in as I walk past tells me it's empty. I continue past as if I'm on a purposeful journey but feel uneasiness forming in my gut. Brent's always on the beach or in the lifeguard's office.

I'm almost at the end of the promenade when loud tapping on the window next to me makes me jump out of my skin.

# CHAPTER 31

With the wind knocked out of my sail once more, I look through the window of a café called The Brunch House. Brent's face looks both amused and apologetic at the same time. Relieved it's only him, I regain my composure and go inside.

At a table tucked away in the back, far from the windows, we order some breakfast and I give him the keys to the beach hut. 'Thanks Brent. I thought I was never gonna find you!'

'Yeah, but then I found you!' he says, and I can't help but feel uneasy over his words. Am I really that easy to find?

He reads my mind. 'But I knew what to look for, didn't I? Almost didn't recognise you yesterday. I was thinking, who's this classy blonde coming towards me?!'

'What gave me away?!'

'I saw your necklace actually.' He points with his eyes at the peridot necklace he bought me for my fifteenth birthday.

'Well spotted.'

'I'm good at paying attention to detail. It's necessary for my job!'

'How come you're not working this morning?'

'I swapped for a later shift. Had a card game with some of the guy's last night and it was a late one. Or an early one, I should say!'

'Oh, did your Uncle Gary go?'

'Nah, he's retired now, but I used all the tricks he taught me! So when will I see you again?'

He drops the question in so casually, but it tugs at my heartstrings as only a childhood sweetheart can. I answer nonchalantly as always and hope he doesn't get fed up of me being evasive. 'Oh, I'll probably just pop up out of the blue some time. You know me.'

His face falls. 'I wish I could see more of you, you know, like the old days.'

His voice is drenched in sadness that I feel too, but can't show right now. We're quietly contemplating for a moment and I fiddle with the necklace to fill the void.

'So where will you be going next?' he asks more brightly.

I smile at him. 'I'm not sure yet. Tend to make my decisions on the spur of the moment.'

He looks disappointed, like he thinks I can't trust him to know where I'm going, but it's for his own good, more than mine.

'If it helps, I know Frazer's due to dock early tomorrow morning. I'm sure he'd love to see you.'

'Thanks Brent, I'll definitely pay him a visit.'

'Oh by the way, there was this weird woman here the other week. She didn't directly ask about you, she was asking about my old school friends, but I sort of got the feeling it was you she was looking for.'

Alarm forms across my forehead, dragging my eyebrows upwards. 'What did she look like?'

'She was late forties or early fifties. Really elegant, smart clothes, smelt amazing. Curly hair, loads of make-up. I thought she looked familiar but I'm not sure where from.'

His description doesn't help me to identify the woman from appearance alone. I need to know more immediately. 'Where was this? What did she say exactly?'

'She bumped into me on the promenade when I was on my way back to the office for lunch. She acted as if it was an accident but I'm sure she did it on purpose. She apologised then said *I know that face, you're Brent Stevens, aren't you?* Before I could answer, she goes; *I haven't seen you in years! You haven't changed much though. My daughter used to go to school with you. Westfield Secondary? You were on the swimming team, weren't you? My daughter had such a crush on you! I'd know that face anywhere.*'

'Did she say who her daughter is?'

'I asked her name and she just said I wouldn't have known her as she wasn't in my year. Before I could ask anything more, she asked me if I still see any of my old school friends. I was getting suspicious so I said no and she looked disappointed. Too disappointed really. More than she should care about a stranger keeping in touch with old school friends.'

'Did she say anything else?'

'Nah, she just said *that's a shame* and then a quick *nice to see you again* and she left.'

'Brent, what if she's watching you?! Oh my gosh, I have to leave.' I grab my bag and ignore his pleads for me to stay.

'This was weeks ago, Layna!'

'It doesn't matter, Brent! She might be following you around, hoping to 'bump' into you again. She could be anyone!'

'Layna, wait!'

'No, Brent! I have to go.'

The lift hurtles down towards the basement, but comes to an abrupt stop on the ground floor above, just as it has many times over. The rag tastes salty from her tears as a few more trickle down from that latest test.

Tiffany watches helplessly as the lift ascends and descends the floors above. Exhausted by the terror that each time it moves could be the end for her, she pushes through the pain to crane her neck over her shoulder, desperately searching the basement for someone who can help her before it's too late.

Fernando the maintenance man has a workshop down here and he hates the lift so always uses the stairs. She can't think straight enough to remember if he's working today or not.

With pain shooting down her spine from her neck, she slowly turns her head back to face the front. She focuses her attention on the plastic ties around her wrists, cutting channels so deep into her flesh that blood-filled bulges flow over the edges. Having made several unsuccessful attempts to break them already she pulls once more, thankful her wrists went numb hours ago, but the plastic holds firm.

Her concept of time is gone, but from the activity of the lift, she thinks the room attendants will be bringing the laundry carts down very soon. That will be the end of her life.

# CHAPTER 32

The bus is stifling and hot, ferociously jerking around the city streets before coming to a halt at a stop in Eastbrook. Even stepping onto the pavement of this notoriously rough area brings sweet relief from the fusion of body odours and bus fumes that have stuck to my skin and entered my taste buds.

I immediately regret not changing into my casual clothes before coming here. Wearing an expensive outfit and carrying a gift bag from Forte Lane, I may as well have stuck a target on my back for the many thieves around here. Although, the thought of someone stealing my 'gift' bag, only to find my battered old stuff inside makes me chuckle.

I pass a group of scantily clad teenage girls, who've likely been out all night otherwise would seldom be up and about at this hour. They stop their chatter and stare intently at me. Worried they are planning to rob me, I turn before I get to them and wait for traffic to pass so I can cross the road. I feel their eyes burning a hole in my back as I head towards a slanted building made from shiny cheap red bricks on the other side of the street.

Ignoring the buzzers on a panel at the entrance, I pull the main door open. Despite being a security door, it's never locked. I glance over my shoulder to make sure the girl-gang aren't following me as I enter.

Climbing the first flight of stairs, I avoid a puddle of what looks and smells like urine on the old greying vinyl tiles. My fancy gold sandals look out of place treading between the many blobs of chewing gum decorating the stairs like polka dots.

After two more flights, I arrive at the third floor and open the door. The corridor before me is dark, so I hold back a moment. The door closes behind, pushing me forward from the doorway, like a shove in the back from someone trying to get me to do something I don't want to do.

I listen for any sounds and hear nothing but the buzzing of the permanently out of order strip lights as they try to flicker to life. Most of the flats are boarded up. Some have been broken into; doors wide open with graffiti jumping out from the walls inside. None of them have numbers, as though they no longer matter and the space no longer exists.

Moving along the corridor slowly and as quietly as I can, I count five doors along the left and put my ear to the door. No sound inside. I check the corridor both ways once more and listen for any footsteps coming up or down the stairs.

Certain I'm alone, I push down on the cold brass handle. The door doesn't open. I hold the handle down and feel along the edge of the door for the weak spot I know is there. I give it a strong shove and it gives way. Held in place by a flimsy chain on the inside of the door, I reach my hand inside the door. The cold, damp air whispers across my knuckles as I curve my thumb and forefinger into half of a heart shape.

Cold fingers that defy the hot summer day touch mine, forming the second half of the heart and then I pull my hand back. The door closes and the chain clunks on the other side.

---

Feeling like an intruder sneaking around the basement, Henry chews his fingernails down to the membrane beneath, as he mentally rehearses the lie he concocted in case he should get caught down here. Going to the linen store is not normally part of his duty, but he will say a guest required an extra sheet and he couldn't find Mary-Ellen.

Creeping along the corridor, he shivers under his uniform. He stops to look around before entering the small room, closing the door behind him. Fresh sheets are folded neatly in piles on the shelves, filling the small room with the smell of laundry detergent and fabric conditioner. Henry kneels on the floor in front of an old wooden chest. The lid is heavy as he reaches inside, retrieving a plastic bag on top of the old disused linen inside.

Quietly closing the lid, he licks his lips as he opens the bag and takes out the sheets inside. Miss Abraham's scent rains down on him like blossoms blowing in a spring breeze as he opens the sheet and lifts it to his face to inhale her presence deep into his lungs.

Amari doesn't flinch when she sees me but I can see my blonde disguise caught her off-guard. I smile to reassure her and she invites me in. With a childish giggle and smiling eyes, she throws her fragile frame around me in an intense embrace that only a good friend can wield.

Laughing along with her, I release myself from her grip to look into her doll-like face. Beautifully clear ebony skin tells me she's well and glowing with health, despite living in a damp, mould infested bedsit.

In her broken English, she immediately fusses over me, offering food and drink that I know she can barely afford for herself.

'I'm so glad you came! It worries me sick when I don't hear from you for so long. Let me go to the corner shop for some lunch and then we can catch up properly.'

'That's ok, don't worry about buying food, Amari. I've had breakfast with Brent this morning.'

'No, it's no trouble. I'll be back in five minutes.'

She's out of the door before I can stop her and I hear her keys jangling from the other side as she locks me in. I wander over to the only chair in the room. Amari's guitar leaning against the arm invites me to pass time in melody, so I comply, gently running my thumb over the strings, feeling soothed by the sound even though I can't play.

The squeaking wheels of the laundry cart, straining under the collective weight of used hotel bedding and towels, comes to a halt outside the lift doors. Mary-Ellen, the room attendant, presses the button and waits.

After a few moments, the light above the door flashes the number seven and the doors open to an empty lift. She pushes her cart inside and presses 'B' for basement.

After a few exhilarating moments of breathing in Miss Abraham's scent and pretending he is lying in bed beside her, embarrassment claws at Henry's conscience.

The little voice inside his head that critiques everything he does and says, is mocking him as always. Then it becomes loud and chastising, telling him this will never happen for real. That this is the closest he'll ever get to lying in bed with her. The shame of what he's doing here, on his knees in the laundry room sniffing her bed sheets, makes him feel like a loser. His lowers the sheet from his face in disgrace.

His breathing is still fast, but that's because he is now more worried about someone finding him here, than being excited over the scent on her sheets. Knowing the longer he is here, the more chance there is of being caught, he packs the sheets away in their hiding place and moves towards the door.

Peering around the frame, he cautiously leaves the room, closing the door slowly and as quietly as he can. Confident he's left no sign he was here, he sneaks along the corridor, away from the linen store.

# CHAPTER 33

Mary-Ellen is surprised as the lift jolts to a stop and the doors open to the lobby on the ground floor, not the basement as she was expecting. She moves her cart to the side to allow a guest to join her in the lift.

'What floor would you like, sir?' she asks as courteously as she can.

'Number four, please.'

'We'll go to your floor first.'

'If you're sure?'

'Yes, of course, no problem. You're our guest!' she says with a wave of her hand to dismiss the notion of any trouble caused by the diversion.

Just as the lift doors are about to close, she thrusts her arm out to stop it. 'Fernando!' she hollers through a gap in the doors.

'My apologies, sir,' she offers the guest, before pushing the cart out of the lift into the lobby. The doors close behind her leaving the guest to continue his journey alone.

'Fernando, just the person! The lamp in room 275 is not working. I've replaced the bulb but it still won't work. Could you take a look at it?'

'Sure, I'll pop up there after I've sorted the radiator valve in room 160. How's Arthur doing, by the way?'

'He's better, thanks. He's not going back to the workshop though. He's got a new business venture in mind. I told him he should retire now, but he won't be told.'

'Bring the cart this way to the basement, I'll carry it down the stairs for you and then you can tell me about this new business venture'

'One of these days, I'll get you in that lift Fernando. It'll save your knees!'

'Never! Don't trust 'em!'

A sound escapes through the gaps in the rag, small but full of emotion. Tiffany shakes all over. Even her dead legs and hands, with blood cut off at the wrists, are trembling. Staring at the bottom of the lift sitting at the floor above, she really thought that was it. The sound of the laundry cart wheeling into the lift was unmistakable.

The last few hours stretched into an eternity of endurance, leaving her at the point of wanting it to be done already, but still terrified in those moments when she thought the time had come. Her cries resound inside her throat and ears, for only her to hear.

Concluding that Fernando is not working today, she's long given up hope that anyone will save her in time. More tears sting her overused ducts and blind her temporarily as the water washes over her tired pupils.

Through the watery vision, a shadow appears on the wall in front of her. For a moment, she thinks the man has come back and braces herself. Instead, a shaky voice calls her name.

'Tiffany?!'

She turns her head as far as her injured neck will let her and cries, this time with relief. Remembering the urgency, she shoots a look upwards to the lift above, telling Henry with her eyes to hurry.

Henry looks up, then flaps about in a panic. 'Oh, oh, wait! I'll get help! Oh no, I'll get... Fernando's room! I'll get cutters.' He dashes off out of sight.

Tiffany tries to rouse her dead legs back to life. They barely take her weight but she manages to stand. At this point Henry returns with wire cutters, entering the lift shaft without a second thought they could both be crushed.

He cuts the plastic ties and Tiffany falls into his arms. Pulling her out of the shaft, he can barely take her weight and they fall to the floor of the basement in a heap. He sits her upright and uses the cutters to snip away at the fabric tied around her head, accidentally cutting the hair that was caught in it too.

Folding over in half, she coughs out the rag and he rubs her back as she chokes and splutters.

Eventually she gathers herself to speak and throws her arms around him. 'Oh, Henry!'

'My goodness, Tiffany! What the heck happened? Who did this?!'

Before she can answer, they both turn and watch the lift arrive on the basement level with mere minutes to spare. The lift doors open to an empty lift.

They are startled again immediately by the sound of voices from the other end of the basement. Mary-Ellen and Fernando are using the stairs to bring a laundry cart down to the laundry room.

'Ssh Henry, don't tell them we're here!' she whispers.

Cowering on the floor together half concealed by a supporting pillar, neither are seen by Mary-Ellen or Fernando who are engrossed in conversation. Once they disappear into the laundry room, Henry helps Tiffany to her feet and they quickly get into the lift.

Still whimpering, Tiffany presses the button for the ground floor while brushing her clothes down and trying to fix her hair in case they should encounter any guests in the lobby.

Henry doesn't say a word, just watches her silently, not knowing what to say or do.

# CHAPTER 34

The sound of crockery and cutlery from the adjacent guest's dining room fills the otherwise quiet and empty hotel lobby. Tiffany slips into the back office, with Henry close behind her.

'Henry, I owe you my life,' she blurts out, as she grabs her bag and frantically digs around for her car keys.

'We need to call you an ambulance! And the police!' Henry reaches for the phone.

She grabs it from his hand. 'No! No, I'm fine. Henry, please don't. I'm just going to take some time off.'

'But you need to go to hospital...'

She cuts him off. 'No, I'm fine Henry. Really, I am.' Keys found, she pulls on her jacket.

'Well, let me take you home...'

'No Henry, I'm good to drive, I swear. Please promise me you won't say anything about this to anyone?'

'But you could have been killed!' He raises his voice above the hushed tones they've been using.

'Ssshh! I know, but you saved me, so it's all over now, okay?'

'But...'

She pleads with her eyes and takes his hands in hers to stop his protest. 'Please, Henry?'

'But... but... Okay. Who did this?'

'I'll explain it all, I promise, but not right now. I just need to go home, alright?'

He doesn't answer but his face tells her he's given in.

'Thanks Henry!'

She looks out the door, making sure there's no one else around before walking out. Legs still unsteady, she weaves a wobbly path through the reception area.

Henry follows as far as the front desk, then watches her cross the lobby and out the main door to the car park. He sits at the desk and puts his head in his hands. Deciding he must call the police, he reaches for the phone.

It rings just as he's about to pick it up, stopping him in his tracks. He stares at it for a moment before his professionalism resumes and he answers. 'Good morning, Hotel Indigo, Henry speaking, how can I help?'

The glare from the sun is blinding. Amari can't see where she's going, so uses muscle memory of the path to the shop. Through the light, the outline of a figure emerges. Sun-drenched eyes prevent her from seeing any detail but the unmistakable yellowing eyes reveal the identity of the young man before her. He circles her on his bike, intending to intimidate her. She holds firm, continues walking at the same pace and stares into his sickly eyes in defiance.

'If it isn't the little African Princess!' he taunts. 'Are you sure you're an adult, you only look about twelve!' The smile at his own joke reveals rotten, browning teeth that clash with his sickly, yellow eyes.

'And you look like you're dying from hepatitis.'

Her quip turns his condescending, smug expression to contempt.

'Keep away from me,' she adds, before he can retaliate.

Taking his anger out through the pedals, he rides directly at her, swerving last minute when she doesn't back down. Turning his face away with shame, he rides off defeated and she watches him disappear down the street.

She's still shaking her head at the encounter as she enters the shop. The cool blow from the air-conditioning just inside the door flutters across her eyelashes as she passes through. The freshness eradicates any lasting thoughts of the sickly boy.

Surveying the aisles she spots Gayle, her nosey neighbour, at the far end of the shop and keeps her distance so as not to invite any curious questioning. She heads to the fresh vegetable aisle and mentally prepares a meal for Layna as she selects the ingredients.

The red sports car offers security as Tiffany slides in behind the wheel and hears the automatic locks snap into place. Fighting the urge to let it all out right here and now, she swallows down the lump forming in her throat telling her she must cry or she'll burst.

Her shaking hands struggle to get the key into the ignition. Finally, after many fumbling attempts, it slots into place. The engine fires up effortlessly and she reaches for her seatbelt.

Backing out of the employee's section of the car park, she frantically surveys all around to make sure the man isn't lurking in wait for sirens to confirm his disgusting deed has been executed. The thought that he could watch her leave and follow her, forces her foot down so hard that she burns rubber on the tarmac, before flying out into the traffic without stopping. Car horns from the angry motorists behind express their animosity.

After a few moments of driving, she settles a bit but that's when the tears flow, obscuring her sight, turning the road into a grey, concrete kaleidoscope of shapes. She dabs at her eyes with the back of her hand, swerving a little, before correcting the car's position between the lines as they start to come into focus.

Traffic lights work against her, stopping her at every junction, where panic takes the opportunity to fill her senses with a desperate need to floor it and ignore the red lights. She chews the skin around her polished nails, trying to persuade the light to change to green with her red-rimmed eyes. When it does, she presses hard on the pedal and beats the BMW next to her in the fastest foot contest, burning rubber once more.

In the distance, the road she lives on comes into sight, making her accelerate towards it. She swerves once more while taking too long to glance in the mirrors to check for any suspicious cars following her.

# CHAPTER 35

The jangling of keys on the other side of the door tells me that Amari is back from the shops. For a moment, irrational thoughts torment me, poking at my nervous disposition in a bid to influence my judgement that maybe it's not her after all. I stand up to prepare myself in case, but soon drop my guard when her smiling face appears round the door.

'Just had a run-in with that awful boy,' she tells me as she unloads the shopping into the fridge.

'The one that offered you drugs when you asked him to call the police the day you arrived?'

'The very one. I wish he would just go away. He's always hanging around the streets, popping up when you least expect him. I see him all the time, watching. He makes my skin crawl.'

'Did he see what your Aunt did to your sister?' I pick up a framed photo from the bedside table. Amari's sister Sekoya looks happy and full of hope for her life, that was taken so shortly after she arrived in the country by her own aunt.

'No, it happened inside the house and I was waiting outside. My Aunt never even knew I was there. She probably thinks I'm still in Somalia.'

'So no risk of the boy telling your Aunt he saw you then.'

'No. I didn't see him until I'd run a few streets away.'

'That's something, at least. Maybe Farrell can help? He wouldn't like to think of you being harassed by this boy. He found you this flat as he thought it'd be safe for you here.'

'I don't want to bother him. He's already done so much for me.'

'Me too!'

'Imagine if Farrell hadn't mixed up our ID's that day?! We would never have even met!'

'I know. It was definitely meant to be.' I put my arm around her for a moment, pulling her close to emphasize the point, before removing it to help chop some tomatoes.

'I wish you'd let him do the same for you. He can get you a place far away. Somewhere they will never find you.'

'Thanks Amari, but I can't leave. My family are buried here and I'm not ready to leave them. Plus, Cliff Garrett has people everywhere, from the city streets to the suburbs, moles in the police forces and banks. The only way I can avoid him is to keep moving.'

Amari's friendship reminds me of how life was before my family were killed. Hanging out with friends, never having to look over my shoulder, sleeping properly. The thought process triggers a spell of broodiness.

'Do you ever get lonely?' I ask her quietly.

'Always. But my life is good now. I'm safe.'

'You're lucky you still have photos.' I look over at the picture frame back in its place on the bedside table.

'You do too.' Amari taps her index finger on her temple. 'In here. Never forget.'

'That's true. Thanks.'

Amari smiles at me. 'That's what friends are for,' and squeezes my shoulders.

'Look here, how I bring the photographs in my head to life.'

She turns my shoulders towards an easel in the corner of the room, next to the tiny kitchenette. The touch-dry canvas on the easel is an African scene. A woman in tribal gowns walks in front of a spindly tree beneath a forbidding, fiery sky.

'Do you think you'll ever return to Africa?'

'No. I'd be stoned to death for running away from circumcision. Sekoya wasn't stoned to death, but I watched through the window as my Aunt cut her throat just to punish her for running away.'

'I'm sorry Amari. It's so wrong. You don't deserve any of it. Neither did Sekoya.'

'And you don't deserve what's happening to you either.'

She brings another painting out from behind the shelf and places it on the easel, covering the African scene. The beautiful blue sky outlines snow-topped mountains that morph into wild flower fields in the foreground.

'One day we will both be free, like the flowers in the mountains!'

'You should sell these Amari. They're so good!'

On unsteady feet, Tiffany finishes her second lap of the block. There's not a soul about, not even any of her neighbours. Certain that no one has followed her home, she uses her security key and goes inside the block of flats.

She listens carefully in the hall for any intruders, before making her way to the back of the building where her ground floor flat is located. Certain she's alone, she unlocks the door and looks in before she enters.

Everything appears to be normal so she steps inside and closes the door behind her. Again, she listens before moving through the flat.

There's no sound.

Only now in the comfort of her own home does she register that she's still shaking and her clothes stink of urine that released involuntarily through fear while she was trapped in the lift shaft. Hot tears of shame fall over her blotchy, damp cheeks as she moves from the spot and into the living room.

A slight breeze blows the chiffon curtain at her window, slightly ajar from how she left it yesterday. The motion makes her jump as her imagination fills the window frame with the man's figure as he climbs through. She rushes over and slams it shut, cursing herself for being so careless in leaving access to her home.

In a race against the nightmarish hallucination of him breaking into her home, she hurries around the flat slamming all the windows shut, turning the tiny keys to lock each one. Then she closes all the curtains and blinds, despite it being daytime.

Sprinting to the front door, the slippery wooden floor almost downs her in the hall outside the lounge. The deadbolt on the front door catches her skin as she pulls it across so fast that her fingers didn't have time to get out of the way.

Backing away from the front door, she turns suddenly when she feels the air behind her moving. Expecting to see someone behind her, she cowers, preparing for an attack but instead is met by the empty room. Ashamed of herself for feeling this way, she locks herself in the bathroom and cries aloud, falling hard onto the cold floor tiles.

# CHAPTER 36

Perched up high in the lifeguard station, Brent watches the swimmers among the soft waves beneath the azure sky. Beside him, Ellis is whistling, as he usually does while watching the water for signs of trouble.

'Penny for them?'

He realises Ellis is watching him instead of the ocean, and it catches him unaware. 'Huh?'

'You look like you've got something more on your mind than the beach-goers. What's up?'

'Oh. I'm just trying to figure out how to help a friend, that's all.'

'A woman?' Ellis surprises Brent with his intuition.

'Yeah. Don't know what to do for the best, you know?'

'Best for you? Or best for her?'

'Both of us?!'

'Well, you gotta be careful, lad. Some women don't want to be helped. You could end up pushing her away if you interfere.'

'I know. She's so hard to read. I always thought I could tell what she's thinking, but not anymore. Don't know if she really wants to be with me or not.'

'If that's how you feel, then you probably know the answer, hard as it is.' Ellis lands a large hand on Brent's shoulder for consolation while delivering the home truth.

'I don't know. It's hard to explain. She's going through some serious troubles, and I'm sure that's the reason she's clammed up. She's just scared. So I figured if I could help her sort those troubles out, then maybe she'll show her true feelings for me again.'

'Sounds like a risky game.'

Ellis's dry delivery hits home for Brent, though his parting word of advice gives him a glimmer of hope.

'Of course, some women are worth the risk, aren't they lad!' before he gets up to stretch his legs.

The sight of a surfer taking a hard knock beneath the strongest wave of the day distracts Brent from his train of thought. Poised to perform a rescue, he quickly relaxes when the surfer emerges from the water and jumps back onto his board for another try, unscathed and undaunted.

The symbolism is not lost on him. He should keep trying with Layna. Ellis is right that she's worth the risk.

The ringing is loud in her ears, amplified by shock that's still resonating through her body. For the umpteenth time Tiffany pleads with the phone for Chloe to answer her call. When the annoyingly pleasant answering service kicks in, she curses, hangs up and hits redial again.

As the ringing starts all over, she grabs a fist full of the fabric from her dressing gown in a bid to pull it tighter across her chest, enjoying the security the warm fleecy hug gives. The hot shower and large gin and tonic have slightly pacified her delicate state. She stares at her face in the mirror, watching the bruises form before her swollen eyes. Her knees knocking together remind her how serious this was and how lucky she is to be standing here at all.

When the ringing stops and the recorded voice thanking her for her call kicks in again, she cuts it off mid-sentence and hits redial. 'Come on, Chlo, pick up!'

As it rings again, her thoughts drift to her unlikely hero; Henry. She shakes her head at the marvel of him appearing at that moment, of cutting her free without any regard for his own safety and then promising to keep quiet about it. She'd never thought of him as brave before.

The answering service interrupts her appraisal of Henry. She hits redial and holds the phone to her ear. This time there's no ringing, just silence. 'Hello?'

The response is not the voice of her sister. It's laughter. A man's voice, laughing at her. Not fun laughter, but sinister and mocking.

Her heart almost stops with fear. She hangs up and throws the phone away. Backing herself into the corner of the bathroom where no one can creep up behind her, she crouches down to become as small as she can and cries uncontrollably, realising this man is not going to go away.

The water is not very hot. I see now why Amari boils her kettle to do the dishes. Following suit, I fill it up and wait for it to boil, before adding it to the tepid water in the sink. While she's at work, the least I can do is wash up from the lunch she prepared.

The notebook is propped up in the recipe stand, full of my scribbled thoughts and emotions at Amari's insistence, as she worries I bottle up too much. Reading it back aloud as I wipe over our plates, I re-live my own words. Despite only doing it to appease her, she was right, it did help.

A knock at the door almost makes me drop a plate. I catch it mid-air, along with my breath.

The male voice, cocky and self-assured, speaks through the flimsy front door. 'I know you're in there! There's someone outside who wants to see you!'

I carefully put the plate on the counter without making a sound, tiptoe over to the door and look through the peephole. His yellow eyes are luminous in the dark corridor, vying for attention with the fluorescent graffiti on the flat opposite. No wonder Amari finds him so creepy.

Immediately, I think he's been sent by Garrett's goons. He's just the sort they'd pick to do their dirty work for them. If they are outside, I'm going to have to find another way out of here. The small and only window is high up on the wall. Being on the third floor means it's too high for me to jump.

Watching the boy through the peephole is eerily frightening. All I can see are his sickly eyes and the outline of his scrawny body against the unlit hallway. I keep watching though, despite the goosebumps tingling all over my body. I see his shape shift as he reaches for the door handle. I grab it from this side and push up with all my might. I also lean forward using all my weight against the door.

He's fooled into thinking the door is too secure and backs off. I see his outline moving down the hall towards the door to the main stairs. I release my grip on the handle and back away. Gathering my few belongings together quickly, I write Amari a note.

After checking the peephole several times to make sure he's gone and there's no one else there, I brave the dark corridor and leave via the fire exit at the opposite end to the main stairs.

# CHAPTER 37

Chloe squeezes Tony's hand and feels the rush of joy when he squeezes hers back. Walking hand-in-hand through Elmhurst Park on her lunch break, her feelings are on display for all to see as she looks into his face while she talks.

'She got my name from another customer, Mrs Kline, while they were at a party at Sherrington Manor. Veronica tried to take over at first, saying her nails should be done by management, but Elizabeth insisted on having me. You should have seen the look on Veronica's face!'

'Sherrington Manor, hey? Fancy!'

'Yeah, they're high society people. Imagine if all her friends start coming in and asking for me too! She said she'd tell everyone she knows.'

'You could be onto something big there, babe. How's your family? Everyone alright?'

'Yeah, they're good, thanks. Look at those people on the boating lake! That's too many in one boat, they'll sink!'

'Oh yeah. Idiots.' He flicks a glance over, annoyed at her distraction tactics, before turning back to her to try again, digging for any clue that she's heard what happened to her sister. 'You made peace with your sister yet?'

Noise from the aviary they're passing means she has to shout her reply. 'No. I don't wanna talk about her, Tone. It depresses me. I want today to be happy!'

She lets go of his hand and slides her arm around his waist instead.

Reeves' mind is in overdrive, wondering if something went wrong. He was expecting to get a call from her in floods of tears saying her sister was killed in a lift accident at work. Instead, she invites him to the park.

It doesn't make sense. He stops the anger brewing by rationalising that nobody went to the basement in the lift yet. That must be it.

He keeps the conversation about her family flowing, so it becomes normal for her to talk to him about them and then he'll hear all about it when the deed is done. 'Maybe life will be happier if you can have a better relationship with her? You should find some common ground, like invite her to your salon to get her nails done.'

'Good idea! I can get my own back for all the times she practiced her make up on me. I'd end up looking like a clown and she ends up looking perfect having honed all her skills on me! I could have a mishap with the nail drill!'

'Ha ha, you've got a wicked side!'

'I *am* the wicked one! To be honest though, she never did anything that bad to me really, I just feel self-conscious next to her. My parents have coated her in gold. And me in mud!'

'So you're really mad at your parents then?'

'I guess.' Her response is quieter, contemplative.

Sensing her mood change, he realises he hit a nerve with that suggestion. He files the information away in the back of his mind as it may come in handy whenever he wants to make her doubt herself again.

For now, he steers the topic back around to Tiffany. 'So how'd she end up working at the hotel?'

Chloe quickly rejects the notion that she should be aiming her anger at her parents instead of her sister. Denial sugar-coats the truth so that she doesn't feel guilty for her attitude towards Tiffany.

Purely through habit, she quickly reverts back to the dismissive tone she uses to downgrade Tiffany's achievements.

'Oh, she used to be a cleaner there,' she answers his question, hoping to sway his opinion of her to that of a lowly cleaner.

Something else is nagging at her though. The fact that Tony pointed out that she isn't mad at her sister really, and got her to admit that it's her own insecurity that makes her feel the way she does about Tiffany, makes her feel vulnerable. She's suddenly scared he won't like her anymore and, worse still, end up feeling sorry for Tiffany and take her side. Before she can think of something to say he catches her off-guard with another question.

'Is she working today?'

Suddenly suspicious why he would need to know that, she keeps the dismissive tone for her response. 'I expect so. Haven't heard from her for a bit.'

She's thankful her tactic worked when he drops the conversation and asks her if she wants an ice cream from a van parked nearby on the road. All of her worries evaporate as he smiles at her, takes a hold of her hand, and leads her towards the ice cream van without even waiting for her to answer.

Amari's skin pricks like hundreds of tiny bugs nipping her with sharp pincers as she enters the flat. The smile that formed just at the thought of seeing her friend again wanes when she realises something's wrong. There's no sound and no Layna.

Securing the door behind her with the chain, she looks all around her tiny bedsit for a clue. Almost immediately, her eyes are drawn to a note on the small table in the middle of the room. As she picks it up, cash hidden beneath slides across the table caught on the static friction of the notepaper. Catching the money as it freefalls, she reads.

Her posture softens as she learns that Layna has come to no harm, but she sighs her annoyance that the nasty boy made her leave early. Disgust for the boy and sadness for her friend entwine, twisting like a helix as each battle to be her sole emotion.

She moves across the room to the kitchen counter to prepare tea quickly as her break from work doesn't allow long. There, she notices the notebook on the recipe stand. Layna's handwriting assures her that she took her advice.

Figuring Layna didn't have time to put it away before she was frightened off, she picks it up. Just as she's closing it to conceal her friend's personal thoughts, the words jump out of the page and tug on her heartstrings with such ferocity that she can't ignore it.

It's a poem. A painful account of Layna's agonising experience, drenched with sorrow and guilt.

*Hot tears fall in shame*
*They're so much more than just pain*
*They come from my heart*

*Borne of guilt that tears me apart.*
*I keep them inside where the tears just lie*
*Soaking my soul, where forever they hide*

*I shouldn't be alive, I should have died*
*It was my turn but I survived*
*They got the wrong girl, for me she died*
*Why, oh why, am I alive?*

*Every once in a while, they escape from my eyes*
*They run down my face and shine in the light*
*I can't bear to speak the reason for tears*
*The words are unspoken, guarding my fears*

*I'm alive and alone*
*Life is so much harder since I had to leave home*
*I keep on fighting, never to cry*
*They won't win, I won't die*

Amari realises she's crying herself when a tear lands on the word 'cry'. Sitting slowly on the edge of her bed, she reads the poem again. So much meaning, so much hurt.

She reaches for her guitar and uses her dinner break to turn the poem into a song, her appetite lost. At the top of the page, she writes the title Uncried Tears and underlines it twice.

The clean and fragrant smell of affluency is just the tonic I need after my time in the poverty-ridden Eastbrook, where Amari lives. As I walk through the upmarket Foxwood Chase, it feels like a world away, as opposed to the five miles up the road that I've just walked in the afternoon heat.

Even though I'm sweating cobs, the air here feels cleaner, perhaps boosted by the many tree's surrounding the large houses secreting more oxygen into the air. Come to think of it, Amari's area is distinctly void of any greenery. A concrete world without a plant in sight. Looking around the gardens as I pass, almost every inch of this neighbourhood is painted with a blend of greens, with dashes of colours here and there from the flower beds of avid gardeners.

The houses give way to a parade of shops, offering the lucky residents of Foxwood Chase a chance to buy groceries, post letters or indulge in takeaway food without leaving the comfort of their neighbourhood. Hunger pangs claw at my ribcage, tantalised by the takeaway cooking southern fried chicken. Having left Amari's after lunch and my watch now showing 7pm, I'm lured inside by the warm, slightly spiced fragrance wafting into the street. With some reprieve from the glare of the sun, I squint at the menu on the wall above the counter.

The woman serving glances at me several times, trying to gauge if I'm ready to order yet. I lean on the counter to indicate I am. My stomach tells me I have room for three pieces of chicken, a large chips and coleslaw. A bottle of water finishes my order and I watch as she piles the chips into the box on top of the chicken. I pay her and leave quickly, hoping to devour the food while it's still piping hot.

An older man entering the takeaway moves aside so that I can exit before he enters. I thank him for his chivalry, but am immediately alarmed as he doesn't go inside, instead choosing to watch me walk away from the doorway. Feeling scrutinised, my heart rate increases with each step. I glance back and sure enough, he's still looking. I cross the street, and go as quickly as I can without running.

A little farther along, I look back again and see that he's finally gone inside. Reminding myself of the extremely devoted Neighbourhood Watch team in this area, I reason that as he was probably no one to be concerned about. Just someone who's filling his retirement days by paying attention to what goes on around his home patch. Although I crave a peaceful life, I hope I don't ever end up so bored that I become one of 'those' people who question every unfamiliar face and gossip with the neighbours over someone new.

# CHAPTER 38

Among the pleasantries presented by Amari's next-door neighbour Gayle, malicious gossiping takes precedent over any genuine attempt at being a good citizen. She's relieving herself of information freely and only stops to enquire why the visit is so late in the day.

'Is it usual for immigration to do their visits out of hours?'

'Oh yes, we do more work outside of normal office hours than we do during the day. It's the nature of the job, you see. We're more likely to catch people home at teatime.'

Marshall does his best to sound as though he knows what he's talking about. He looks over at Reeves, who nods along in agreement.

'I see. Well, you'll struggle to catch this girl home. She works funny hours, that one. Mostly two to ten pm it seems.'

'She's working, you say?' asks Marshall, playing along.

'Yes, at a factory. I'm not sure if she's allowed to work there, but she does. I don't know where she's from, but she has an African accent. I was always suspicious of her, right from the start.'

'Why's that then?' Marshall shoots Reeves a look of interest as he speaks.

'Well, she's always alone. Usually these illegals cram as many people into one flat or house as they can fit. But not this one. Always by herself.'

Marshall sinks back into the sofa in disappointment. 'I see,' he says quietly.

As if reading his body language, what she says next has him sitting upright as quick as the soft cushions will let him.

'Until yesterday, that is.'

She stares at him hard, indicating this isn't a waste of their time after all.

'Yesterday?' he asks, with a casual tilt of the head.

'Yes, well, I knew something was different when I saw the girl with...'

Reeves cuts her short. 'Another young girl?'

'No. A huge basket of food at the shop.'

Marshall and Reeves share a look, frustration followed by humour, betraying their charade of professionalism. Before each can set the other off laughing, they look away.

Reeves converts the laughter forming at the back of his throat into words. 'Really? Is that unusual then?'

'Yes, it is,' she says very seriously. 'She usually only buys one of everything, you know, one apple, one banana, one tomato...' Gayle continues as if it's one of the world's biggest conspiracies. 'But this time, she bought two of everything!'

'Two?!' said Reeves, going along with Gayle's conspiracy theory.

'Two, yes,' she confirms with authority, unaware of the mockery she's facing as she's too happy to tell her story to notice. 'Then I knew I was right when I heard two voices.'

'Oh?' Reeves was suddenly glad Marshall had talked him out of punching the woman's lights out, and to try and get her to talk first. Maybe she has useful information after all.

'Yes. I wasn't listening at the wall or anything,' she adds quickly in her own defence.

'No, course not,' Marshall genuinely supports her to keep her on side, but a visual of the nosey cow with a glass to her ear at the wall sprang into mind.

'I just happened to hear two of them,' Gayle adds.

'Did she have a fella then?' asks Reeves.

'No, no, it was definitely a woman.'

'And what were they saying?' Reeves wishes she would stop giving these short sentences and not expanding until they push further.

'Oh, I couldn't hear what they were saying at all,' annoyance shrouds the words as her thirst for other people's business had gone unquenched. 'Their voices were so small I could barely hear them,' she went on.

'But there were definitely two in there?'.

'Oh, yes, most definitely.'

'Just yesterday?' Reeves voice came out a little louder than he intended while pushing for the information.

Gayle nods as she takes a sip of her tea. 'There's not now, though,' she deflates them once more. 'They each left in turn earlier today.'

Then she leans in closer as if the walls have ears and she doesn't want them to hear her theory. 'I heard the door go twice.'

'Oh, I see.' Marshall plays along with the theory once more.

'I mean, she might've had other people there before, but that's the first time I noticed. She normally gets home around ten-thirty though, from work that is,' she adds. 'I've no idea if her employers know that she's here illegally, but surely they must do?'

This time the question is aimed at them and neither were expecting it, distracted by the information about when they can catch the girl at home. Gayle's enquiring face prompts for a response.

Marshall can see that Reeves' manner has changed and he's no longer in the role of immigration officer, but is reverting back to his usual callous self, so he fields the question in as non-committal fashion as he can. 'Oh, that's something we will be looking into. But I'm afraid we're not able to say anymore, you know while there's an investigation going on.'

He stands up, indicating the conversation is coming to an end. Reeves stands up also, and although quiet, he snaps back into character just in time. 'Thank you for your time, Mrs Winslow.'

As Gayle's door closes, they're left in the dark, deserted corridor. The overhead light flickers a strobe effect across the words sprayed on the flat opposite.

'What do you think Reeves, shall we try to befriend the girl and trick her into divulging when her little friend will visit next?'

'No. I've got a better idea.'

# CHAPTER 39

I've concluded that suburbia makes me just as nervous as the rougher parts of the city. Eager to get off the main road, I hurry towards the turn off that takes me down a dirt path between two houses before the Neighbourhood Watch team has time to spring into action.

The stickers are on every door and window, declaring their intent to challenge anyone considered a stranger in the midst. The anxiety almost suppresses my hunger, until my body reminds my stomach that I've been walking for hours and my energy needs replenishing. My tummy rumbles at the thought of the moist, hot chicken in my bag, waiting for me to devour it.

The dirt path leads me out of sight and with that comes a little calmness to placate my anxiety, knowing I can soon be hidden away completely to eat my meal. Following the dents in the soil made by wheelie bin wheels on waste collection day, the path leads me to the back gardens of this row.

Gaps in the fence lining the path offer striped glimpses of an immaculate garden beyond; lime green grass and cerise blooms. I round the corner where the path gives access to the garden gates.

Soft, delicate pink petals caress my cheek as I push through the branches of a tall hydrangea bush growing at the back of the first garden. The centre of the bush offers not only concealment but also the remnants of a child's den, with a homemade lantern hanging from a branch and a tree stump stool. It reminds me of a den I made in my own garden when I was little.

Ignoring the invite to dine in the centre of the hydrangea, I get as close to the fence as I can and peer through. There's no sign of anyone in this garden or near the windows. I pull one of the boards aside. It's hanging from only one nail at the top and creates just enough of a gap for me to slide through. Thankfully, I'm still concealed by another shrub on the other side.

From behind the branches, with leaves scented like a herb I recognise but can't place, I scour the garden to make sure no one's around. The conservatory on the far corner of the house is in use as a dining room. The family of four are passing bread rolls in a basket around the table. In a flash of opportunity, when all heads with the purest white-blonde hair lower at the same time, I leave the cover of the herbaceous shrub and slip inside the nearby summerhouse before anyone sees me.

Ducking down below the windows, I spread my denim jacket over the polished oak floor and pinch a cushion from the wicker sofa to lean on. Safely in the summerhouse, the uneasiness fades and my hunger kicks back in fully when a waft of chicken escapes from the bag, so I start my own evening meal in suburbia.

My mouth waters with the first glorious bite of the juicy, lightly-spiced chicken. The skin comes off in one piece, loaded with fat and carcinogens, and I relish it unashamedly.

I'm startled as the door shakes and there's a scratching sound on the other side. The chicken skin lodges in the back of my throat. I gulp to avoid choking on it, before staying perfectly still.

For a few seconds there's no sound at all.

Then it happens again.

Quietly, I curl my knees beneath me so I can raise myself off the ground just enough to look out the window of the door. I see the top of a blonde head and sink back down to the floor quickly.

The heated debate bounces off the car interior as words are thrown around over whose plan is likely to work the best. The Mercedes is parked in a dark corner of a residential parking area, behind a set of garages. The car is dark but the conversation is alight.

'I'm telling you Reeves, your dirty little plan to break the girl is only going to piss Garrett off!'

'He might be momentarily pissed but he'll soon come around when we present Layna on a platter for him!'

'But if this girl don't talk, like the last one, you're just gonna push Layna further underground. At least now we know most of the places she stays, we just have to get the timing right.'

'Timing?! It's all a bloody waste of time, Marsh! One punch and this girl will cave, I know it!'

'You're insane! You said that about the last one!'

'Your ideas ain't exactly bringing home the prize either, are they?! You playing card games and me playing the kid sister is getting us nowhere!'

'You've just got to be patient! This lad will break first, I'd put money on it. The women are too strong Reeves, none of them will give her up, I'm certain. Let me have a bit longer to play this lifeguard kid and plant a few seeds of doubt in his mind, and he'll turn!'

'Are you going soft?! You think women are too strong?!'

Marshall holds his hands out but says nothing.

'Alright, Marsh, I'll take that bet. A thousand pounds says one of the women will break first.'

'Deal.' They shake on it.

'As you're in a gambling mood, let's toss a coin. Heads your way to playing the little African chick or tails my way to break her into little pieces.'

With a sigh of resignation, Marshall speaks. 'Go on then.'

Reeves flips the ten pence into the air. A nearby streetlight catches the edges of the silver coin rotating, shimmering as it decides Amari's fate. Reeves catches it and turns it over onto the back of his hand. They both lean in as Reeves unveils the verdict.

# CHAPTER 40

The door handle squeaks as it presses down slowly and the door inches open just a crack. From my position on the floor, I find myself nose-to-nose with the fifth blonde member of the family. The golden retriever pushes her way in, all tail-waggy and friendly, and settles on my jacket before pawing at me for strokes. Conveying her wish to join me for my meal, she licks her lips and sniffs the bag expectantly.

A voice comes from behind the dog. 'Honey, you've just eaten! Greedy dog. Hello, love. Are you alright?'

Theresa's calm disposition tells me it's ok for me to be here tonight. 'I'm good thanks. Everything ok with you?'

'Yes, everything's fine, thanks.'

'I saw Angel the other day.' The mention of Angel lights up her mother's face, filling the summerhouse with a mother's love that clings to me, the only other beneficiary available.

Her voice is awash with pride, even at the pure mention of her oldest daughter's name. 'I spoke to her this morning. Glad you got to see her.'

'It's never for long enough though.'

‘Oh, I know how you feel, love. I wish I could see more of her too. With her living on the other side of the city and working, living her life, you know...’

‘Yeah, she’s doing good. Is Aaron still at Uni?’

‘Yes, he is and it’s going very well. He switched to the graphic design course. It’s much more up his alley.

‘The kids are looking more and more grown up every time I see them.’ I nod in the direction of the conservatory where they are still eating their dinner.

‘Yes, they’re not so little anymore. Molly’s twelve, going on eighteen. Honestly, she’s in too much of a rush to grow up, that one! And Matthew’s just turned fourteen. I’ll be glad when his moody teenage years have passed, I’ll tell you that!’

I smile at her, as even though it sounds like she’s complaining, I can see in her face she’s happier than she’s ever been.

‘Do you want a drink with that?’ Her eyes point to my takeaway box. ‘I can bring you a glass of water?’

‘Thanks Theresa, but I have water here.’ I pull out the bottle from the bag to show her. ‘I don’t want to cause you any bother.’

‘It’s no bother at all. I just wish I could have you in the house, but I can’t guarantee one of the kids won’t tell someone about you. And you know Keith, he’s as strait-laced as they come. I'm certain he'd call the police immediately, thinking he's helping.'

'It's ok, I understand, really. And it's fine out here. Better than a lot of places I spend the night!'

'It doesn't seem enough...'

An expression passes across Theresa's face that I can't read. It was only there for a fleeting moment, before she checked herself. Was it pity, maybe? I'm not sure.

The sense of shame swells inside Theresa's chest, expanding it into a sudden onset of heavy breathing. She hopes the knowledge she's hiding isn't visible on her face. The horrible truth eats away at her every time she sees this poor girl. It stabs at her heart like a razor sharp knife that could cut her open and reveal what she's been concealing. She's not sure Layna would understand, or even want to be around her or Angel again if she knew.

Helping her out with a place to stay every once in a while is pitiful compared to the enormity of what really happened. And it kills her that Layna is so sweet and appreciative of her too, jabbing the knife in further.

'Theresa, it's fine,' I assure her with another smile. 'You're doing all you can. I'm thankful for you letting me sneak in here occasionally. You're lucky you got a second chance with Keith, he's a good man. No need to spoil it over me.'

A few moments of quiet consideration pass.

'Okay, well I'd better get back inside before they notice I'm gone.' She turns to leave then stops. 'Oh, before I forget, a woman came to my door asking the whereabouts of Angel's old childhood friends.'

Having already taken another bite into my chicken, I stop mid-chew. 'Oh?'

'Yes, she just knocked on my door one afternoon. She didn't ask for you specifically, but she was digging for information without asking what she wanted outright. Before I could get to the bottom of it, she said goodbye, thanked me for my help and was gone as swiftly as she appeared.'

'What did she look like?'

'She was about late forties or early fifties, light brown curly hair, quite long. She was very attractive and glamorous; her hair and makeup looked like she'd just come from a salon.'

'Sounds like the same woman who asked Brent about his school friends too. I should take off, it's probably not safe here.' I gather my things, ignoring Honey's disappointed face.

‘Oh no, this was a fair few weeks back.’ She puts her hand out to stop me. ‘She hasn’t been back since. You’re fine here, I promise.’

I slowly sink back down onto my knees, as my mind explores a thousand thoughts simultaneously. Flitting between the notion of needing to run away immediately, to the fact that I don’t have anywhere else nearby and it’s getting dark already, I finally settle on staying put. Much to Honey’s delight, displayed through a toothy dog grin from ear to ear.

‘Just relax here and enjoy your meal, love. Come on Honey!’

Honey doesn’t budge.

Theresa rolls her eyes at her furry friend’s determination. ‘Looks like you’ve got a companion for the night! Goodnight, love.’

Theresa closes the door, leaving us to devour the rest of the chicken together. Snuggled up on my jacket, my dinner guest and I are happy to share the food and each other’s company. My stomach cramps as a piece of chicken fills the space that’s taut with anxiety.

Having been sat in the car all day long and the Oceanside Shopping Centre long emptied of shoppers, Jamie is as uncomfortable as he’s ever felt both physically and emotionally. Playing this game of watching and waiting is tedious, and with dead legs and a stiff neck, he looks over at Peter.

'Let's go home Pete. I could use a shower and sleep in a proper bed.'

'Jay, what's the matter with you?! Why don't you wanna put the work in? We're bound to spot her soon, and it'll all be worth it!'

'But Pete, I don't think....'

Peter cuts him off. 'You're always so bloody negative!'

'All I was going to say is that I don't think we're gonna spot her tonight. Look, these are the last people coming out now. Looks like employees as the security are locking the doors after them.' He gestures towards a girl with bright pink hair and a well-dressed young man in a suit, who split up and head for the last few cars dotted around the car park.

Peter looks over at them. 'Well, yeah you might be right about that, but there's no point going home. We're not far from the dock. Let's keep watch on the boat for the night.'

Tongue-tied over saying the wrong thing again or making things worse, Jamie resigns himself to even more hours sitting in the car and starts the engine. He follows the pink haired girls car out of the shopping centre car park, and turns into the lane that will take them to the dock. Broodiness takes over his mood in anticipation of another night trapped in the car with Peter.

Her footsteps are quiet on the thickness of the beige carpet. At the top of the stairs, Theresa encounters Keith coming out of the bathroom fixing his watch into place, having taken a shower after dinner.

'The kids doing their homework?' she asks, as he picks the towel up off the floor and hangs it on the rail.

'Um...yes, I think they are. I've been in the shower.' His hesitation tells her to check.

She puts her head around Molly's bedroom door. Amidst the twelve-year-old birthday cards standing proudly across the desk, Molly is quietly writing in her notebook, with her laptop open in front of her. 'All ok, sweetie?'

'Yeah, I'm almost finished.'

'Lights out soon then.'

'Okay.'

She blows her a kiss and closes the door.

Along the hall, she knocks and opens another door. Matthew's headphones tell her he didn't hear her knock and that his subject matter is more in the gaming category than the homework category. She stands in his eye line with her hands on her hips and he pulls the headphones around his neck.

'Matthew, didn't we talk about this? Homework first, games second, please!'

'Okay, okay! I'm fourteen, I can decide what I do for myself, you know.'

'Then decide better!'

He switches his screen to a word document with a couple of paragraphs of typed text.

'Thank you, love. Shout if you need a hand?'

'Alright.'

Her bedroom offers a cool blast from the ceiling fan. Wandering over to the window, she starts to remove her jewellery. Looking down to the summerhouse in the garden, she drops her earrings with alarm, spotting movement across the fence in next doors garden.

# CHAPTER 41

There's something about gardening at night that Estelle finds invigorating. Once her eyes adjust to the dark, it's no different to daytime really, but for the moths, midges and snuffling sounds from the hedgehogs in the bushes.

The water she pours glimmers in the light shining from her kitchen window. The smell of wet earth on a summer evening takes away all the stress from her day as she peers through the fence to Theresa's garden next door.

She can't see the girl but she's definitely still there. When Theresa comes for a cuppa tomorrow, she'll entice her to share the story behind this fascinating girl that sneaks into the garden to stay in the summerhouse every so often.

A rustling in the bush makes Amari move a bit faster. Walking home along the path next to the dark woods, she searches the mysterious, navy-blue cavities between the trees for anyone lurking.

Illuminated only by the occasional streetlight with a bluish tint, supposedly emulating daylight, it only succeeds in making the woods look more sinister. She can't see anyone, but can't be sure either. Her shoulders shudder, even though the night air is warm, as she re-lives many of her nightmares through the reality of these woods.

There are people in Eastbrook who are willing to commit crimes in broad daylight, let alone under the cover of night. The knowledge encourages her on this longer route around the woods, instead of her usual shortcut through the middle that she does in the light of day.

The feeling of not being alone compels her feet to move quicker, until she is jogging, then running at full speed. She can't tell if the sound of footsteps behind her are the echo of her own or someone else's.

The ocean is as dark as the night sky, with reflections from the city glowing as molten gold across the surface. The Blue Star bobs up and down slowly on the relatively calm water.

From the corner of the Fisherman's Club car park, Peter and Jamie Lawrence have a perfect view of the boat. All along the dock, boats sway back and forth against the jetty, quietly tapping the concrete edge in a sedate rhythm. The hypnotising effect is not lost on Jamie, who uses the peaceful setting to pose a question to Peter, hoping for a calm response.

'Don't get mad, Pete, but I've always wondered what the plan is for when we find her? How're we gonna get her in the car? She's not likely to come quietly.'

'We'll cross that bridge when we get to it.'

Jamie sits back against his seat, trying to accept the reply. 'Do you think she'll sneak onto the boat while it's dark?'

Peter still doesn't give him many words, despite being given a possible scenario to play to. 'Yeah, she might do.'

'So you're sure you want to stay here then?' Jamie tries again to convince his brother to go home, in the form of posing a question rather than telling him that's what he wants to do.

'Yeah, we're staying here.'

Jamie holds his hands up in defeat. 'Okay. It's worth a shot.'

'Yes, she is.'

'You're not really gonna shoot her, are you?!' Jamie's voice was a little louder to express the humour intended, but the joke immediately falls flat when Peter's response is dry and genuine.

'Yep. Guns in the boot.'

A moment of sickening silence passes before Jamie can speak. 'Seriously? You bought a gun?! I thought we were just gonna take her to the police when you said you wanted her to pay!'

'Police?! Nah, Jamie-boy. An eye for an eye, tooth for a tooth, and all that.'

As she opens the door to her flat, Amari sighs with relief for getting home safe from the monsters prowling around Eastbrook. She crosses the threshold and turns to close the door.

The man is hiding behind the door and before she can scream, a large, firm hand covers her mouth. Her arms flail as she's pulled back into the flat.

Another man appears, pushing the door closed with one fingertip slowly for dramatic effect, forcing her to watch as her only way out is blocked. For a fleeting second of desperation, she almost wishes that horrible boy would appear from the depths of the dark corridor and intervene, but her sensibility soon puts that unlikely scenario back into its place of insanity. As the door clicks shut, the man smiles at her, a pleasantry so out of place in the scene unfolding.

Amari struggles for breath as the other man's hand clamps her nose shut with his thumb and forefinger, while still keeping the rest of his hand over her mouth. She wriggles with the discomfort of feeling his hand on her lips and has no choice but to suck air through his sweaty palm, tasting his vulgar odour on her tongue.

The smiling man gets in her face. She closes her eyes and braces herself as a low, husky voice taunts her. 'Evening, Sweetness!'

She opens her eyes and tries to kick out at the wall to alert her neighbour, but the man holding her pulls her back before her foot can make contact. With the strength of just one hand, he holds her arms firmly behind her back, sniggering at her attempt to get help.

'Nice try, sweetness!' he taunts.

The other man is still smiling, beaming as if there's a joke that she's not privy to. He walks intentionally slowly towards a sharp knife on the kitchen counter, purposely giving her time to evaluate what he's doing.

She struggles against the force with which she's held, as the blade is lifted high to show his exaggerated interest in its sharp edge. The silver blade reflects on the wall, and she follows its trail across the floor, rather than look at the disturbing, smiling man.

After walking back over to her, he holds the knife dangerously close to her right eye. She blinks frantically, trying to scream, but can't find her voice.

Marshall speaks through his smile. 'Ah, now that's very dangerous to keep a knife as sharp as this just lying around.'

He can tell she understands just what's happening as she starts wriggling and almost gets free of Reeves' grip.

'No, no! Nice and still, please!' Reeves adjusts his hold and pulls her arms tighter behind her back as he speaks.

'You'd better listen,' says Marshall. 'One more move like that, and myself and Mr Reeves here will be the last two people you'll ever see!'

'And if you don't tell us what we wanna know, then we WILL be the last two people you'll ever see!' Reeves shouts, gratified with her flinch.

Marshall turns the knife over once more. The reflection shines into her eye drawing her attention back to him. 'Layna was here, wasn't she? Just a nod or a shake will do?'

She shakes her head.

Marshall shrugs his shoulders dramatically and looks down to the floor, and then up at Reeves.

Reeves spits over the side of her face as he speaks. 'She obviously doesn't think we're serious. I think she's questioning our sincerity, Marsh. Do you think she's questioning our sincerity?'

'Yeah, I think she is!'

'I find that quite insulting, don't you?'

'Yeah, I find it insulting!'

In a swift move, Reeves uses his whole body weight to force her arm further up her back than it can naturally go. Her muffled scream vibrates against his hand as all three of them hear the crack of her bone shattering. Reeves sweeps his eyes over her features, creased with pain and feigns sympathy. 'Oh dear, is the arm broken?'

'Well, I guess you won't be needing this anymore then.' Marshall picks up the guitar from the corner of the room. Holding one end, he uses all of his strength to bring it down on the floor, smashing the guitar into pieces like an overly aggressive rockstar. What's left of the guitar is held together by only the strings, which he throws onto the pile of debris.

'I've always wanted to do that!' he declares through a self-satisfied grin.

# CHAPTER 42

Gayle bites down on her palm as the crashing resounds on the other side of the wall. The glass pressed against her ear offers only muffled voices. She mollifies her lack of action by assuming the girl is putting up a struggle, though she hopes they're not using excessive force for the sake of it, she's only small after all.

Disregarding the glass as useless, she takes it back to the kitchen where she puts it away in the cupboard. She flicks the kettle on and takes some milk out of the fridge to pour into her teacup. She prepares a tray with biscuits while waiting for the kettle to boil.

Returning to her armchair, she settles back with her cup of tea and digestive biscuits. Ignoring the commotion next door; she also ignores the tiny fleck of conscience telling her that on the one occasion when she should be interfering, she isn't.

No longer comforted by the bobbing boats in the bay, Jamie is desperately trying to hide the panic that's swimming around his body at the thought of them killing Layna. He fidgets in his seat while trying to come up with a solution.

Visions of his sister fill his mind, smiling at them, then frowning when she realises what they are about to do. Her face then morphs into that of their mother, the unspoken anguish written across her face every time he looks at her. Then finally thoughts of his father, once outgoing and outspoken, but now too grief stricken to even leave the house.

He struggles to understand why Pete thinks killing Layna will help, nor can he think of a viable angle to stop Peter from going ahead with his plan. Driving Peter around the city was his way of reassuring their parents that he would be keeping an eye on his brother, but now it's turning into something completely different and he doesn't know how to stop it.

After a few moments of tapping his foot to an anxious rhythm, he takes his phone from his pocket and pretends to read a message. 'Pete, mum wants us to go back and have a late supper with her.'

'Tell her we can't J! We're busy!'

'She said dad's in his office and she doesn't want to eat supper alone.'

'Well tell her to knock on the office door, dad will probably come out if she asks him.'

Jamie knew this wasn't true. Barely anything could lure their dad out of the sanctuary of his office these days. And if Peter was being honest, he knew it too.

Out of ideas and not wanting to push it, Jamie utters a feeble; 'Okay,' and pretends to type a message back. He puts his phone away without hitting send, and takes a side glance over at Peter to check he hasn't caught him out, and is relieved to see he is none the wiser.

He looks out over the bay, contemplating and plotting, but noticing how all of a sudden the ocean is not so calm. A swell has developed, sending the boats around the dock into a turbulent rocking action. Similar to the swell of violence that has escalated in his brothers intentions, he watches as the water is controlled by the dangerous undercurrent, feeling as helpless as the boats docked in the bay as they're thrust around.

Reeves throws Amari on the bed, enjoying the sound of her crying out in pain as she lands on her broken arm. He flips her over and duct tapes her mouth and hands.

Her small body writhes with agony on the bed and her eyes roll back in her head as if she's passing out, so he leans down and shouts in her face. 'No sleeping now! We don't want you missing out on all the fun!'

Her eyes open wide with fright and he laughs. 'You know Marsh, my old mum used to say a splash of cold water on your face will keep you awake.'

'Yeah, good idea Reeves!'

Reeves drags Amari off the bed by her arms, once again laughing at the hearty growl of pain that came all the way from her stomach, before coming to a halt when it hits the duct tape across her mouth. Under his grip, he feels two parts of the bone moving separately inside her arm. Her petite body crumples but he doesn't stop. He hauls her over to the kitchen sink.

Marshall turns the tap on and puts the plug in, watching the sink fill with a swirling, powerful flow. When the sink is full, Reeves grabs a fistful of Amari's hair and plunges her head under the water.

With the duct tape over her mouth, the water gushes up Amari's nose, down her throat and into her stomach. She swallows quickly to avoid it going into her lungs. The pain in her arm is making her woozy.

Her mind, overcome with terror and pain, takes her to a surreal, dream-like place. She's swimming in a turquoise ocean. The soft, warm water is soothing as she floats through red corals towards a sun-bleached path of white light shining down from the sky. The hazy underwater world is so far removed from the one she's living at the kitchen sink, it helps her to disassociate from what's happening.

A burning sensation in the back of her nostrils ends her daydream as she breathes in, filling her lungs with water. The burning continues down her throat and into her bronchioles as she drowns.

# CHAPTER 43

Reeves pulls her head back just as she goes limp. She's barely conscious as he rips the tape off her mouth. She gasps for air and projectiles the water she inhaled over his legs and feet. She's coughing and spluttering for what seems like an eternity.

Sensing the girl isn't going to take much more, Marshall speaks up before Reeves can do anything else. 'Let's try again, shall we? When's Layna coming back?'

'I don't know... what you're talking... about.'

Marshall watches the tears roll down her face and the tap water spill from her mouth as she speaks. He looks at Reeves and recognises the expression he has come to know so well and braces himself knowing what's about to happen.

Reeves punches her hard in the face. Her head recoils and her lip splits, spurting blood into the air as she falls backwards. Her light frame hardly makes any sound at all when her body hits the floor.

A sound like a bomb exploding reverberates as her head hits the ground. The lights go out completely and Amari's world is dark for an indeterminate length of time.

She's roused ever so slightly to a semi-conscious state by a strange weightless feeling. A distant thought gradually strengthens as it comes closer to the forefront of her mind; she's being lifted up to Heaven.

Feeling calm and ready to go, she drifts back into unconsciousness, allowing the angels to take her wherever they want.

The tray of crystal glasses on offer beneath the chandelier sends even more shimmers of light flickering around Cliff Garrett's opulent lounge. The prisms catch on the diamond necklaces, earrings, cufflinks and bracelets of the guests he is entertaining this evening.

With his glass in one hand and his phone in the other, Cliff addresses each of his guests with a passing comment to make them feel welcome and important, as he makes his way through the room to take a step away from the party for a moment.

The number on his phone screen was enough cause for concern for him to abandon his revered role as host for some very important guests he's hoping to do business with very soon. Closing the door to the den behind himself, he descends the few steps down into the room and sits back in the large leather chair behind the captain desk to take the call.

'What do you want?' he demands.

'Can you talk?'

'If you make it quick, Harry, I'm hosting drinks here at the house with some friends from Morrocco. What's up?'

'It's more a heads up actually. This new Chief Inspector seems hell bent on digging around your businesses. I've tried to steer him off but on a separate note, he's also asking for a new cold case taskforce to be set up over the Raye family murders. I'm not sure how much longer I can keep them from finding out the truth, you know?'

Cliff smashes his whisky glass down onto the desk with such force it sends the liquid splashing over the mahogany wood. 'What do you mean you can't stop them?! That's what I'm paying you to do! Sort it out Harry! Or do I need to find someone else? Plenty of other bent coppers I can buy! I chose you because I thought you had brains enough to manipulate your superiors. You came with an exceptional CV in that regard. So just fix it, will you!

'But Mr Garrett it's become impossible...'

'What do you mean impossible?! You had them believing the girl was the shooter, so you need to give them the evidence! Pay someone to say they sold her the gun, anything!'

'But this new Chief Inspector...'

'I don't care Harry! Plant something on him to discredit him. Whatever you've got to do. Just sort it out, or they'll be investigating *your* murder next! Do you understand me?'

'Yes, yes, I get you. I'll, well, I'll see what I can do.'

Cliff hangs up and throws the phone onto the desk. Anxiety makes his palms sweat, sending him over to the drinks cabinet he keeps here in the den for occasions such as this. Pouring himself a double, he downs it quickly, hoping it will calm his nerves.

Remembering his special guests, all waiting for his presence in the other room, he cuts off the anxious thoughts racing through his head by reminding himself of his own importance. These people are here tonight to see him. They could bring a whole new empire of business, and with that will come more power, enough to rebuke any attempts from some hyped-up police inspector trying to bring him down.

With that resolve, he stands up to full height, straightens his shirt and utilises his well-practiced fake smile before re-entering the party room.

The sound of the Mercedes engine echoes in the dark alley next to the fire escape stairwell. Reeves looks all around to make sure there's no one to witness what they are about to do.

He opens the boot as Marshall emerges from the fire escape with the bound and broken Amari in his arms. He scoffs when he sees how Marshall is handling the girl so gently.

Marshall places her in the boot like he's putting a sleeping child to bed while trying not to wake them. He even takes a second to put a hoodie he keeps in the boot under her head, before closing the boot slowly so as not to make too much noise by slamming it.

Reeves shakes his head. He'd have thrown her in and slammed the boot shut quickly.

'Hope she can breathe in there,' Marshall says as he looks all around for anyone who could be watching them.

'Who cares!'

'I care, Reeves!' His voice was a little louder than he intended.

'Sshhh! Keep it down!'

'We can't have another body on our hands, or else you and I will be the next two bodies that turn up in this city! Mr Garrett's gonna skin you alive as it is!'

'Only if he finds out! Are you gonna tell him?'

After staring at him for a few moments, Marshall responds. 'No, Reeves. I'm not gonna tell him.'

‘Then what’s the problem?!’

Marshall rounds the car to the driver’s side. ‘Let’s just get out of here.’

The St Ives Hotel boasts all that is luxury for a city centre host. Doing a three-sixty degree turn as he speaks into the phone, the man feels his blood rush past his eyes as he tips his head back to describe the artwork adorning the ceiling.

‘Yes, Mr Brooks, the hotel is great, even more lavish than the charming little bed and breakfast.’

He picks up a statuette of a dancing couple and checks the bottom for the name of the artist. ‘Yes sir, I believe she’s back here in the city but I haven’t caught up with her yet.’

He puts the statuette down and walks towards the bathroom, where he turns the light on ready to take a shower and call it a night. ‘I know, sir. If only she knew we mean her no harm, then perhaps she’ll be willing to sit down and talk.’

He flicks his shoes off and hooks the phone between his shoulder and his ear to free both hands to remove his watch. ‘I will absolutely keep trying. I haven’t lost one yet, so I’m keen to keep that record! Thank you, sir. Bye now.’

This isn't Heaven.

Amari's eyes flicker as they try to adjust to the pitch black that tells her the angels didn't take her after all. Entombed in darkness where the air is tight, she senses she's enclosed even though she can't see. Her mouth has been taped again so she can't speak or call out for help.

A bump in the road shakes her to a full state of awake, underscored by searing pain from her arm and her head. She figures she's moving so must be in the boot of a car or the back of a van without windows.

The assault in her flat plays through her memory in colours more vivid than reality and with the volume unrealistically high. She closes her eyes, listening to the almighty crack of her bones breaking, then the mellow sound of the ocean, and the explosion in her head. Her eyelashes tremble with the weight of her tears as they fall rapidly from her eyes. Lying still, crying silently in the dark, there is nothing she can do but wait.

# CHAPTER 44

High-beam headlights distort the white lines into zigzag shapes. There are no other cars on the road, no streetlights, just the silver Mercedes and its three occupants.

'You're enjoying this, aren't you Reeves?' Marshall speaks quietly.

'Aren't you?!' He fires the question back.

'No, Reeves, this is not what I signed up for! You better hope the girl ain't hurt enough that she can't speak.'

'She'll speak, don't worry.'

'You said that about the last one! How's she gonna speak if she's unconscious?!'

'She'll soon wake up when she sees what I've got in store for her! Head to the golf course.'

'Are you mad?! That's a bit too close for comfort, ain't it?! You really have got a death wish!'

'Trust me, she'll be so scared, she'll be begging to tell us where Layna is.'

'You're a piece of work, Reeves, you really are!'

'What, and you ain't? You're as much a part of all this as I am.'

'Yeah, that's what I'm worried about! You taking me down with you!'

The blow to the back of her head catches her off guard and sends her hurtling forward. The dinner plate falls from her hand, smashing on the kitchen floor. Tiny pieces scatter over the tiles. Her cheek lands in the middle of the shattered ceramic, scraping across the sharp splinters as she slides along the floor.

Terry is drunk and yelling obscenities, blaming her for something Angel said or did. Before she can pull her body off the floor, Theresa hears Angel's cries as he unloads his punches on her instead. Every pounding thump her daughter takes hits her soul as if she is the one receiving them.

Just as she gets to her knees, Angel screams. A piercing sound that shatters Theresa's heart into pieces, replicating the shards of plate strewn across the floor.

She awakes with a start, throwing back the bed sheet and looks over at her new husband, Keith, peacefully asleep and unaware of her torment. Although this was a dream, it was no nightmare. It was a re-run of her past reality.

The car jolts to a sudden stop, tipping a few reluctant teardrops over her lash line. Instinctively, Amari puts her bound hands out to stop herself from rolling forwards, but instantly regrets it when searing pain rips through her broken arm, up and over into her shoulder blade. An excruciating reminder of what occurred only a short while ago but of which her mind is already trying to protect her by glazing over the memory, turning it hazy, muting the colours and sounds, to lessen the distress.

She bends her knees to stop herself from rolling forward and take the pressure off her arms. Being in the foetal position provides a small sense of comfort in such an alarming environment of a dark boot of a car, being driven to goodness knows where.

She begins to cry again, afraid that she is on her way to meet the end of her life. In the midst of her physical assault, she had been ready to let the Angels take her in order to end it. But here, in the dark confines of the enclosed space, her conscience is telling her that's she's alive and still has a chance to survive. No longer able to accept her fate, she shakes her head and whispers behind the duct tape across her mouth; *I'm not ready. Please, I'm not ready!*

The car stops.

Almost immediately, her tears stop too. Listening hard for any sound or clue what's happening, she holds her breath with anticipation and fear. After a few moments, the clasp in front of her face clicks. The boot opens only enough for her to see a terrifying pair of eyes peering in at her.

'Wakey, wakey!' Reeves uses a singsong voice, loaded with artificial joviality. Opening the boot fully, he teases more. 'Time to rise and shine, sweetheart!'

He starts to drag her out of the car by her broken arm.

Marshall quickly jumps in. 'Careful!' He takes over, lifting her gently out of the boot.

'You really have gone soft, ain't ya?!' Reeves slaps another piece of duct tape across Amari's mouth unceremoniously. The first piece had come loose around the edges from her tears.

Marshall doesn't respond verbally, but shoots him a scornful look beneath asymmetrical eyebrows, as he places Amari on her feet. She's very unstable, so he keeps hold of her.

Seeing how wobbly she is, Reeves uses the opportunity to torture the girl further. 'Let's take a little walk, shall we?'

Marshall half drags Amari along the path as her legs move slowly against Reeves' deliberately fast pace. With his arm around her tiny waist, he lifts her so that she doesn't have any weight to bear on her shaky legs.

Reeves leads a path through the empty golf course. The occasional light shines from the tall lamps, picking out the perfect green grass, contrasting against the dark purple sky dotted with white stars.

At the edge of the course, Reeves slows a little. Basking in the sick mood that he's in, he gives Amari a mock tour. 'Now this, my little friend, is the Kings Park Golf Course. Splendid, ain't it?!'

He points to a house high up on a hill that overlooks the golf course. 'You see that house up there?'

He grabs her from Marshall's grasp and roughly spins her around so she can look. 'That's Mr Garrett's house. You'd love Mr Garrett's house, you would. He's got a swimming pool, a cinema room, tennis courts and even this very golf course you are standing on belongs to him.'

'You see, he's quite greedy is Mr Garrett,' Marshall adds, hoping to keep the chit-chat going so she talks before Reeves can do her any more harm. 'He was an only child, you see. Always got what he wanted and he doesn't like to share, you know? He's a bit spoiled.'

'Yeah, spoiled!' Reeves smiles at Marshall, enjoying that he's finally joining in the fun. He pushes Amari to the very edge of the golf course where it overlooks the ocean.

All three stand in a line looking out for miles, in a poignant moment of acceptance over what's likely to happen. It's silent but for the crashing waves below and Amari's weeping from behind the tape.

# CHAPTER 45

Reeves laughs at the girl, who's shaking so hard she has to lean against Marshall to stop herself from falling over. He eventually contains his laughter enough to speak.

'You see, Mr Garrett, that's Cliff to his friends, doesn't look too kindly upon people who get in the way of what he wants. In fact, he personally asked us to introduce you to another of his friends, also known as Cliff!'

He nudges her towards the edge of the cliff. 'Don't you love it, Marsh?!'

Marshall can't help but snigger. 'Yep, I love it!'

Reeves gives Amari a bigger shove but holds onto her so he can drag her back. He leans in close so his lips are only a few centimetres away from her face. 'Enjoying the view?!'

His spit hits her eyeball, and she closes her eyes in response. 'Good idea. Don't look down, whatever you do!'

Marshall laughs along, glad the conversation is still flowing, prolonging the inevitable.

'Now, I'd love to stand here taking in the view with you, sweetheart, but business has to take over I'm afraid.' Reeves grabs a fistful of her hair and whispers into her ear. 'I'm going to take the tape off and give you one last chance to tell me where Layna is. Ain't that nice of me?'

Marshall chips in, knowing Amari cannot answer the question aimed at her. 'Yeah, I think that's pretty decent of you, Reeves!'

Though he's playing along, Marshall is desperately trying to think of a way to stop Reeves from pushing the girl over the edge without getting into a physical fight of their own. Before he can come up with anything, he realises Reeves is untaping her and he hopes to God she will talk and save her own fate instead.

Reeves peels the tape off slowly, relishing the pain it causes her as a piece of skin comes off her lip that's stuck to the tape. She cries out.

Reeves grabs her jaw and forces it shut. 'No! No screaming now.'

He rolls up the tape in his free hand and throws it to the ground. 'Now then, where is she?'

Marshall looks at her with pleading eyes. The desperate look she fires back at him doesn't convey any clue if she will tell or not.

Reeves, losing his patience, gives her another little shove forcing her to look at him and not Marshall. 'Well?'

Her voice is small but clear, despite the evil eyes burning holes into her soul that warn her to tell them where Layna is or she will die as a consequence. 'You will never find Layna.'

Amari stares him down, finding assurance from within that surprises even herself. She watches his reaction closely, as his pupils first dilate then shrink as the anger at her response kicks in.

She feels his fingers curl into a fist full of her clothing in the small of her back. The cool ocean breeze catches her mid-air as she's launched over the edge, carrying her away from the cliff and out into the ocean. The stars swirl around in the sky as she drifts, making her dizzy, before everything goes dark when she hits the water. She's helpless as the waves wash over her broken, limp body, sweeping her against the rocks as they crash and tumble.

The cliffs surrounding the dock area protect it from the hum of city life on the other side of the hills. The quietness of the dockside at this hour is having little effect on Jamie.

Pretending to be vigilant in watching out for the Blue Star masks the worry he's internalising over what Peter is planning to do to Layna. It's been eating away at him all night.

Normally he would've had a snooze by now, but sleep is the farthest from his mind than it's ever been. Racking his brain for an idea on how to stop him has given him a thumping headache, and no real solution either.

In contrast, Peter seems to have allowed the calming effects of the night time harbour to lure him into slumber. Jamie stares at him as he tries to comprehend the conundrum of Peter being so angry and ready to kill, yet able to sleep so easily, when he himself cannot sleep even at just the thought of it.

Peter startles him as he speaks with his eyes closed. 'She ain't here is she, Jay.'

Jamie wonders how he can make such an assured declaration, seeing as though his eyes have been closed for most of the time they've been here, but plays along. Anything to avoid actually running into Layna so Peter cannot carry out his plan. Acknowledging that this really is his only viable option, he vows to do everything he can to make sure they don't find her.

Buoyed by this new found goal to keep them from catching Layna, he hides it by deliberately keeping his voice low and flat. 'Don't think so, Pete.'

'Let's go to another retail park. She's bound to pop up at one of them sooner or later. Let's try The Lime's so we can be there when it opens.'

Jamie starts the engine, plotting how he can drive slowly enough to delay their arrival, maybe stop for petrol somewhere and deliberately take his time. Then he'll try to make sure they have a terrible vantage point for watching the doors to the shops at The Limes Retail Park. If he sees Layna, or anyone that looks like her, he will try to distract Peter with something in the opposite direction.

Marshall stands open-mouthed, staring over the edge of the cliff, where he sees the girl's body being thrown against the rocks by the pounding waves. He looks up at Reeves, who shows no emotion as he walks away.

Marshall follows, seizing the chance to voice his dismay, if only to the back of Reeves' head. 'You really have lost your mind! Mr Garrett's bound to find out and he's gonna wring your neck! I'm telling you, Reeves, you've just signed your own death warrant!'

Reeves keeps walking ahead, where, with every step his momentary joy over what he just did turns to annoyance as the reality sets in that she didn't talk. By the time he can bring himself to respond to Marshall, his mood has turned into that of a sulky teenager. 'She was pissing me off.'

'Oh so, because you got pissed off, you decide to launch the girl over the edge of a cliff?!'

Reeves doesn't respond.

The two men walk in single file across the golf course towards the Mercedes. Striding, but without confidence.

As he walks, Marshall loosens his tie. 'I'd better get to my card game then, hadn't I? Seeing as though your tactics ain't working.'

He walks around Reeves to get in front, swinging his car key around his finger, an act meant to remind Reeves that he's still in the driving seat of the games tactics they've been playing.

The bravado isn't lost on Reeves, who drops his head at the dig, knowing his violent strategy hasn't worked, yet Marshall's game with the lifeguard is still on. He's sullen as he gets into the passenger seat, dreading being shut in a car with the gloating Marshall.

# CHAPTER 46

The doorbell breaks the concentration around the table. Ellis takes his cards with him as he walks through the dimly lit house towards the porch. Slotting his cards into the front pocket of his shirt, he unlocks the front door and pulls it open.

The outline of the coast hovers in the background behind the large figure filling the foreground. A few twinkling stars catch his eye from the dark sky above, before he focuses on the face before him.

His voice is friendly but surprised. 'Hello Cavan, mate.'

'Evening! Sorry to show up so late. Is it too late to join the game?'

'No mate, come on in. Your timing's impeccable as we're just about to start another round.'

Marshall slides into position at the table and evaluates the situation. Brent looks like he's had a few beers tonight. Alcohol helps people become loose-lipped, so he quickly kicks off a conversation to get everyone talking. Once the chatter is flowing, he's able to steer the conversation to women.

'No use asking him, mate, he's as single as they come!' says the guy with short, cropped, grey hair and acne-scarred skin. He nods towards Brent as he speaks.

Marshall looks at the guy as he tries to remember his nickname to reply. It's something like Gator or Crater, but he's not sure, so he directs his response to Brent instead. 'I find that hard to believe! A good-looking young lad like you?! Bet they're all over you at the beach!'

'They are, but I'm happy being free!' Brent slurs his reply to the ribbing.

'Really? I'm sure I saw you with a hot brunette, a small girl?'

'Nah, not me mate. You probably mean Billy. Me and him look alike apparently.'

'Yeah, Bill's always got a woman on his arm,' Ellis adds.

The conversation turns to Billy's new car and the subject of women is dropped. Marshall nods along, quietly frustrated but determined to find another avenue to get this kid to talk, or else Reeves is going to carry on hurting the women and Cliff Garrett will have them both on the chopping block for disobeying orders.

Seeing the effect of alcohol on those who were here before him, he watches the red, drunken faces stare at their cards, taking longer to assess than when they're all sober. The pile of poker chips rattles as more are added and he joins in, waiting for another opportunity to get this kid to spill the beans.

The torch beam moves slowly over the sofa and its floral cushions. I watch as the delicate flowers are highlighted in sections, while I crouch under the window of the summerhouse as close to the floor as possible. Someone is shining the torch right in, so they must know I'm here.

I may be frozen still on the outside, but on the inside the food is lurching around in my stomach, still undigested, as the anxiety tosses it around like clothes in the washing machine, ready to project it back up at any moment. Swallowing down, my gulp sounds louder in my own ears and I worry, unrealistically, that someone outside may have heard it.

With my irrational fears at full height, I dare myself to look up. My eyes strain into the far corner of their sockets as I look for a reflection of someone peering in the window above me. There's no bullseye of light on the glass so I theorise that someone is shining the torch from a distance. The beam is shaky as it moves around. Honey left a while ago so it's just me and whoever is shining the torch.

As quickly as it appeared, it's gone. I wait for a while without making a move, hoping against hope that no one is coming to investigate in person. Then, when I'm sure the coast is clear, I grab my things and leave.

She knows it's wrong and that she's supposed to be asleep, but she can't help it. The book is so exciting, she just can't put it down. Her mum will be mad if she finds out she's still awake.

Under the bed covers, Molly follows the torch along each line as the words come to life in her imagination. She worries the light will shine under her bedroom door, so she turns the torch down to the lowest setting and adjusts the duvet over her head to make sure there are no gaps it can seep through.

Picking out the brightly coloured illustrations, she smiles as she takes in the adventures of the main character, Celeste. Reading fantasy books like this one called Nightlife, is something her mum wouldn't approve of, so when she's finished, she'll hide it back under the mattress until she can give it back to her friend Kayleigh at school.

The shed door squeaks as Estelle pulls it open and leans a garden fork against it to stop it from closing. She puts her watering can away for the night and hangs her torch on a hook, thankful she found one with such a powerful beam that when she moves away from the kitchen window, she can see right down the back of the garden.

A noise behind her makes her jump. She spins around but sees only darkness outside the shed.

'Who's there?' she asks with a shaky voice.

Silence.

After standing still for a few moments, listening hard, she relaxes in her stance, theorising that it must've been a hedgehog. Or a mouse. Her gardening gloves are not too dirty, so she takes them off and leaves them on top of a box in the corner, before locking up the shed for the night.

She walks through the dark garden back to the house and in through her French doors, locking them as she double checks for any movement through the darkness. Certain there's nothing out there, she pulls the curtains across, closing out the night and the mysterious behaviours in the gardens this evening.

# CHAPTER 47

The streetlights leading downhill to the harbour twinkle beneath the dawn sky. I never bore of this magnificent view of sunrise over the ocean. It's invigorating after another night of walking into the early hours that's left me feeling weary and in need of a proper rest. It's usually quid's in at Theresa's but the torchlight made me too nervous.

The old castle ruins watch over the bay from the cliff opposite. Their position, elevated compared to my own, tells me I'm getting closer to the bottom of the hill and my achy feet are relieved.

The smell of a nearby bakery lures me with its tantalising scent of fresh bread and sweet doughnuts. It's the only business open at this hour along the winding cliffside road that leads down to the bay. The cakes in the window remind me that today is a special day.

Without hesitation, I go inside and pick out a single cupcake which they kindly put in a box that I tuck away inside my bag for later.

The collage of bruises across her face reflects back from the unforgiving bathroom mirror. Tiffany flinches at both her appearance and the memory of yesterday. The bags under her eyes from a lack of sleep further add to her battered exterior. Her earlobe is hot and red from the amount of time she's held the phone to her ear while trying to get through to Chloe. The voicemail clicks in again and she curses through plump, blood-filled lips.

The sound of the kettle clicking draws her attention, but she immediately regrets the swift action of turning her head when pain shoots from her neck down to her feet. Feeling her back distort as her muscles cramp, she holds onto the bathroom counter for support while she dials again. She's startled when a voice other than the voicemail service shouts through the phone.

'WHAT'S UP?!'

'Chloe! Why aren't you answering?!'

'Sorry Tiff, I was in the bathroom!'

'Listen to me, this is important. That guy you're seeing, he's bad. Chloe, you have to stay away from him!'

'What are you talking about? You don't even know Tony! He's a good guy.'

'No Chloe, please listen. I've never done anything against you our whole lives. I have no reason to lie to you. He's dangerous! Please stay away from him, promise me?'

'No! You don't know what you're talking about. Why do you think he's dangerous?! He's harmless. You'll like him Tiff, I'm sure.'

'No Chloe, listen to me. I've already met him, he's evil and he's setting you up! Please, Chloe, I wouldn't lie to you.'

'What do you mean, you've met him? I don't believe you! You're just jealous because something good is happening to me for once! You can't bear that mum and dad might actually look my way for their prized daughter for a change.'

'No, Chloe, this has nothing to do with that. When are you going to stop with this rivalry thing?! I've never once been in competition with you.' Her voice becomes quieter. 'He's bad. Please listen to me. You're gonna get hurt. Stay away from him.'

'You're insane. You're just trying to spoil things for me!'

The phone goes dead.

'Chloe!' Tiffany's voice bounces off the phone now there's no open line.

After a few moments standing quietly trying to control her emotions with a breathing technique, she dials another number. Her fingers tap nervously against the bathroom counter as she waits for a reply.

It's early at The Lime's Leisure Complex, as indicated by the morning birdsong filling the airwaves with summer melodies. Parked under a canopy of lime trees that the complex is named after, sticky buds shower the Honda Civic under a light breeze.

Jamie switches on the windscreen wipers and wash function, but the soapy liquid struggles to remove the residue of honeydew and aphids. He tuts, and turns the wipers to the fastest setting.

After another night in the car, Peter fidgets as cabin fever pokes at his early morning temper. His jaw clicks as his teeth grind, chewing over words he eventually spits out. 'I hate these places, J.'

Jamie almost bites back that it was his idea to come here and that he had wanted to go home, but at the last minute opts for a less provocative response. 'Me too.'

Peter tilts his head to one side, before making a calm statement, out of character for the mood he's in. 'I think we should go back to following Garrett's men.'

'What?! We only stopped following them a few days ago!' The words were out before Jamie could stop them. He quickly backtracks before Peter can retaliate. 'I mean, why the sudden change, Pete?'

Smugness spreads across Peter's ruddy cheeks as he nods towards the row of retail units near to where they're parked.

Jamie follows his eye line. 'Oh, I see! That's one of Garrett's guys coming out the pharmacy!'

'Yep, it is! You see who he's with, J?'

'Ain't that the lifeguard that works with the kid Layna went to school with?'

'Yeah, it is. Garrett's clowns have shown some nuance for a change.'

'You think he's onto something?'

'Yeah, I do. Let's follow him for a bit. Wherever he goes, we go. He might just lead us to her after all.'

# CHAPTER 48

The pharmacy is beginning to fill up with people collecting prescriptions. Having paid at the counter already, Marshall is glad to be leaving as he pushes through the door. His head hurts and he was feeling claustrophobic in the small pharmacy full of sick people. He's just enjoying the fresh air outside the door when a voice interrupts his thoughts.

'Morning mate! Looks like you and I have the same idea!' Ellis looks at the boxes of paracetamol in Marshall's hand.

'Yeah, mate. I'm suffering!'

'Regretting challenging young Brent to that drinking game now, I bet?! Told ya you'd feel it in the morning!'

'Yeah, I really am. Next time I do that Ellis, just pour me water instead of vodka, will ya?'

'Ha ha! No problem, mate. Get a good fry up in you, that'll help!'

'Thanks Ellis. See you again.'

'Yeah. Hope you feel better, mate.'

Eager to continue with his plan to avoid capturing Layna if at all possible, Jamie waits until the guy is in his Mercedes before he starts the engine. Once the Mercedes starts to pull out, he pauses before moving off, feigning looking around for other cars pulling out or to avoid shoppers.

'Come on, J! Get going or we're gonna lose him!' Peter's voice bounces off the windscreen and into Jamie's face, reprimanding him for dawdling.

And with that, he has no choice but to pull out and follow the Mercedes. But he'll do his best to lose him along the way without making it too obvious.

A break in the amplified bass riff filling The Calypso Inn with reggae, gives the ringing phone a chance to declare a call.

'Yo!' Farrell greets the caller.

'Please can I speak to Farrell?'

'This is Farrell.'

'You don't know me but I know you help Layna. If you know where she is, I need you to get a message to her for me. Tell her the Hotel Indigo is no longer safe. Can you do that?'

'What? Who is this?'

'Please, I know you can help!'

'I'll try, but who is this?'

Click.

He cradles the phone in his hand for a few moments before placing it slowly back on the base. The woman didn't ask him to tell her where Layna is or divulge any information, just to warn her not to go to the Hotel Indigo.

The music booms in the background, accompanying the customers who are here for breakfast. Deep thundering base drives the thoughts racing through his mind about where Layna could be right now and how he can contact her. He looks around for Davies.

'Can you watch the bar for a bit? I need to pop out.'

'Yeah. You alright?'

'Yeah.'

Davies' raised eyebrows tell him he doesn't buy it, but before he can ask anything more, a customer appears at the bar. When Davies turns to deal with them, Farrell takes the opportunity to leave without further probing from his cousin.

From across the bar, The Watcher sees the exchange between Farrell and Davies. Having become hard of hearing lately, his mastery of lip reading and judging facial expressions has developed.

Sensing something is going on, he downs the last of his orange juice and grabs his car keys, ignoring the others at his table who offer enquiring looks at his sudden urgency. In the moment, he is too consumed with his new tactic to follow Farrell instead of those other two, to bother explaining.

Outside in the balmy morning air, he slides in behind the wheel of his Volvo and waits for Farrell's car to exit the parking area behind the Calypso Inn. He follows along a few cars behind to make sure he is not seen.

Something he learned long ago is that moving in the shadows is the best way to find the opportune moment to exact revenge. Making a big song and dance of it will only alert those to your plans. So he quietly waits and plots, while driving carefully so as not to draw attention to himself.

Reeves lets the phone go to voicemail. It takes several minutes for the notification to come through, so he knows she left a long message. He clicks on it and listens.

'Tony?! It's Chloe.' She's sobbing down the phone. 'Please can you call me back! I need to speak to you right away! Please

Tony. Please call me back when you get this message. It's about my sister Tiffany!'

Reeves laughs at the distress in her voice, happy his deed was finally done at the bottom of the lift shaft. After a few more minutes of her crying down the phone and begging him to call her, he deletes the voicemail and relaxes knowing he will never have to see the stupid cow again.

# CHAPTER 49

The weathered wooden boards of the jetty feel soft under my feet. The water is calm beneath, softly splashing against the posts. It's early but it's already very warm and my skin feels clammy.

The Blue Star sits proud among the other boats. Always immaculate, the navy-blue hull looks freshly painted under the white capital letters. The orange and white life ring makes it picture-perfect.

No sign of Frazer. He must be down in the cabin, though its unusual as he is usually up and pottering around the boat well before dawn. I climb aboard and open the hatch. There's no sound from inside. Stepping down into the living space carefully, I feel the eerie emptiness, as he's clearly not here.

The boat bobs up and down under the gentle waves as I drop my bag down onto the chair. A silver picture frame on the shelf catches my eye. I pick it up and smile at my father standing next to Frazer's old boat, The Silver Moon.

Suddenly the hatch opens and large, booted feet traverse the narrow steps sideways so they fit. Frazer's cumbersome build fills the space and his closed-lip smile tells me he's pleased to see me, as always.

'Do you miss The Silver Moon?' I ask to kick off the conversation, holding up the picture.

'I'll let you into a little secret.' He takes the it from my hand and stares at his old boat. 'She ain't really dead.'

He laughs with a chesty bellow at the astonishment on my face, his grey-blonde sideburns framing his open mouth.

'She's on Sinclair Island,' he says.

'I remember Sinclair Island.' I say, as I'm catapulted back to a time when I was sitting beneath a blue and white parasol with my family at a restaurant called The Palm Tree, the only building on the island. The memory wipes the smile from my face.

Sensing my sadness, Frazer's voice softens. 'I figured she could use a bit of the quiet life in her retirement. The island's uninhabited, apart from the restaurant in the summer months, so she spends her days resting or taking the kiddies on short trips around the island when the restaurant is open.'

'I love how you speak of her as if she's a real person. It's sweet.'

'Well, my boats mean a lot to me, girl. They're my family.'

I suddenly feel sad for him. Frazer's never been married or had any children, and here I am mourning the loss of something he never got to experience.

His words break my thought pattern. 'Nearly didn't recognise you as a blonde. Suits you.'

'Thanks.'

'So, I guess I got myself a deck hand for a while?'

'Only if that's alright?'

He doesn't reply but his smile, this time open and warm, fully reaching his eyes, gives me his answer.

The binoculars hone in on Layna boarding the Blue Star and then disappearing out of sight into the cabin below. Knowing where she is and that's she's safe brings a sense of comfort, if only for a few days.

Brent is supposed to be keeping an eye on the early morning surfers from the lifeguard station, but the Blue Star is the only thing he's been interested in since it docked. Ellis returns with two coffees so he quickly shifts the binoculars back to the ocean in front of him.

'You're quiet today, kid.' Ellis hands him his coffee. 'Still pining after that girl?'

'Yeah. She's in town visiting a friend. I wish I could see her, just to talk, you know?'

'Why don't you take a longer lunch and go by? You're not going to settle till you do. I'll cover for you.'

'Thanks Ellis. I might just do that.'

Farrell leans on the counter of the reception desk at the Hotel Indigo. After a few moments, a young guy comes over and asks how he can help.

'Yeah, I wonder if you can. Someone called me from here a short while ago. A lady. Do you know who that would have been?'

Confusion overlain with suspicion spreads across the face of the boy behind the desk. 'I'm the only one here on admin today,' he says. 'The other lady is off sick,' he adds reluctantly.

Sensing that must be her, Farrell presses on. 'Maybe it was her. Could she have called me from home do you think?'

'Umm, I doubt it. What did she call about?'

Farrell is searching for the right words to use next, when another man, apparently a guest who's checking in or out, leans over and fills in the blanks.

'I know who you mean! Gorgeous girl, she is. Tiffany's her name, isn't it Henry?' he says to the boy behind the counter, though he doesn't wait for a response before turning back to Farrell. 'Yeah, she lives up on Queens Avenue, drives a fancy red sports car too. Lovely girl.'

The boy behind the counter is motionless and his mouth is open, as if he wants to object to this breach of data divulsion, but it's too late. Just as he starts to fluster, the other man continues by way of explanation.

'I stay here a lot, see,' he speaks to Farrell, before looking back to the receptionist. 'Don't I, Henry?' Again, he doesn't wait for a response before continuing. 'I know everything there is to know about this place. Did you know the limestone they used to build it was quarried not far from here? I'm right, aren't I, Henry?' This time he waits for a response.

'Oh, um. I wouldn't know about that.' He clears his throat and turns back to Farrell. 'Sorry I can't help anymore.'

Feeling dismissed but having everything he needs, Farrell heads out, with a nod to the man who gave him the information for Tiffany.

# CHAPTER 50

Queen's Avenue looks just as nice as the name suggests. Farrell eyes the immaculately kept buildings and impressive collection of pricey cars in the parking area.

The only red sports car jumps out from a spot towards the far corner of the dead end street. As he approaches he sees the numbers of the flats they belong to painted on the ground. The one's either side of Tiffany's car are empty, showing him the numbers one and three. She's in the second flat.

Farrell heads to the building that the parking spots belong to and approaches the door. He presses the button for the intercom for flat two and waits. No answer. He presses again and waits once more. Still nothing. Then he sees the services button. He presses it and the door clicks, indicating he's in luck. He pulls it open and enters the building.

Looking around the ground floor, he quickly finds the door for flat number two at the back of the building and taps lightly on it with his knuckle. No answer again. He looks around to make sure no one else is present, before speaking quietly to the door, hoping she will hear if she's on the other side looking through the peephole.

'Tiffany? My name is Farrell. You called me at The Calypso Inn? About Layna. Please, if you're there, can I talk to you?' He waits a moment and is met with nothing but the sound of his own breathing. 'Please?' he adds as gently as he can, in barely more than a whisper.

The unmistakable sound of the lock turning answers his question. In the few seconds it takes for her to open the door just a tiny bit, he is suddenly very conscious of his size and wishes he could make himself smaller and less imposing. This woman has obviously had a run in with Garrett's men and is probably frightened.

With the chain still on the door, the view of her beaten face and terrified eyes slowly emerges in the gap, telling him he is right. Poor girl. His shoulders slump at the sight of her.

Cliff Garrett's name jumps out from the ribbon beneath the news reporter on the TV screen in the corner of the Calypso Inn. Davies reaches for the remote and cranks the volume up to the max. The reporter shuffles some papers before she launches into her bulletin.

'*Questions are being asked today of local businessman and philanthropist Cliff Garrett, after a young woman was found floating in the water at the bottom of the cliff on which his golf course sits. She had been bound before apparently being thrown over the edge. Police are appealing for witnesses and for anyone who was at the golf course yesterday afternoon to come forward.'*

Davies's chest expands as his lungs fill from the deep breath he needed to process what he just heard. He shakes his head as he exhales slowly. 'This can't be good,' he says.

The cushions are bouncy behind her back as she settles on the sofa, with a cuppa in hand. Theresa enjoys the view through the patio doors into Estelle's garden, full of greenery and bursting with colour.

Similarly, the inside is also alive with vibrant colours in teal and raspberry, orange and blues, matching Estelle's bright personality. Theresa thinks of her own decor in neutrals of grey and beige as homage to her new-found calm lifestyle, as opposed to the harsh black, white and red of her past home she shared with her ex.

'Penny for 'em?'

'Sorry, Stel, I was miles away, admiring your garden and thinking how decor reflects our lives.'

'Yes, I suppose it does. Is everything alright? You seem a little distracted.'

'I'm just a bit tired. I didn't sleep well last night.'

'Are you worried about anything?'

'Nothing in particular. Just life. Things from the past keep popping up to remind me they haven't gone away.'

Estelle assumed she meant the girl in the summerhouse. 'Do you talk to Keith about your past?'

'No, not really. He's a good man, but I'm not sure he'd understand. He's sailed through life without any real problems to face, so to him it's all very simple. But life isn't simple, is it?'

'No, it's not. I'm here if you ever want to talk, Theresa, we've been friends for a long time now. If you can't talk to Keith, you can talk to me.'

'Thanks Estelle,' she squeezes her arm. 'The garden's looking lovely, by the way.'

Estelle finds it hard to hide her disappointment but allows the conversation to change to the garden. Theresa will tell her in her own time, now that she's planted the seeds for confiding in her.

Still on the hunt for Layna, the dilapidated state of the building shocks Farrell. This used to be a nice block and he immediately feels bad for housing Amari here. The dark corridors are creepy even for him, let alone a young woman coming through here alone. A bad feeling settles over him when he gets closer to her door. It's ajar and she's not inside.

Just as he's getting his phone out to call her place of work, a woman comes out of the flat next door. She doesn't say anything but folds her arms showing she's not pleased at his presence.

'Sorry to bother you. I'm looking for my little sister,' he lies, thinking the real story of how he knows Amari will not help matters. 'Have you seen her?'

The woman scowls indicating she doesn't believe him. 'I wasn't aware she had any siblings.'

'I haven't seen her for a long time,' he lies once more. 'I don't live in this city, you see,' he offers through a third lie. 'Do you know where she is?'

'Well, they might have made a mistake then, if she really is your sister, that is...' Her voice trails off as the worry becomes evident by her hand splaying across the top of her chest.

Farrell takes a few steps towards her. 'Who made a mistake?'

She starts to answer, but stops herself.

It takes him all of his might not to grab the woman's shoulders and shake her until she tells him what she means.

Instead, he forces a meagre smile, to encourage her to trust him.

Finally, after battling with her thoughts, her incredulous thirst for gossiping wins. 'The two men that were here. They were from immigration. They thought she was one of them illegals, you know. I mean, I told them she couldn't be and she's the sweetest girl...'

Farrell cuts her short. 'Lady, what did they do with her?'

'They took her away with them.'

Farrell feels the blood drain from his body, making him unsteady. He rubs his face with his palms to bring the feeling back to his skin, while processing the information. Before he can form another question to ask, the woman spills more of her own accord, though it's not words he wishes to hear at all.

'I don't think they were too rough with her, if that's what you are worried about.' The guilt evident across her face exposes her words as untrue.

Farrell barely hears her through the fog of fear clouding his brain, but at the same time, her words are loud and clear. He turns on his heels and runs down the corridor. Taking the stairs down two at a time, he's out of the main door before Gayle even gets back to her armchair.

# CHAPTER 51

Vintage jazz spills from the speaker beneath black and white photos of Hollywood golden era stars and a large picture frame of the Eiffel Tower. Glamorous dressing table lights shine a spotlight on shimmering tears pouring down her face, pooling in the wrinkles that appeared overnight when her daughter was murdered.

Lavinia Lawrence looks at the framed photo of her family on the dressing table. It was only taken a few weeks before Stephanie died, so she looks just as she remembers her last and even more tears prick her eyes.

Completing the family portrait, Peter and Jamie look so light-hearted and carefree standing behind Stephanie like the proud brothers they were. A far cry from the tormented, grief-stricken masks that adorn her boys faces now. Some days she can barely bring herself to look at Peter, such is the devastation he displays for them all to see; watching, waiting, wondering how he will react to even the slightest comments.

Still hurting from the loss of one child, each day her sons live out their vendetta to bring Layna to what they see as 'justice', feels like they're slipping away from her too. She must get to her before they do. If she can't save her own child, then she must save this one.

Another pang of grief grips her and she leans on the dressing table while the emotion racks through her body. Careful not to make too much noise, she takes a tissue from the sequined box and dabs at her tears.

Seeing that she's cried off all her mascara for the second time today, she reaches for the wand to re-apply it before her husband sees her. After a few dots of extra light concealer around her eyes, she judges herself acceptable, then picks up her pen.

On the note paper, she looks through the list of names. She's already put a line through the lifeguard's name and Angel's mother, so she circles the Hotel Indigo where Layna's mother used to work.

Through the throbbing in her head from trying to internalise her crying so her husband won't hear, she presses herself for an idea on how to approach the staff at the hotel without setting off any alarm bells. So far, everyone's been too guarded, and her offer of help is redundant.

Her planning is interrupted by the doorbell, followed by her husband's voice calling out from his office room for her to answer the door. Ignoring her concern that he barely leaves that room, spending every waking hour buried away in books instead of dealing with his grief, she responds in a calmer voice than even she expected to hear in that moment. 'I'll be right there.'

She puts the list into her makeup bag, somewhere her husband will never go, nor her sons. She goes downstairs, leaving the jazz to play out in the empty room.

Farrell enters the bar as it's in the full swing of lunchtime. It's loud and bustling, and he feels out of place with his solemn disposition.

'Hey, you're back! Did you hear...'

Davies is cut short as Farrell interrupts.

'Amari's missing. Two men took her apparently. It's got to be those same two goons Garrett sent here.'

Davies rubs the back of his neck as it breaks out into a troubling sweat. 'Oh no, I see what happened!'

'What?'

'While you were out there was a report on the news. A young, unidentified woman was found at the bottom of the cliff near Cliff Garrett's golf course! They said she was bound and thrown off the cliff. That can't be a coincidence, can it?'

Farrell feels the acid from his stomach reaching for his throat, burning and corroding as he swallows Davies' words. 'No, it can't.'

'They were asking for anyone who had been at the golf course that afternoon to come forward.'

'Garrett won't be happy with that!'

'No, he won't!'

After a few moments of watching the sorrow form lines across Farrell's face, aging him within seconds, Davies asks; 'What can we do?'

Having seen Farrell turn back into the Calypso Inn car park, The Watcher is just about to follow when, by pure chance, he spots the silver Mercedes he was following the other day come flying past.

In a split second decision, he turns out of The Calypso Inn and tries to keep up with the Mercedes instead. He tuts his disapproval as he watches it swerving around the cars deemed to be travelling too slow, then ducking in and out of lanes.

His driving reflexes are a little slower than they used to be so he has trouble keeping up. Though he can tell they appear to be heading towards the sea front. Pulling hard on the steering wheel, he feels the heaviness of the old rubber tires resisting.

In a quick assessment of the way the guy is driving, at such speed and with such aggressiveness, he can tell the mood has changed and that things are about to heat up. He swallows down a gulp of something that tastes like trepidation mixed with anticipation for the moment to finally come. It tastes sweet and sour at the same time.

He has a hard time keeping up with the Mercedes, hearing the whirr of his engine turn more to a grunt as he tests the old Volvo. 'Don't let me down now,' he mutters, without taking his eyes off the silver Mercedes ahead.

# CHAPTER 52

Brent takes a bite of his sandwich while keeping his eyes on the sky to watch for seagulls that might be tempted to rob him of his lunch. Juggling walking and eating, he navigates through the car park away from the lifeguard's office on the promenade, and heads towards the dock.

He doesn't notice the Mercedes at first, then just about gets out of the way in time as it swings into a space next to him. He's about to yell at the driver, but then sees who it is.

Cavan is laughing as he gets out of the car. 'Hey-hey, almost got you!'

'Hello, Cavan mate!' Brent laughs good-naturedly and shakes his friend's hand.

'How're you feeling? I've been struggling today, mate, I tell you.'

'Oh yeah, me too. I had to do the early shift as well, so I didn't bother going to sleep in the end.'

'Oh boy, no sleep at all?! I used to be able to do that. I'm getting too old for all-nighters!'

'What brings you down here?'

‘Well actually, I thought I’d better talk to you about yesterday,’ Cavan says as he slams his car door shut.

Brent racks his brain for something that might’ve occurred that he’s forgotten through liquor-induced memory loss. The way Cavan said it, suggests there was a problem.

‘What happened yesterday? Apart from a lot of drinking.’

‘The reason I was late for the game yesterday is that I was talking to a young woman about a mutual friend of ours.’

Brent relaxes a little, glad he hasn’t done anything to offend his new friend. But as the words register, he’s now searching his mind for a mutual friend.

‘A girl called Layna Raye?’

Brent’s heart lurches at the mention of her name. He can tell Cavan sees the recognition and is waiting for a reply, but he daren’t speak.

Cavan fills the void for him. ‘You see, I didn’t get to find out where Layna is because another mate of mine, Mr Reeves, well, he got a bit overzealous and chucked one of her little friends off a cliff.’

Brent’s eyes widen at hearing what happened to Layna’s friend. Still though, he can’t find any words that will sound believable. Realising that Cavan is not who he thought he was, and is as dangerous as he just suggested, he mustn’t let on that he knows Layna at all.

Cavan removes his sunglasses and wipes them with a cloth from the top pocket of his shirt. To Brent, the act seems so casual and out of place following the declaration he just made. He tries to think of a response that is strong enough to defy the obvious effect Layna's name had on him. He swallows hard, before opening his mouth to speak, but is cut off.

'And I'm sure you've already heard what happened to her other little friend too?' Cavan puts his sunglasses back on as he speaks.

Brent stares at the shades knowing the eyes hidden behind the dark lenses are looking directly back at him. The words he planned to use are stuck at the back of his throat, remaining unspoken.

'Blonde bird from the hotel? Copped it at the bottom of a lift shaft, as I heard it. That was down to Mr Reeves too. Got some anger issues, he has.'

After a short pause to allow the words to sink in, he continues. 'I like you, Brent, mate. I don't want to see the same thing happen to you.'

Brent understands the threat but still thinks his best bet is to plead ignorance. He finally finds some words from somewhere. 'Look, I think you've got the wrong guy...'

Cavan cuts him off again. 'No mate, that won't work. We know you were her childhood sweetheart and you've been helping her hide out ever since. No need to deny it. I can see it written all across your face. You blushed when I said her name! There you go again!'

Brent instinctively looks down, searching for an imaginary hole in the ground that he hopes will open up and swallow him. He's always found his feelings for Layna so hard to control, and this moment is no different.

'Bet she's told you she still likes you and made you think you have a chance? I hate to break it to you, mate, but we've seen her with a lot of guys and she looks very cosy with them all, if you know what I mean.'

Brent physically jolts at this information. A scowl forms as he tries to fathom if this could be true or just another tactic. Even if it's not true, jealousy still rouses inside the pit of his stomach. Scratching at his insides, it claws away at his rational thoughts, turning them irrational in a way that only the green-eyed monster can.

He starts to question everything. Could that be why she never sticks around and is so non-committal when he asks to see more of her? Or was she genuinely trying to keep moving around? He isn't so sure anymore. She does keep coming back to him though, doesn't she? But that's because she needs his help. Is Cavan right? Is she just using him and his feelings for her, for her own gain?

No, Layna isn't like that, he pacifies. She's kind and would never do that to him. Though she's been through a trauma and that changes people. Not always for the good. Has she changed and he just didn't notice? The jealousy won't let go of the internal debate, tugging away at those delicate heartstrings that have suddenly become taut and ready to snap at the idea that maybe he has been blinded by his love, all this time.

Marshall, in his role as Cavan, lets the notion of Layna being with other guys sink in. He watches Brent's eyes searching some imaginary world where the truth has become tangled in a web of lies, and sees he touched a raw nerve. He looks over the top of his sunglasses so that Brent can see his ridiculing eyes. 'She's been leading you a right merry dance, mate!' His belly laugh emphasises the mockery.

Brent now has a new emotion to contend with. Embarrassment. Has he really been a fool? Cavan laughing at him in such a manner makes him feel stupid. Has Layna really done this to him? The shame eats away at his integrity as he tries to make sense of it all and find a way to save face.

Cavan stops laughing suddenly and becomes very serious. 'She's using you, Brent. I know you think you're helping her, but really all you're doing is prolonging the inevitable. She can't run forever. And the longer she's on the run, means Mr Reeves is likely to hurt more people. You, my friend, are getting people hurt.'

Brent's jaw feels tense as he grinds his teeth, where the remnants of his sandwich squish into gooey dough that he swallows, but it gets caught in his throat that has gone so dry from a mix of shame and anger. Mostly anger, though. From being made a fool of and the idea of Layna with another man. He's never thought of her with someone else before and it fuels the resent that's swimming through his veins. Sweat seeps through his t-shirt on the front of his chest displaying his jealous rage.

Cavan notices right away, and continues to pick at the thread. 'She's stringing you along, mate. Don't let her get away with that. You need to show her that she can't be leading you on like this when she's out there sleeping around with other guys, and not facing any consequences. It's better you tell me where she is now. It'll stop Mr Reeves from hurting anyone else. Including you, my friend! You know, one life in exchange for several others?'

Brent runs his hand through his hair and purses his lips, before eventually speaking. 'Look, mate....'

The Honda Civic circles around the car park just off the promenade, without entering. Jamie drives as slowly as he can, while Peter leans over his seat in every which way as he can to keep his eyes on them.

Jamie sees the opportunity and tries swinging the car abruptly to throw Peter off balance. Unfortunately, Peter is unphased and keeps his eyes glued to the two men talking in the middle of the car park, next to the Mercedes.

‘He’s well in with them lifeguards, ain’t he J? He’s talking to Layna’s old lovebird now.’

‘I doubt he’d give her up though, would he? They were childhood sweethearts.’

‘It’s hard to tell. Garrett’s guy looks all smiley but the lifeguard looks a bit tense to me. His fists are clenched by his side and he don’t look happy at all. Circle round again J, I wanna get a better look at his face.’

# CHAPTER 53

The crisp, fresh salad offers the only colour among the cold, stainless steel decor of Cliff Garrett's kitchen. Resembling an operating theatre and in the polar opposite of the rest of his luxurious house, the emotionless atmosphere is only interrupted by the crunching sound of vegetables.

Cliff takes another bite as Anna, his housekeeper, refills his orange juice before scurrying away. The phone rings loud on the table next to him and he grabs it up, annoyed at the interruption. 'What?!'

'It's Kevin, Mr Garrett. I looked at the security camera footage like you asked. It was definitely them, Mr Garrett. And they had the girl with them, so they must have thrown her over the edge. Or maybe she fell. But it was definitely Marshall and Reeves.'

'Those fools. What did they think they were doing?!'

'I managed to wipe it before the police took it, so nothing should come back to you, Mr Garrett.'

'Good man, Kevin. I owe you one, but not before I skin those two alive.'

He hangs up and slams the phone on the table, before scooping up another mouthful, stabbing at a piece of tomato when it won't balance on his fork.

Anna makes herself busy in the background, not wanting to get in the way, but also needing to stay nearby in case Mr Garrett needs anything else. She quietly starts to prepare the afternoon tea, trying not to rattle the cups and saucers.

The Mercedes brakes just about hold on the steep hill opposite the dock. Facing forward so they have a good view of the Blue Star, Marshall has his foot poised to jab the foot brake, in case the hand brake fails and they go hurtling down the hill.

'Here look, Marsh. Frazer Ryan's just appeared. Don't look like there's anyone else with him though. You sure this kid's good for the info?'

'Well, he said she was thinking of going to see him once he's docked and he's been there for a day.'

'We can only see one side of the boat from here, though.'

'Don't matter. If she's down in the cabin, she'll have to come up to the deck at some point. She can't stay down there forever.'

'Maybe after dark. She'll think she's safe, but then BAM!' Reeves punches his own palm.

Marshall jumps in his chair.

'We'll jump on board and snatch her!'

'Reeves, you're a lunatic! What about Frazer Ryan?! He ain't gonna let us 'just snatch her' is he?!'

'We'll throw him overboard!'

'He can probably swim, you fool!'

'Yeah, but we'll be long gone with the girl by then!'

'Alright, Reeves! Whatever you say...' His smile suggests humouring over belief.

The battered old Volvo edges to a stop further up the hill, on the same side of the road to the Mercedes but several cars back so he can't be seen. The car judders as he removes his foot from the brake and the handbrake reluctantly takes over. He hopes it will hold.

The Watcher switches off the engine and grabs his binoculars from the passenger seat so that he can watch their every move. He doesn't know why they're here but they haven't got out of the car again, so he figures they must be watching the dock. It's the only thing in view.

His senses are on high alert, waiting for the right moment. He licks his dry lips and settles back in the driver's seat to wait it out.

The Honda Civic is also parked on the same hill but on the opposite side of the road to the Mercedes and further back.

'See, J, I told you he was onto something. That kid obviously told him the Blue Star was here.'

'You think she's on board?'

'Yeah, I think she could be.'

Jamie raises his binoculars and hones in on the Blue Star. 'The old man's there on the deck but I can't see Layna.'

'Don't mean she ain't there though. She might be in the cabin or on the other side of the deck. Or maybe she's due to arrive later, after dark. It's nearly six thirty so we've got a few hours to wait if that's the case.'

Realising they will be here for a while yet, Jamie lowers the binoculars and adjusts his position to get comfy.

'This is it, J. I can feel it!'

'You think so?' Jamie can't hide the disappointment from his voice, but thankfully Peter doesn't notice.

'Yeah, I do, J.' He claps his hands together and rubs them, smiling at himself in the wing mirror.

# CHAPTER 54

Marshall's phone rings, breaking both his and Reeve's concentration on The Blue Star. He looks at the caller ID and throws his head back against the headrest.

Letting out a long sigh, he answers. 'Evening, Mr Garrett.'

'Did I not make my rules clear?!' he barks down the phone.

'You did, Mr Garrett. I'm sorry...'

'That's not good enough! How dare you bring this to my doorstep!'

'I'll let Reeves explain that one to you, Mr Garrett.' He casts an accusatory look over at him as he speaks. 'But since then, we've got a good lead. I got her little boyfriend to talk and we know where she is. We're just waiting till we can put eyes on her to confirm.'

'Where are you?' Cliff's voice was softer.

'We're on Primrose Hill, watching the dock.'

'Don't move. I'll be right there. Don't do anything till I get there!' he barks again, then hangs up.

'Shit, Reeves. You've really done it this time. We are as good as dead if this lead don't turn out; we might as well say goodbye to each other right now!'

'Calm down! He'll settle down when he realises we're onto something. I'm telling you Marsh, he'll have no choice but to pay us that money! We're gonna win!'

'Think about it though. I get the lead from this kid, then he sweeps in at the end to claim the victory for himself, then he'll say we didn't do our job as he had to do it himself! I'm worried he ain't gonna pay us a penny!'

'Nah, you're wrong. He's good for it. He wants the girl gone. We're gonna lead him to her. Then we get paid for it. You'll see.'

Marshall leans his heavy head against his palm with his elbow on the window, unable to share Reeves optimism. He can't shake the feeling they're being set up, so his thoughts turn to self-preservation as he plans his next moves.

At the top of the stairs, I open the hatch and step onto the deck. The sunset immediately engulfs me as I join Frazer in a chair on the deck.

'Just relax, girl, you're safe here.'

I smile. 'These sunsets never grow old, do they?'

'No, they don't. Seen many in my time. Every night is different. You see how the ocean soaks up the colours? Affects everything beneath the surface.'

'You love the ocean, don't you?'

'Aye, it's been my home since I was a boy.'

At the mention of the word home, I am once again catapulted back to thoughts of my own. My family. Steph. And then I remember the cake.

I take it out of my bag and open the box.

'You celebrating something, girl?' Frazer asks.

'Sort of. Today would be Steph's seventeenth birthday.'

'You still got her brothers on your tail?' he asks.

'I think so. To be honest Frazer, I have so many close calls, I'm not even sure who's who anymore.'

I close my eyes and pretend there's a candle on the cake. It's not my birthday wish to make, but I say one on behalf of my best friend who can no longer make wishes. Something I think she would want. Then I blow out the imaginary candle in solemn celebration.

The limousine pulls alongside the Mercedes. Instead of waiting for the chauffer to let him out, Cliff Garrett jumps out quickly and climbs into the back seat of the Mercedes.

'Is she on the boat?' He fires the question at them without so much as a greeting.

Marshall replies before Reeves can try and take any credit for finding her. 'Yes sir. We believe she's on there right now,' he exaggerates. 'Frazer Ryan is on the deck, he went round the other side so we can't see him at present, but he's been pottering about. We think she might be down in the cabin.' He looks over at Reeves to check he'll go along with this glorified version of the truth, and is assured when Reeves nods along.

Cliff is not that impressed though, glazing over the fact that Marshall just declared they have found her. 'Well, what if the boat takes off with her on it! Go and hire us a boat.'

'Ah... Yes. Good idea, Mr Garrett.' Marshall gets out of the car and walks down the hill to the promenade.

Just as darkness takes hold in the sky, agitation takes hold of Peter's dwindling patience, subduing the jubilance he felt just a short while ago that this could be it. Preparing for more disappointment, another outburst festers away inside his body, bubbling and ready to burst out, but then he sees the limousine arrive. Immediately, the agitation dissolves and is replaced with exhilarating hope beyond anything he ever felt before. He sits up straight in his seat.

'Well, well, well! Look who's just turned up, J!' He nudges his brother and points over to the Mercedes.

Jamie lowers the binoculars just as Cliff is getting into the back seat. 'Cliff Garrett himself!'

'Something's definitely going down, Jamie-boy! First that one was talking to the lifeguard, now they are here at the boat and Cliff Garrett turns up. The lifeguard kid must have told them she's here.'

Jamie points the binoculars back to the Blue Star. 'I'm not so sure. There's no sign of Layna, but that Frazer's got a blonde bird with him. I doubt Layna will be there if he's got a date.'

'A blonde bird?!'

'Yeah. She's sitting on the deck chair next to him. I can only see her from behind, but she looks too classy and a bit young for him.'

He passes the binoculars to Peter, who checks out his brother's theory through the magnified world and scoffs. 'Dirty old man!'

'Here look, Pete. One of Garrett's guys is heading over to Atlantis Boat Hire.'

Peter lowers the binoculars. 'So he is. They probably can't see Frazer's hot little date from where they're parked. But it's not a bad idea actually, in case she does turn up and they take off. Go and hire us a boat, J,' before adding, 'Cut through that alley so they don't see you.'

The Watcher sees the acquisition of a boat and readies himself for movement. His old bones have locked into position, his muscles tense and cramped.

The smartly dressed gentlemen in the limousine seems to be propelling the action and The Watcher suspects something heavy is about to go down. He reaches for his phone on the passenger seat. His fingers, not so dexterous anymore, take a few moments longer than most to dial the number.

'You know who this is?' he asks the person who answers. 'Trouble at the dock. Think they found the girl. You better get here now.' The person on the end of the line is still talking as he ends the call.

# CHAPTER 55

Looking down his nose, Cliff Garrett takes a hanky from his top pocket and wipes it over the bench in the boat Marshall has hired.

'Why didn't you get a bigger one!' he yells, more of a statement than a question, before continuing. 'And cleaner! It's covered in fish guts and looks like it's never seen a mop in its life!'

Marshall tries to appease him. 'Sorry Mr Garrett, but it's late in the day and all their boats have just been returned from a day of fishing, so they haven't had time to clean them.'

'Plus, it'll be faster than the Blue Star as its smaller, see?' Reeves shoots Marshall a look confirming their unity to win Cliff Garrett over as he speaks.

'You'd better be right.'

Reeves continues with his positive proactive approach to further impress him by making a suggestion. 'We still can't see the side he's sitting on. Shall we try moving the boat further up the dock?'

'I'm hoping we won't have to go anywhere on this measly little boat!' Cliff fires back.

'Me neither,' Marshall admits hesitantly.

'Please tell me you two idiots know how to operate a boat?!'

Marshall moves his hands over the controls, trying to work out their function. 'I do, Mr Garrett, sort of. I'm sure I can figure it out.'

'Is this what my money pays for?! Incompetence!'

'We're good for it, Mr Garrett,' says Reeves, desperately trying to keep him on side.

'Well hurry up and figure it out, or I shall really lose my patience with you!'

The smallest and lightest boat at the dock bobs up and down dramatically with each wave, unable to absorb them as well as the bigger boats.

Jamie struggles to keep his balance as he adjusts to life at sea. Spending his days sitting in a car has left his standing muscles weak.

'This boat stinks, J!'

'It's all they had left. Garrett's guy took the only other boat that was back from the fishing trip.' Jamie lied. He had deliberately asked for the smallest, least powerful boat they had on offer.

'This thing don't look like it's gonna cut it against the Blue Star. It's puny!'

'Do you remember how to drive it?' Jamie tries to change the subject.

'Yeah, sort of. It's been a long time though.'

'Remember when dad used to bring us all out fishing in the sea? Steph hated the cold. Mum always felt sick, and you only ever caught crabs!'

'Yeah, they were good times.' Peter doesn't sound happy, despite his words. Then he continues. 'Dad barely leaves the house now.'

'Maybe we can bring him out for the day? Try and get him back out into the world?'

'The only thing that can help him is knowing that girl is DEAD!'

Peter shouting shocks Jamie.

'Sorry, Pete. I didn't mean to upset you.'

'Let's just concentrate on the task in hand. Keep your eye on that boat.'

'We can't see the old man from here, but at least we can see Garrett's boat as well as the Blue Star. We can watch them both from this position, hey Pete?'

When Peter doesn't respond, Jamie looks over at him. Beneath the steely moonlight reflecting down onto the boat, Peter's face looks old, grey-tinged and haggard under the weight of vengeance. Jamie, feeling sorry for him, gives up trying to lighten the mood and leaves him be.

Stars have replaced the sunset and I find them just as mesmerising as the rainbow spectrum that adorned the sky not too long ago. The sound of chugging boat engines nearby is relaxing.

I look over at Frazer. 'I understand why you like living on the ocean so much.'

'You could get a boat of your own, you know.'

'If I had the money, I think I would!'

'Maybe one day, girl.'

Both of us fall into silent contemplation of Frazer's words, as we allow ourselves to be hypnotised by the stars in the black sky. My hypnosis is broken not by a snap of someone's fingers, but by a voice, and it's not Frazer's.

'Stay very quiet!' He whispers his demand from over the side of the boat.

I freeze.

Frazer sits up suddenly. 'What the devil is going on?!'

There's a pair of eyes looking at me through the bars on the side of the boat and I jump up to my feet.

# CHAPTER 56

After a double take, I find my words. 'What are *you* doing here?!'

'Saving your bacon! Again!' Farrell uses his loudest whisper.

Davies playfully salutes me from his position at the helm of a speedboat idling at the side of the Blue Star.

'Come quickly. They're watching you!' Farrell says, and I look at Frazer for help.

'Take her to the Silver Moon. On Sinclair Island. They won't find her there.'

He gives me a hand to climb over the side and I drop down into the speedboat as quietly as I can. Then Davies carefully turns the speedboat away from the Blue Star.

'How'd you even know I was here?' I ask Farrell.

'I got a tip off.'

'From who?!'

My question goes unanswered as we move off slowly and quietly. We disappear into the midst of the dark ocean and pick up speed when the engine kicks in, sending my wig flying under the force. I look back to see it falling into the ocean and catch sight of the two boats chasing after us. 'They're coming!'

Farrell looks back over his shoulder. 'Let's go!'

We're already going as fast as we can, cutting a trail in the water for them to follow. In the distance, Sinclair Island looms, a dark and forbidding silhouette against the night sky.

I look up to the stars and say another silent prayer for help. It's always worked for me, though I'm afraid I've reached my quota for answered prayers, with the amount I've said over the last year. *Please just one more*, I whisper. This can't be the end. It just can't.

All three men hunch over the controls of The Onyx fishing boat as it tries in vain to keep up with the speedboat.

'She's getting away!' Cliff's spit flies back into his own face. He wipes it away with a swipe of his hand. 'Told you we needed something better than this!'

'We can still catch them!' Reeves yells. 'Just keep it on max speed, Marsh!'

Marshall pushes the throttle as far as it'll go. 'Looks like they're heading to Sinclair Island!'

'Good. We'll corner them there! Don't you two dare let her get off the island! You hear me?' Cliff warns.

Reeves takes the warning with a pinch of salt, enjoying the knowledge he can do what he likes to the girl when they catch her. 'No, Mr Garrett. We'll make sure she never steps foot on the mainland again!'

Marshall casts a quick look at Reeves upon hearing this and sees his eyes sparkling with intent through the dark. He shakes his head in disbelief. Reeves is so caught up in his own agenda to realise they are likely to have the rug pulled out from beneath them very soon.

Anger fills the sea air between Peter and Jamie on the smaller Shore Seeker fishing boat. The spray hits both of their faces as it cuts a path through the dark ocean.

'You said a blonde bird!' shouts Peter.

For once, Jamie allows his temper to spill out. 'How was I supposed to know she changed her hair?! I was looking for a brunette!'

'Well, now they're getting away!'

'We're still ahead of Garrett and Co. Just go as fast as the boat will take us!'

'This *is* as fast as it goes, J!'

Jamie's feet slip on the wet surface of the boat, causing him to fall forward into Peter. The motion makes Peter momentarily let go of the throttle and they slow for a few seconds.

'Damn it!' Peter is as furious as the ocean gets on a stormy day. 'Come on! Come on!' he shouts, as the boat slowly builds back up to its full speed again.

Pushing The Onyx so hard makes it glide across the top of the water, but also means less stability and it rocks from side to side, almost throwing Cliff Garrett off his feet.

'Careful, you idiot!' he yells at Marshall, as if he has any control over it. Before he can berate him anymore, The Shore Seeker racing ahead of them distracts him. 'Who the hell is that?'

Reeves squints to train his eyes on the boat in the dark. 'That's the Lawrence brothers!'

'Well, what are they doing here?!' Cliff demands but doesn't wait for an answer. 'Stop them before they get to her first!'

Then adds coldly. 'She's mine.'

Sinclair Island is much less inviting at night than it is in the daytime. Normally an island full of fun and pleasure seekers, I can't help but feel it's about to become our prison. Trapped by the water, with no way off.

Farrell and I jump out of the speedboat as soon as it gets close enough to the jetty. Davies somehow manages to lasso the rope over the post while running, like a seasoned cowboy securing the bull by its horns.

Farrell grabs my arm. 'I don't think the Silver Moon is going to be safe for you now!'

'What shall we do?'

'Head for the restaurant.' He points over at The Palm Tree restaurant and bar.

We reach the doors, which of course are locked as the restaurant is only open during the day and no one lives on the island. Davies manoeuvres me out of the way and uses his elbow to smash the glass door and reach inside to unlock it. All three of us hurry inside. Thankfully no security alarms go off.

It's unnervingly empty and quiet. Eerie shadows dance across the walls and tables, like a ghostly celebration of souls lost at sea is taking place after dark. Frantically looking around for somewhere to hide, I can't help but panic. 'We're trapped now!'

'Davies and I won't let anything happen to you!' Farrell's voice is strong and reassuring.

A voice on the other side of the room makes all of us jump.

'Now how can you make a promise like that?'

# CHAPTER 57

I see the gun before I see Peter. The moonlight shining through the window reflects off the metal casing. When I finally find the courage to look at his face, he looks older than I remember. Accompanying age, pure hatred shapes his expression. I wait for the gun to fire but it doesn't happen.

Farrell finds his voice before I do. 'Why are you after the girl? It makes no sense!'

'*SHE* is the reason my sister is dead!'

I grip my stomach as the guilt cramps take hold and my eyes fill with burning tears of shame. Peter's words hurt more than his bullets ever will.

'What are you talking about?! Layna was as much a victim as your sister! She was a child, still is! How could she stop it?!'

'My sister would still be alive if it weren't for her! She hid herself away and left everyone else to die!'

'No, it wasn't like that...' My voice is small and feeble, and only succeeds in angering Peter further as he screams at me.

'I LOST MY SISTER AND NOW YOU HAVE TO PAY!'

His voice ricochets all around and I feel each of his words as they deflect onto my skin, tarnishing me with labels like guilt, shame and regret. Even though he has misunderstood what happened that day, I understand how he feels. I feel the same; Stephanie shouldn't have died. It should have been me. Still, I can't find any words of my own to put him straight.

I'm thankful when Farrell steps in again as his voice is more authoritative than mine. 'Well so did she! She lost her whole family and her best friend too. You're grieving, but so is she! Even more so!'

I watch Peter for a sign Farrell's words have reached him, but he's not even listening. The words travel right through him as if he's transparent, and they fade away unheard.

Instead, he continues with his accusations. 'If it weren't for her father and his dodgy dealings then it would never have happened! But he ain't here for me to blame, so you're it!'

He looks me dead in the eye and cocks the gun in readiness to pull the trigger. I grapple between the fear of him actually firing and the bolt of lightning he just fired at me from his lips.

'My father? My father has never been involved in anything dodgy! What are you talking about?'

'Come off it....you know full well!'

'Listen to yourself!' Farrell jumps in once more. 'Whether her father was involved or not, you're talking about killing a young girl for something she had no control over!'

'JUST SHUT UP, WILL YOU! SHUT UP!'

From behind, Jamie's voice reaches over Peter's shoulder and fills the room just from the magnitude of what he's saying, even though he speaks quietly. 'But Pete, the guys got a point. She is only a kid...' His voice trails off as he runs out of courage mid-sentence.

Peter turns to his brother but keeps the gun pointed at me. He's about to speak but Jamie takes a deep breath, inhaling another shot of confidence. 'She can't be expected to take responsibility for what her old man did.'

'Our sister is dead because of her!' Peter's voice breaks a little under the weight of the emotion it carries.

'No Pete! She's dead because of someone else, but not because of Layna. I know you're angry. I'm angry too and I've supported you on this for the last year, but killing Layna ain't gonna bring Steph back. It's not gonna make the anger go away. It's only gonna make you as bad as the men who did this in the first place. It's gonna kill what's left of mum and dad. Please give me the gun?'

Peter looks back at me and I feel the heat of his imaginary target on the middle of my forehead. His lungs are heaving like a drowning man, full of hate and no oxygen. His face tells me the story of his emotions, like a silent movie, and the gun in his hand starts to shake a little.

Jamie pleads with him. 'Think about mum, Pete. It'll break the rest of her heart if you become a murderer. Don't do it!'

Peter wipes the sweat from his face with his free hand. His whole body is shaking now, so much so that I think he might drop the gun or shoot me by accident. Broken and pale, the moonlight now shines its spotlight on the tears streaming down his face.

After what feels like forever, he lowers his arm and hands the gun to Jamie, who opens it and lets all the bullets fall to the floor. The clinking sound as they scatter has us all captivated, in joint solidarity of relief it brings.

I look over at Farrell and he looks as relieved as I feel. Davies' stance visibly loosens too. Jamie takes a hold of Peter, who weeps in his brother's arms.

'Touching!' Cliff Garrett startles us all.

# CHAPTER 58

Another gun is pointed at me.

Looking up from the barrel, I meet the eyes of the man who ordered the killing of my family. Chills shoot up and down my spine, making me shake all over from the cocktail of emotions I'm experiencing in one intense rush.

There's no remorse in his eyes. They're brown but with no warmth, just cold icicles draped around his pupils. A deep-rooted anger that I didn't realise I've been suppressing comes to the surface of my skin. An angry rash spreads across my chest, hot and itchy, and I'm no longer afraid of dying.

Farrell is the first to speak once more. 'These are the real killers of your sister!' His voice is loaded with disdain as he cleverly tries to get the Lawrences on our side.

'Quiet, Farrell! I'm not interested in your little anecdotes.'

It's the first time I've heard Cliff Garrett's gravelly voice, as he dismisses Farrell's attempt at mediation. He looks back at me with a smirk on his face. 'You have been most troublesome, young lady.'

His patronising tone, speaking to me like a naughty child only angers me more. My breath comes faster as my heart rate increases. I think about running at him with all my might, but the two men from the market lingering behind him remind me it's a terrible, impulsive idea.

'DON'T EVEN THINK ABOUT IT!' Cliff shouts.

Startled, I wonder how he knew what I was thinking, but then I see that he's looking at Davies. He must've been contemplating a move too.

'Stand over there.' He motions for me to move away from Farrell and Davies. I'm rooted to the spot, unable to move, just like my sixteen-year-old self, too frightened to move from the treehouse.

'Don't do this! Haven't you caused these people enough pain?' Farrell looks over at the Lawrences and then me, in another attempt to draw them onside for the inevitable battle.

Cliff fires the gun over Farrell's head as a warning.

Everyone flinches.

'I SAID BE QUIET FARRELL!' he shouts again. 'This doesn't concern you.'

I reason with myself that if I die now, at least I can be with my family again. The pending reunion makes me tremble even more and my words come out shakily. 'My father would never have been involved with someone like you.'

He doesn't reply, but his unfriendly smile, more of a grimace, tells me he's enjoying the doubt in my voice over my father's innocence. It's infuriating that I can't speak clearly and strongly, like Farrell, as it undermines my whole argument.

Pulling my shoulders back and tilting my chin up, I try again. 'Even if he was, what could he have possibly done that was so bad that you would kill *CHILDREN*?!'

I surprise even myself by shouting, but the tears pouring from my eyes, gushing like a waterfall after heavy rain, once again defy my quest to show strength.

He laughs at me.

I shake my head in defiance. 'I don't believe it. He was a good man.'

'He meddled in my business! Poked his nose in where it didn't belong.' He taps the side of his nose with his index finger.

'But, why would he...'

Losing his patience, he cuts me short mid-sentence and blurts out more.

'My business was not with him, you stupid girl! My business was with the other old guy! Your father stuck his ore in, thinking he could help. Well, I tell you, he shoulda kept his nose out! So don't give me all these tears and the 'you killed my family' nonsense! You wanna pay a visit to Colonel Bond if you're looking for someone to blame!'

The room starts spinning, like I'm on a carousel at the fair, except this isn't fun. Off balance, I fall backwards a little, but Davies catches hold of me with a large, warm hand in the small of my back, keeping me upright.

Once stable, I find some more words. 'What was that?'

'I said you can blame COLONEL BOND!'

Farrell turns to me. 'Who is Colonel Bond?'

'He's...He's Angel's father, Theresa's ex-husband. He's my dad's friend from when they were in the military together.'

Finding an inner strength from somewhere deep within, I turn back to the man who's twisted enough to think this rationale justifies his actions. 'You're saying my father was killed because of some business you had with Colonel Bond?'

'He came around trying to sort out his old pal's cock ups! It was none of his business. So he asked for it! That's what you get when you mess with me. You ought to take heed and learn from your fathers' mistakes, Little Miss.'

My fury allows the derogatory comment and warning to bounce off me like a shield of protection, and I continue to challenge him. 'You shot him because he was trying to help a friend?'

As I say it out loud, I process the meaning. Then I'm shouting again. 'You shot my whole family because my father was trying to help a friend?! WHO DOES THAT!' My voice breaks like an aged rock musician that's screeched into a microphone one too many times.

Cliff fires another warning shot.

The bullet grazes my cheek ever so slightly as it whizzes past. It's surprisingly delicate, like a graceful hand stroking the side of my face, as opposed to a murderous metal assassin sent to end my life. It leaves a tingly sensation on my skin for several seconds and I'm thankful for Davies' strong hand on my back, or I may have fallen down by now.

The sound of the bullet echoes around the room long after the shot. The atmosphere is charged for all of us, like a hundred volts surging through the air that makes hairs stand on end and goosebumps rise on normally smooth skin. Peter and Jamie are cautiously looking around, to determine if this man intends to shoot them too. Both look worried.

As if reading their minds, Cliff pipes up. 'Don't worry boys, I'll get rid of her for you.' He made it sound like a game between kids in the school playground.

The taller of the two men standing behind Cliff Garrett speaks for the first time. 'I suggest you all clear off home in your little boats.' He looks between the Lawrences, then Farrell and Davies.

Taking his cue, the other one with dark hair chirps in. 'Yeah, that way you won't end up dead like her other little friends!'

He looks at me as he says it and the blood drains from my body as I realise what he's saying. Before I have time to react or recuperate, he sticks the knife in deeper.

'You know, Blondie at the hotel? And the little African chick?'

Bile burns the soft tissue in my oesophagus as my body starts to heave up the contents of my stomach. I wrap my arms around myself tight and fold over in two.

Davies rubs my back in a comforting gesture.

The laughter from all three of the men sounds distant as the lights go out in my head. I barely register when Cliff announces my time has come.

He prepares the gun for another shot. 'That fifth bullet was meant for you, Little Miss. Not the Lawrence kid. So now it's your turn.'

# CHAPTER 59

The shot rings out much louder and clearer than the others. It sounds more like a cannon, and takes me a few moments to register that it was from a different gun.

Terrified for our lives, we all duck down, as primal instinct takes hold in response to such a deafening boom. It snaps me out of my fainting spell like a clap of thunder on a clear summer day.

Cliff Garrett doesn't die instantly. His body keeps him alive just long enough to look into the stranger's eyes and for confusion to display over the motive. His very last expression before passing is that of astonishment, that someone actually had the guts to shoot him in the heart. He falls to the floor, clumsily crashing into one of the tables on his way down.

I jump back to avoid him landing on my feet.

As everyone else slowly rises to their full height, we silently watch the large red stain appear on the front of Cliff Garrett's pristine white shirt. In almost choreographed synchronisation, we all look to the old man holding the gun.

Cliff Garrett's men look at each other. The taller man throws a wide-eyed look of accusation at his accomplice. In response, the dark haired one smirks and turns to the old man. 'You missed me, you fool!' he sneers.

The old man scowls as he raises his arm again, aiming at the mouthy one. Everyone prepares to duck again.

Except Farrell.

'NO! No, Dexter!' He puts his hand on the old man's arm to dissuade him from firing another round.

I look around at everyone, confused, as they all seem to know who the old man is. The Lawrence's are the only ones who's expressions are hard for me to read. From the corner, they're still silently watching on, making no attempts to intervene, likely to avoid getting shot themselves.

The old man speaks with a rasp. 'He hurt my granddaughter! In the bar! He cut her throat!' He points the gun at the man with dark hair, ready to take another shot.

'I know,' Farrell says, softly. 'And he will get his comeuppance, I promise you.' He glowers at the man staring down the barrel, before continuing. 'But this isn't the way. Let it go, man. He's not worth it. You've killed his boss. You don't want his blood on your hands too.'

'I got to protect my own!' The old man jabs himself in the chest with his other hand as he speaks.

'And you are! They won't bother you again.' He looks over at Cliff's men, inviting them to comply with his eyes.

Both men raise their hands, feigning surrender.

'See?' Farrell reasons with the old man.

We can all tell that the men are clearly playing along, but thankfully the old man doesn't appear to notice. Though I see that Farrell's chest is heaving, indicating his anger towards the men he is trying to save.

'Let this be the end.' Farrell gently takes the gun from his hand.

Davies speaks for the first time. 'Come on Dexter, let us take you home to your family.' He guides the man towards the door. 'How did you even get here?'

'I've been following them for days.' He points at Garrett's men. 'I climbed into their boat when they weren't looking and hid under a tarp.'

'A real-life stowaway!' Davies attempts to ease the fraught atmosphere with humour.

The dark haired man can hardly contain his distasteful chuckle over the old man's easily foiled vendetta.

Farrell shoots him a look. Normally chilled, his blood is boiling, burning his limbs as it pumps around his body. His emotions tangle up inside, creating a knot that builds up into a raging ball of fire. The fireball grows until it's as big as he is, filling his whole body, creating a fiery outline around his tall, muscular frame.

Dealing with an out of body experience for the first time, he sees the flaming version of himself step aside to become a separate being. Ties are severed and he can no longer control this version of himself as it raises old man Dexter's gun and shoots.

# CHAPTER 60

I've never seen this side of Farrell before. His eyes are alight with a mix of abhorrence and satisfaction, replacing the usual empathy and kindness.

We're all ducked down once more, including Davies and the old man in the doorway. The dark-haired man is writhing around on the floor in front of me, screaming and holding his knee. An old gun that size will have shattered the bones on impact.

I can barely look at him. There's such an amalgam of emotions rolling around together inside my head; hatred from knowing this man has hurt my friends and disdain that he made another of my friends behave so terribly out of character. But the human being in me hates to see someone hurt or tortured in this way. I just can't bear the sight. With my head spinning even more, I daren't try to stand up for fear I'll fall straight back down.

Eventually, Farrell speaks. It still doesn't look like him, but it sounds like the Farrell I know.

'That's for Amari.'

My tears flow freely as his words hit the sore spot in my heart.

The icy fear of crossing a line to shoot someone is enough to tame the heat that's been flowing through Farrell's veins. As he cools down, the heat inside of him diffuses and the fiery version of himself disintegrates into thin air.

Looking down at the smoke billowing from the old gun in his hand, his attention is drawn to the lips of the man rolling around on the floor in agony. He's trying to say something.

He leans in. 'What was that?'

After a few moments of grimacing, the man spits his response. 'I'm not sorry!'

Standing up to his full height, the raging ball of fire returns quickly and the fiery man once again steps into the foreground, equipped with even more strength having crossed the line once already. He takes aim, as visions fill his mind of the women this man has hurt. They're frightened instead of pretty. Bruised and battered, instead of happy and confident. It incites him to pull the trigger once more.

Through the gunpowder fumes, he hears his own voice speaking to the man who is no longer writhing, but silent and still that only death can bring. 'That one was for Tiffany.'

Even though we all saw it coming, everyone jumps again. My legs are weak from the trauma of the last few moments and I'm sure my eardrums have burst. I fall out of my squat position onto my knees.

Through my swollen and puffy eyes, I look up at Farrell. From my position on the floor, he looks even taller than he already is. Formidable and powerful, but yet now that the man on the floor has gone completely still, the normal Farrell starts to return once more and his body relaxes. I watch his transformation, curious how he can morph into such a destructive force and back again within seconds.

The man on the floor is gone. With his passing, he's taken the anger from Farrell with him, it seems, as he lowers the gun and looks at me with his usual soft and compassionate eyes. He hands it to Davies and walks over to me.

His hands are heavy and hot on my shoulders as he lifts me to my feet. 'It's over, girl. It's over.'

'Come on Pete, we should go. He's right, this needs to be over now.' Jamie, being the strong one for a change, takes charge and starts to lead his brother out.

Peter starts to move, but then stops and stares at Layna. Jamie nudges him along but he doesn't budge. He's anchored to the spot and for a second Jamie worries this isn't over after all.

My fear returns as Peter stares hard at me. He's been so quiet through this whole episode that I genuinely don't know what he's thinking.

His eyes are searching my soul, looking for a reason to hate me. Feeling scrutinised, I can only plead with him with my own eyes to understand that I'm hurting just as much as he is.

'Pete?'

Jamie gets no response. 'Pete, come on. We need to go home.'

Peter shrugs himself free of Jamie's grip. The intensity is still written across his face. Jamie searches Peter's eyes and sees something he's not familiar with. Tiny flecks of softness appear in his pupils, spreading an expression that travels around his face. His lips part and in a gentle voice, Peter utters one word as he looks Layna dead in the eye.

'Sorry.'

It was an apology that sounded as though it came from a belligerent three-year-old, but it caught Jamie off guard altogether. He feels his eyes widen, mirroring Layna's surprised expression.

After a few seconds to absorb what just occurred, Layna nods her acceptance, seemingly unable to speak. Peter lowers his head in very apparent shame. Though he does finally allow Jamie to guide him out of the restaurant, back to their boat. As they walk down the path lined with tall palm trees, Jamie embraces the new feeling that washes over him, and speaks to Peter more freely than he ever has before. 'Things are gonna be different now Pete, for the better.'

Peter only nods, like he ran out of words to say after "sorry".

Jamie presses on, keen to voice his thoughts now while he can. 'I think we should spend more time at home, with mum and dad. It will help them to heal if we're more present.'

This seems to encourage Peter to find more words from somewhere deep inside. 'I miss Steph.'

To Jamie, he still sounds like a young child instead of a grown man. 'Me too, Pete.'

Back inside the restaurant, Marshall allows his tense body to relax a bit after hearing the others talk of this being over. It seems he will be the only one spared. With the Lawrence's gone, he watches the dark outline of Farrell, Davis, Layna and the old man disappear through the door too.

He can't say he's sorry Reeves is gone but with Cliff Garrett dead too, he'll never be paid for the time he spent working on this. Unless he could convince Kevin, Cliff's accountant, to pay out still.

In complete silence, he stands over the bodies of his former boss and colleague. Alone with two corpses, he shakes his head as he struggles to process the severity of what just happened here and what he needs to do next.

# CHAPTER 61

The dimly lit car park gives me goosebumps as I walk through. Under the only streetlight, my shadow stretches out in front of me, leading the way to the other side.

Rows of Victorian townhouses line the car park on two sides, giving way at one end to a contrasting 1970's building with greying Formica panelling. The neon sign above the main entrance is sparking from a faulty wire, sending me rushing over the threshold, as I don't want to linger beneath.

Inside, the stark waiting room full of plastic chairs and people with pained, worried expressions feels cold in comparison to the warm summer ether outside. The smell of bleach is overwhelming.

Behind the counter, a receptionist in the zombified state of someone who's been on shift for more hours than is legal, clicks away on her mouse. She doesn't even see me come in, let alone ask if she can help, so I please myself and walk past her.

The gloomy corridor is long and surprisingly windy, leaving me baffled as to its presence considering there are no windows and no wind blowing outside tonight. My breathing is heavy and loud as I walk to the end. The first set of double doors leads to an even longer corridor.

Halfway along is a small lobby from a side entrance, where a gang of teenage girls are messing around with an abandoned trolley bed. I can't help but wonder what they're doing out at this time of night. It's way past midnight. I was never allowed out after dark with friends, let alone to be in the city centre at night. They're being disrespectfully loud too, and they look at me as if daring me to tell them off. I deliberately ignore them. I'm not here to do battle.

At the end of the corridor, I hover outside another set of doors which are controlled by a code lock. After a few moments, footsteps approach from the other side and the door swings open. Standing back, the tired looking nurse coming through doesn't see me as I slip inside before the door shuts.

The atmosphere on the ward is totally different to the greying, dull corridors that led me here. It's low lit, almost cosy lighting, with white surfaces, blue curtains, clinical but warm. The staff here are very calm and at ease, considering the high dependency ward. No one questions me or why I'm here.

With trepidation, I approach the bed in the middle of the row. The occupant is deadly still. I can't tell if it's from sleep or unconsciousness. Amongst the tubes and wires, I see both legs in plaster. There's a bandage around the jaw and one arm is in plaster too. I get as close as the bed barrier will let me.

'You're so lucky to be alive.' I whisper.

I catch a tiny movement out of the corner of my eye. The free arm is moving. The index finger curves and the thumb remains straight. I complete the heart shape with my own hand.

'You're going to be ok, Amari. You're a survivor. Cliff Garrett is gone. There'll be no more violence now. No more running.'

I take hold of her hand in both of mine. Her fingers are small and cold. 'I'm going to find us somewhere to live together. I'll take care of you, Amari. We'll have a good life from now on. I promise.'

I know she can hear me as she squeezes my hand.

# CHAPTER 62

I emerge from the cabin to see the hands of dawn stretching over the ocean, gently rocking the boats to awaken all onboard from their slumber. I join Frazer on the deck and sit in the deckchair facing the horizon.

Perched on the edge of the seat, I watch the sunrise unfold over the first day of my new life. Everything feels strange and I don't quite know what to do with myself.

Frazer expertly reads my body language. 'You'll find your place in the world, girl. Give it time.'

I nod and relax back into the chair.

'How about some breakfast?' he asks.

We bring a tray of croissants and orange juice up to the deck to enjoy under the rising sun.

'How'd you sleep?'

'Not great. The events of last night are still too fresh in my mind and I couldn't switch off.'

'It's understandable.'

'It's the sounds that repeat on me. The gunshots. Then the two splashes in the water that we heard from the other boat behind us as we came away from the island.'

'I wondered what would happen to the bodies.'

My shoulders shudder and I spill some of my orange juice. Then a voice surprises me and I almost spill more.

'Knock, knock!' The tall man is dressed sharply in a suit and tie, and his briefcase looks heavy. He's smiling at his own joke about knocking on a vessel that has no door.

Frazer jumps up. 'Can I help you?'

'Yes, I believe you can!' The man is very sure of himself as he turns to me. 'Are you Miss Layna Raye?'

Cautiously, I rise to my feet and battle with my engraved habit to lie about my identity. It shouldn't be so hard to simply confirm my own name, but I have to force the words out through my reluctant lips. 'Yes, I am.'

'Maybe this game isn't over, after all.' Frazer says, curling his fists ready to defend me.

'Please, relax.' The man puts his hand up, palm towards us, to emphasize his words. 'I mean you no harm, Miss Raye.'

He's unaffected by the prospect of being beaten up by a heavyset sailor, and swings his briefcase up onto the ledge on the side of the boat to remove some papers.

'Miss Raye, my name is Lincoln Schwartz. I'm an investigator for a law firm called Smith & Brooks. Mr Brooks asked me to locate you so that he can execute your parents' Will.'

He hands me the paperwork and a business card. 'I wonder if you'd be so kind as to make an appointment at your earliest convenience.'

I appreciate the pause he offers at this moment to let the information sink in. 'Yes, I'll make an appointment.'

'Great!' The smile returns to his face as he looks over the Blue Star with obvious envy. 'Shall I assume this to be your contact address?'

I look at Frazer, who nods and writes the post office box address he uses for his own mail on a piece of paper for him.

'Thank you very much!' He puts the paper in his briefcase and snaps the clasps shut. 'Right then, I shall leave you to your breakfast. Good day to you both.'

As we watch him leave, Frazer voices the notion that I almost daren't accept for being too good to be true. 'See girl, things will fall into place.'

'I hope so. I could use the money to help Amari.'

With just a seconds hesitation, he signs his name on the bottom of the written statement, and slides the paper across the desk.

For all the turmoil this will cause, the almost mundane unimportant thoughts are overriding his fear of what the future holds, such as why are we still using paper statements in today's digital world?

The new Chief Inspector has his arms folded across his chest where he sits across from Harry. A scathing look of distaste is portrayed through his staring eyes. Without unfolding his arms, or even blinking he speaks with the authoritative voice only someone in his position could possess.

'Is that everything?'

'Yes, sir.' His own voice quiet in meek submission.

'All the details? I want every last detail you can think of in that statement, Harry!'

'Yes sir, that's really all of it. I don't know what occurred last night, but I've put everything that happened before that, leading up to it. How the department came to think of the oldest daughter as the shooter. I've got all my bank statements to show how much he gave me. Cliff Garrett, that is. There's nothing else to tell, sir, really.'

'Right then. Let's get you booked in.'

Both men stand, similar height, though one standing taller than the other. The Chief Inspector holds the door open for Harry.

'Just one more question, though, Harry. Off the record.' He pauses in the doorway and waits for Harry's response.

Harry doesn't speak though, just looks at him expectantly for the question that's coming.

'Was it worth it? I mean, losing your career, your lifelong work, just for the money?'

Harry takes a deep breath in through his nose and out again, before answering. 'No, sir. It wasn't.'

In the tiny room, below sea level, I empty my bag onto the small bed and survey my few belongings. Selecting a floral gypsy top and skirt from my pitiful collection, I turn to take my fresh outfit to the bathroom but stop when something catches my attention.

Dropping the clothes onto the bed, I pick up the map that Virginia gave me. Once again, the mystery of what is located at Barley Lane has me baffled. I unfold it and take another look, but nothing new jumps out. Still just a highlighted street and an extra entry on the key.

I look through the round porthole window at the sea-green water as a few strands of seaweed float by, trying to figure out what it all means, to no avail. With an unsatisfactory sigh that comes only when one cannot figure out a riddle, I fold the map back up and grab my clothes to get ready.

# CHAPTER 63

Having finally succumbed to sleep, Tiffany is woken with a start by her door buzzer. Her heart races as she jumps out from beneath the pile of blankets she had buried herself under on the sofa in an attempt to form a protective shell of safety.

After releasing her legs from the grips of a blanket that had wrapped itself around her ankles, she eventually breaks free and cautiously approaches the intercom at the front door. She hopes its Chloe, she really needs to show her the bruising so she'll believe her about Tony being bad.

Nervously, she presses the intercom with a shaky, bruised finger. 'Hello?' Her voice is feeble and tentative.

'Flowers for Tiffany, from Blooming Fresh?'

It takes her a second to register and reply, her mind is still half enthralled with much needed sleep which is fighting against the post-traumatic stress that's still very much alive and running through her veins.

Eventually, she finds her voice again. 'Okay, come in.'

She doesn't understand who is sending her flowers. Would Chloe do that? She didn't think so.

Feeling unnerved, she peers through the peephole to make sure it's not another trick, and is reassured to see the unmistakable logo of the flower shop embroidered onto the man's shirt. She takes the chain off and opens the door, trying not to let him see her face. But, inevitably, she senses his shock at her appearance without even having to look at him.

Avoiding eye contact, she takes the large bouquet of flowers and thanks him as she closes the door as quickly as possible. Standing still for a moment, she stares at the beautiful blooms.

After checking the door is locked, even though she knew it was, she takes them through to the kitchen and places them down on the draining board. The card is attached to the outside in a tiny envelope. She slides it out and reads;

*Feel better soon Tiffany. The game is over, Layna is safe forever and you won't be harmed any more. Farrell xxx*

Two squirrels play chase around the tree trunk. I smile, feeling as free as they do for the first time in more than a year. I watch them for a few moments, enjoying their frivolity, before turning back to the large headstone with the words *Raye Family* engraved across the top in ornate writing.

I fidget as I try to get comfortable, both physically and emotionally. The soft lawn beneath my knees offers a cushion of solace.

'I'm going to be okay now,' I tell them. 'I'm going to the police tomorrow. Frazer's coming with me.'

A wood pigeon calls from a tree nearby in response to my news, making me wonder if it's a sign from my family. I look up at the huge fir tree, but I can't see it. The ghostly cooing echoes out from the depths of the branches where it is surely perched deep within the tree's embrace.

Hoping for more signs, I continue to speak with my family, as if they're all here sitting beside me on the lawn. 'It's really different here in the day time. I've only been able to come and see you when it's dark and creepy. It's actually very charming,' I say, looking up at the chapel nestled among the trees, keeping watch over those sleeping under its protection. 'And peaceful.'

The scent of honey and lemon fills the air from the yellow rose bushes planted either side of the headstone, the vines trailing around it in a ring of reassurance. A peacock butterfly, one of my mum's favourites, flutters over to inspect the roses. In the same moment, a robin appears on the ground next to me. He looks at me before singing his song with a voice much louder than you'd expect for one with such tiny lungs.

I accept their appearance as further signs that my words have been heard and allow the knowledge to comfort and heal my soul. I stay a while just sitting quietly, enjoying being close to my family without the terror of being caught.

At the edge of the plot, some stray daisies that were missed by the lawnmowers catch my attention. I pick a couple and set about re-living a childhood memory of making a daisy chain. I surprise myself at how adept I am with this task, considering the amount of years that have passed since I last made one. It helps to keep my focus in the here and now, as opposed to what will happen next in my life, or to brood over what's happened in the past.

With a passing breeze, the peace and tranquillity are swept away momentarily, when thoughts of last night filter into my new-found placid state of mind, to once again bring turbulence and unrest. The events on Sinclair Island, Amari in the hospital, the fitful night of no sleep, tossing and turning, and in an instant the exhaustion hits me and I suddenly feel as though I could sleep for a hundred years.

With tiredness comes tears. Just a few at first, then more. I'm careful not to lose it too much though, as I really don't want to cry in front of my family. I know it would hurt them to think of me upset, so I try to put the brave face on that I've become so well-rehearsed at over the last year. Raiding my pocket for a tissue, I dry my eyes and blow my nose.

After a short while of reigning in my emotions, another breeze sweeps in, caressing the yellow petals of the roses. It disperses as quickly as it came, gathering up all of my emotions and taking them away with it, so it seems.

Feeling somewhat human again, I find more words to share with my family. 'I told you I would never leave you, no matter how hard it became. There are some amazing people I owe my life to, who really helped to keep me safe. Farrell, Amari, Tiffany, Corey and Virginia, Theresa and Angel. And Brent, of course.' I wipe a few more tears, this time of gratitude, from my face. 'I'm sure it was all orchestrated by you, from up there.'

The sound of people nearby interrupts me, but this time I don't flinch. I look around to see another family laying flowers and then turn back to make a final promise to my family. 'I'll be able to come and see you more frequently now. I promise.'

I peel my knees off the grass and stand up. There's someone else I need to visit while I'm here. Blowing a kiss to the grave, I walk a few rows through the cemetery. The butterfly flutters alongside me, accompanying me to another grave marked with a dozen pots of colourful flowers, brightly coloured pebbles and windcatchers. I perch in front as I read her headstone.

*In Loving Memory Of Our Daughter, Sister, Granddaughter and Niece. Taken Too Soon. Stephanie Lawrence.*

I cry out as I fall to my knees. 'Oh Steph! Do you blame me like your brothers did?' I ask her out loud for the first time.

'I didn't hide on purpose. You know that don't you? You heard my mum asking me to untangle Lyle's kite from the tree, didn't you? I was hidden but not hiding.' I sniff back more tears, but they inevitably still fall into my lap. 'They killed you because they thought you were me. I should have died, not you.'

A couple nearby look over at me. My sobbing has become out of control. I put my head in my hands to muffle the sound as I let everything out. My palms are sodden from my tears, my cheeks clammy from the burden of guilt. It takes a few minutes of racking sobs but eventually I feel like I'm settling into a normal rhythm of breathing again. The muscles in my stomach that are only used when crying so hard begin to ache, for they can cry no more. Removing my hands from my face, another whispering summer breeze dries my tears as it wafts over my skin. I relish its freshness.

Once I've regained my composure, I sit quietly for a while. The robin appears at my side again. He looks directly at me, as if evaluating my mental health state. His compassion makes me smile.

Gathering my thoughts, I speak to Stephanie once more. 'I think your brothers forgave me. At least it seemed that way. I'll try and visit your mum soon, if she'll see me.'

Then I make my second promise of this cemetery visit. 'I promise I'll do what I can to help them heal.'

# CHAPTER 64

Summer rain falls gently outside, stirring up the pollen that gives even those without allergies the sniffles. The softness of its droplets as they caress the outside world with their moisture is emulated on Tiffany's face. And mine. We have both shed tears, hugged, and then cried some more.

Despite it being the height of summer, she's wrapped up in fluffy blankets on her sofa. Curled up next to her, I feel her heat radiating towards me. The heavenly scent of lilies in a vase on the coffee table draws me to lean forward and breathe in their floral delight. 'These are beautiful.'

'Aren't they? Farrell sent them.'

I smile. 'Sounds like something he'd do.'

For the first time since I got here, Tiffany smiles too. 'He's such a kind soul. How did you meet him?' she asks.

'A girl in my class used to go clubbing even though she was only fifteen. She was always bragging how her cousin got her a fake ID. The name of his bar stuck in my head, so I went there not long after I left home, and asked for a driving licence.'

'And he just did it?! Without question?'

'Well sort of. He did ask some questions, but he still got me one. Over time I ended up telling him everything and he got me more ID's in case one of them got hot.'

We're both quiet in a few moments of reflection, as we sip the tropical juice Tiffany poured for us. 'That's how I met Amari too,' I add, mostly to fill the silent void. 'Farrell was giving us both a new ID once and got them mixed up, and gave me hers. We had to meet to swap them and have been friends ever since. Her life is so tragic.'

'So is yours,' Tiffany adds.

I can't answer. Truth is hard to speak. Instead, I deflect onto the Lawrence's. 'Same for Steph's family too.' I must be displaying the guilt I feel every time I think of Stephanie all too evidently.

'Layna, what happened to Steph isn't your fault.'

'I know. But it doesn't stop the guilt. It won't go away, no matter how much I try to reason with it.'

'I think you should speak to a therapist. I know a good one.' She unravels herself from several layers of blankets and fishes around in a drawer for a business card.

'Did you speak to Theresa or Angel yet?' she asks as she hands it to me.

'Not yet,' I say as I look at the therapists name on the card. 'I'm not sure what to say to them.'

'Talk it over with Colette,' she nods toward the card in my hand.

'I will, thanks.' I reach over and squeeze her hand.

'You're so much like your mum.'

Her comment catches me off-guard, and I jolt at the mention of my mum.

'Sorry, I didn't mean to upset you. It's just that you're so alike, in looks as well as personality. She was exceptionally empathetic, like you are.'

I look down into my juice, hoping that breaking eye contact will stop the next few tears from forming. My long lashes hold them in, like steel bars on a prison door.

Tiffany continues in her gentle calming voice. 'You know, I was so very painfully shy when I first started working at the hotel. I had zero confidence. And now here I am on the management team, and I have your mum to thank for that. She just had a way, drew me out of my shell and built me up into someone I never thought I'd have the strength to be.'

The tears break free and escape from my eyes. She just described my mother perfectly. 'That was her,' is all I can manage to say.

The piano key patterned awning invites Farrell inside the music shop. Stepping inside feels like he has joined an exclusive club where musicality is the only requirement to join, and he feels somewhat of an imposter.

Looking around at the various drum kits, keyboards and woodwind instruments on display, he is distracted when another customer in the far corner begins to play the keyboard that's on display for people to try out before buying. The rifts fill the small shop as his hands expertly trail up and down the chords.

Farrell approaches the man at the counter in the middle of the shop, noting that he has a piano pattern tie that matches the awning of the shop front outside. After a few moments of pleasantries and a brief description of the requirements, the shop owner, who makes jazz hands when he talks, places the brand new guitar into its case and slides it across the counter to Farrell.

'I'm sure your friend will find many hours of musical pleasure with this little beauty! It's a step up from the one you said had been broken. Makes a gorgeous sound, I hope she'll be pleased with it.'

'She will, I'm sure it'll bring her a lot of happiness once she's out of hospital and her arm is mended. It'll give her incentive to heal quickly.'

The sprinkling of summer rain we had earlier has stopped and the sun has already dried the pavement. I'm standing next to the street sign for Barley Lane. It's a long straight road, mostly residential and not too busy with cars. Virginia's map indicates number seventy-eight, so I look to see if the street is set in odds and evens, or just a straight run down each side. It looks to be a straight run, so I stick to the left side of the road and follow the numbers.

Part way along, the aroma of fresh-caught fish and chips sets my stomach rumbling. The takeaway sits in the middle of a small parade of shops featuring Archers General Store, a butchers and greengrocers.

Just as I'm contemplating picking up a takeaway on the way back, a small building appears on the left with a brass plaque displaying the numbers seventy-three to seventy-nine. This is it.

I walk up the drive, which has off road parking for around four vehicles at a squeeze. The front entrance is open and I walk inside.

The grey carpets are thick and lavender cleanses the air as I get my bearings. The door to my right says flat seventy-three. There's one other door on the ground floor for number seventy-four, so I head up the staircase, finding another two flats on the first floor and finally come to seventy-eight on the top floor.

There's a book on the floor, leaning against the front door. I pick it up and a key falls out of the sleeve. I feel weird just letting myself in, but that's obviously what Virginia wants, so I put it in the lock and turn it.

Poking my head inside, I call out. 'Virginia?'

Silence.

'Virginia, are you here?'

Still no reply.

I push the door open further and look around the hall without stepping across the threshold. There's a bright and sunny kitchen to the left and a bathroom to the right. Down the hall is a set of steps leading up into a lounge. There's no sign of Virginia. Worry creeps in, sending shivers down my spine that maybe I'm too late and they hurt her too.

With a little more courage, I step just inside the door and call her name once more. The only sound is whirring from the fridge in the kitchen. I take a few more steps and poke my head right into the kitchen to have a proper look. The counters are clear with the kettle tucked neatly away into the corner.

I go across the hall and into the bathroom. A free-standing tub with Victorian feet and gold taps fills the space beneath a round port-hole style window. The tub and the sink are dry, indicating a lack of use today. The towels are neatly folded over the rack and the pot plant in a wicker basket looks well-kept.

Frowning, I approach the steps up to the lounge, wondering where she can be. After a quick look back to check the front door is still open for escape, if need be, I dare myself to walk up the steps.

On the top step, I once again poke my head in to look around without committing to entering the room. I'm greeted by a cosy space surrounding a cream leather sofa with a dark wood frame, covered in cushions of brown and gold. The antique furniture smells freshly polished and the wood floors squeak beneath my feet. I tread a little way into the room to allow a view into the two rooms coming off the lounge either side.

Both are bedrooms. I check the one on the left first. Not surprisingly, it's empty of people but full of more beautiful furniture. I tiptoe across the lounge floorboards to avoid the squeaks, feeling like an intruder, and check the second bedroom. A four poster bed takes up most of the room. There are flowers in a vase on the bedside table and a carved wood wardrobe, but still no sign of Virginia.

I turn back into the lounge, not knowing what to do next. The decor looks like Virginia's style but I've never been here before so she must have moved since the last time I saw her.

Then I remember the book in my hand. Looking down, I notice its title for the first time. It's called Home Sweet Home. I open the book and on the inside page, Virginia has written a note.

*I hope you'll be happy and safe here, love Virginia*

I slam the book shut and look around.

'No! Really?' I say aloud to no one but myself.

I open the book again and read the words over and over until they sink in. My tears land on the page with a thud as I'm overcome with the emotions of the past twenty-four hours.

Dropping onto the sofa, I sink back into the pile of cushions and allow my tears to flow freely once more. I didn't think I had anymore left, but they come one after the other in a constant stream. Several minutes pass with me just sobbing what's left of my heart out. Virginia's kind gesture has broken me. Truly broken me.

It's only once I've cried myself dry that I notice the skylight above the sofa for the first time, surrounded by exposed beams. The blue sky sends fluffy white clouds rolling by, gentle and wistful such as life is meant to be from now on.

Sitting up, I lean on my knees while I gather myself. Looking down the steps towards the front door, I remember it's still wide open. I leave the book on the side table and walk down the steps to close the front door, accepting now that I'm not an intruder. As the lock snaps into place, I pocket the key.

I lean back against the door and survey the flat from the viewpoint of someone who has just returned home. I still don't know what to do with myself. It's unnatural for me to stay in one place long enough to feel connected, but it's so beautiful and relaxing here. My heart does a little happy dance and I feel a smile forming, a smile that has for too long been oppressed by fear.

Instead of returning to the lounge, I'm instinctively drawn to the porthole window in the bathroom that reminds me of being aboard Frazer's boat. I have to go on my tippy toes to see out, but the expansive ocean calls to me from the vista view.

I hardly recognise this relaxed version of myself in the ornate gold mirror hanging over the sink. After tidying my hair a little, I reach into my pocket for the key and leave the flat, locking it securely. I take the stairs down to the street two at a time and almost skip down the street like my old childhood self before life changed so dramatically.

The bottom of Barley Lane opens out onto sand dunes with a small trail leading through to the beach, delicately lined with tufts of scorched grass spiking out from the sandy path. I sit at the top of the tallest dune and breathe more freely than ever before. The salt softens my lungs as I watch a family of mum, dad and son walking their dog along the beach.

As the waves gently wash ashore, I imagine bringing Amari here to help with her recovery. Another smile comes as I think about her also being happy and free here, away from that damp bedsit and that awful boy who torments her.

At this moment, the family's dog runs over and sits next to me in unconditional friendship. His silky fur slips easily through my fingers as I stroke his head.

I look back at his family, expecting them to call him back, but they don't. The boy is flying his kite along the beach where it rides the sea breeze, symbolically representing the end of my journey in exactly the same way that it began.

Printed in Great Britain
by Amazon

50078224R00205